RELIC HUNTERS

EAGLE OF THE EMPIRE

MARTIN FERGUSON

Eagle Of The Empire
Relic Hunters
Copyright © 2017 Martin Ferguson
SECOND EDITION
All rights reserved.

No parts of this book may be reproduced in any form without written consent from the author. Except in the use of brief quotations in a book review.

This book is a piece of fiction. Any names, characters, businesses, places or events are a product of the author's imagination or are used fictitiously. Any resemblance to persons living or dead, events or locations is purely coincidental.

This book is licensed for your personal enjoyment only. This book may not be resold or given away to other people. If you are reading this book and have not purchased it for your use only, then you should return it to your favorite book retailer and purchase your own copy.

Thank you for respecting the author's work.

Cover by Tom Roberts of Zoom Illustration
Editing by Karen Sanders Editing
Formatting by Pink Elephant Designs

ALSO BY MARTIN FERGUSON

<u>Relic Hunters:</u>

Eagle of the Empire

Curse of the Sands

War of the Damned

Blood of the Dragon

To all those who have made this journey possible

1

MATT—The Highlands, Scotland

'Run! Run! Get out of there!' the headset screams in my ears as I dive through the waterfall. Soaking to the bone, I land hard on the rock of the cavern floor, the bite wound at my arm searing in agony. Around me, the cave tremors; stalactites crash down from the ceiling. I duck away from the cascade, rubble striking me, but I don't slow, heart thundering in my chest as adrenaline and sheer will to escape forces me on.

My predator leaps after me, jaws snapping wildly as it emerges from the water, fangs dripping crimson. I run on without pause, clutching at the deep bite to my arm, blood flowing through my fingers.

Despite my agonising wound, I have no choice but to carry the torch with that side. The torch is the only source of light in the cave. I feel the hot breath of the creature behind me, too close now to escape. I turn, slamming the flashlight across its skull, hoping that my surprise attack will be enough to give me an advantage. Howling in pain, the creature crashes into the wall behind, blood drawn above an eye to stain the white and grey fur. Tremors ripple through the cave and I take flight once more.

Emerging into the widest cavern, flanked by the graves of the dead, I run for the entrance I used less than an hour before. In the distance, I see the great stone door begin to fall, threatening to trap me in this desolate place forever. Sprinting with all the strength and energy I have, I charge, arrows soaring from the walls and spears rising from the floor to stop me – punishment for disturbing sacred ground. I duck and dart away from the iron points which seek to tear my flesh. Many come close – too close – and my baseball cap flies from my head across the cavern, impaled on an arrow.

'No! No! NO!' I yell as the rock door continues to fall, knowing I am not fast enough. The door hits the floor just as my fingers touch it.

Trapped.

Slamming my fists uselessly on the stone, I swear loudly, my curses echoing throughout the dark cavern.

'There must be another way out!' the voice on my headset cries frantically. 'Don't give up! Look around you!'

'There is no other way out,' I mutter back in defeat, sweeping my torch back across the chamber.

The light begins to flicker and dim, my torch failing as the batteries die. I'm slowly plunged into darkness. Just as my vision is taken, I hear its clawed steps across rock.

Closer.

Closer.

I can almost touch the menace.

'I'm not alone in here,' I whisper. Terror seizes me. There is no escape.

I have a terrible choice. Light a flare and give away both of our positions, or play guess in the dark. There isn't time to over-think it. From my pocket, I pull free a flare and ignite it. Red sparks burst from the tip, giving hellish light to the cavern. I hear the roar of the beast, shaking the catacombs around me. I see it then – properly, for the first time, demonic eyes glowing as it circles nearer. I struggle to control my fear. All I can do is breathe deep, readying myself for one last fight I have no chance of surviving.

'Are you sure there's no way out?' the voice in the headset pleads.

'There isn't,' I say, resigned to my fate. The red eyes of the monster are curious; it's as if it's waiting to hear what my last words will be. 'Can you call Kat for me? Can you put me through to her?'

All I want is to hear her voice one last time, to tell her I love her. To tell her I will always be with her. To tell her I'm sorry.

'I've tried to contact Kat already, but she isn't picking up,' the voice informs. 'I'm sorry, Hunter.'

'Typical,' I say, forcing a laugh. 'She never picks up the phone when it's important. Tell her for me, will you? Tell her I... Tell her...'

I struggle to find the words to say my goodbye.

'I'll tell her,' the voice says, and I can hear the sadness and devastation.

My final thoughts are of my family; my brother, my mother, and of course, Kat.

'I'm sorry,' I whisper to them, knowing they will never hear my last words.

The beastly roar grows deeper, louder, as the creature paces towards me. It is preparing for the kill.

I will not fall without a fight.

'Come on then!' I urge, but it only roars again, as if playing some kind of game. 'Come on!' I yell.

A deep, menacing voice calls out to me from the shadows. It echoes throughout the chamber, giving it an unearthly quality. 'You are right, my friend. You are not alone.'

'Who are you?'

I am answered by the sudden flare of blue flames at the centre of the chamber. They grow with astonishing speed, rising high and filling the cavern, surrounding me.

'You are not alone,' the voice states. 'You are never alone.'

The flames grow closer, as if reaching for me; their heat licks my skin. There is nowhere to run, nowhere to hide.

'I sense it. Your past, your tragedy.'

The blue flames surge towards me, engulfing me. All defined senses are lost as I scream in sheer agony.

'HUNTER!' the voice in my headset cries. 'HUNTER!'

2

ADAM—Richmond, London, England

My classmates are cheering me, 'HUN-TER! HUN-TER! HUN-TER!' as I pull myself up from the windows to the drainpipe and then to the top of the building.

Standing on the rooftop of the college, grin broad across my face, I raise a finger to my lips to hush the small crowd on the playing field. They don't stop. Their cheers grow until I give up my protests and lift my arms high in triumph.

My name is Adam Hunter, and I am a failing student at the Kett Sixth Form College, dreaming of a life beyond text books and classrooms. Sixteen years old, a week shy of my seventeenth birthday, and always daydreaming of escape and freedom. Handsome, with a perfect athletic build and a dazzling smile with dark spiked hair and blue eyes –

that's me. Modest too. Careless, reckless, always distracted; those are just some of the words used to describe me, and to be fair, they're probably spot on.

I stand and salute my adoring fans one last time before backing away from the edge. The smile is still at my lips but I can't help it. The challenge has begun.

I am wearing the usual jeans, ripped at the knees, a red hoodie, faded grey leather biker jacket, and old trainers, muddy and faded with use. I cross the roof, vaulting over all obstacles and then leap to the next building, unhindered by the effort needed, and fearless of the gap, height, and potential fall – and probably death. My friends call it parkour or free-running but I simply see it as making the world my own private playground.

I drop out of sight as I see teachers pass the windows opposite to where I prowl the rooftops, lingering for a few seconds before rising again. The way is clear and my presence unnoticed.

'Get the prize and get out,' I say to myself, pulling the hood over my head, concealing part of my face in case of discovery or being captured by the CCTV cameras. 'No worries.'

One more time, I cross to another rooftop before nearing a skylight, popping its lock open with my trusty pen-knife – my father's gift from long ago. I wait and listen for signs of discovery, but no alarm is raised. Opening the skylight as wide as it'll go, I squeeze through and drop to the classroom below.

As I fall, my jacket catches on a chair and sends it tumbling towards the floor. My reflexes are, thankfully, quick enough, catching the chair before it can crash to the ground and betray my location.

'No worries,' I whisper to myself in relief.

Carefully, quietly, I put the chair down, but I hear an approaching voice from outside coming closer. Quickly, I duck down behind a desk as a teacher walks past the room. She speaks loudly on her mobile phone, complaining relentlessly about her terrible students and our misdeeds. I know the voice all too well; it belongs to Mrs Rhodes, known as 'Spike' to her pupils. Peering through the window, I see her; a tall woman, big, dolled up grey hair, and a damning stare that would terrify most. Not me though; I just find it funny and struggle not to break down in laughter each time she yells at me. Her hair is nearly all gone but for one solitary lock that won't settle, no matter how much she tries to brush it down. Unsurprisingly, she hates the name.

'...and the Hunter boy! He's getting worse by the day. Nothing like his brother before him. They're the sons of a teacher, did you know? Who would've thought he'd turn out like this! Mind, they're often the worst.'

My mother certainly knew, despite her best efforts. She is glad she never had to teach us, especially me.

'Not only did he unscrew every nut and bolt in my chair so that it collapsed when I sat down today,' she continues, 'but I am certain it was him who broke into my cabinet, stole my test papers, and replaced those I was to hand out today with the answer copy. Unsurprisingly, they all scored a hundred percent!'

I struggle not to laugh until Mrs Rhodes passes on.

'Yeah, it was me,' I whisper once out of earshot, grinning still. 'Another bout of detention on its way, I guess.'

Moving to the doorway of the classroom, I crouch again, looking down the deserted corridor. My mobile phone buzzes twice in my pocket and, making sure no one is approaching, I quickly look to its screen, two messages showing.

Hurry up
Duncan

You're running out of time
Sara

'Nothing like pressure,' I say, returning the phone to my pocket.

Checking the corridor one last time, I set out, running quickly and silently. I stop a few times, listening for approaching footsteps, and peer into classrooms, but just as I am nearing my destination, I see the door before me swing open. Spike emerges; she is still ranting on the phone. I dive towards the nearest set of lockers, pulling myself up and atop them, out of sight. I try not to move; the lockers creak under my weight.

'...and he messed around with the presentation for my ten o'clock science class! Instead of the different categories of rocks, there were pictures of me on my beach holiday! I've never been so embarrassed and...and sickened in all my...'

'Neither have we,' I think, struggling again not to laugh. She disappears around the corner, her tirade unending.

My phone buzzes with another text message.

C'mon Hunter, hurry up!
Everybody's waiting
Duncan

Before I can put the phone away, it vibrates again, another message received.

I'm guessing you don't want your motorcycle kets
back then? I wonder how much I can sell the bike
for????? Sara

Lowering down from the lockers, I move quickly along the corridor, nearing Mr Beckett's classroom; my target. The man stands before the entrance, talking with another teacher I have not seen before. Mr Beckett's untidy beard and creased clothes add to his tired, miserable appearance. He has a stern look on his face as always.

'Wait here while I grab my lighter,' he tells the other teacher.

Mr Beckett raises his staff badge to the door handle, a fob activating the lock, the only way inside. As I wait, I pull a fresh green apple from my pocket. Mr Beckett takes no time at all, emerging quickly with lighter in hand. Once the two teachers begin to walk away, I roll the apple across the floor, wedging the door open just as it's about to close. I smile with satisfaction.

Running forward, I silently enter the room, heading straight over to Mr Beckett's desk. I produce a set of keys from my pocket, a keychain image of Mr Beckett and his wife and children and the teacher's car keys are attached.

'Next time you confiscate someone's football, keep a better eye on the keys in your jacket pocket,' I murmur, before unlocking the desk drawer. I could've picked the lock on the desk easily enough – a skill my brother taught me years ago – but it was much more challenging and fun to *borrow* them from Mr Beckett as he berated me. Always that extra challenge.

Inside the desk drawers are mobile phones, iPads, and a dozen other confiscated items from my classmates. In the deepest drawer at the bottom is a football – Duncan's football – but there is also one more item of note, one that I can't forget. A silver chain with a rose pendant. Hurrying, not knowing how much time I have left, I return all the items to the desks of their owners until I hear the door handle turn.

'Just got to get my keys!' Mr Beckett calls as he enters the classroom.

Ducking beneath the tables and desks, I run unseen, sliding through the now ajar doorway and leaping through the open window on the far side of the corridor. I fall amongst bushes, tumbling through the foliage with branches whipping my body and face until I hit the ground. Rolling as I land, the impact is still enough to drive the air from my lungs. Coughing and gasping for air, I stagger up and jog on, football still in my arms.

I head towards the playing field but I am brought to a sudden stop as three figures emerge before me. I know them; guys from my class. Thick, stupid, always eager to fight and steal – this is far from our first run in. I have no idea why they are still in college; their grades are as bad as their stench. There has been a rivalry between their leader, Shane, and I for years. It's been going on since way back to primary school. I can't even remember how it all began – probably over a girl.

'Hey, Hunter,' Shane, the tallest and broadest of them says. 'I was hoping we'd run into you. Time we had a little *chat*. What you got there for us?'

Tracking his eyes, I see he is looking at the thread of

necklace looping out of my pocket. In the sunlight it is shining brightly.

'Nothing for you morons,' I say, hiding the silver chain away.

'Oh, I think you're wrong,' the tall and stick-thin Frazer replies, face marked with acne and the odour of cigarettes about him.

'How's the head?' I ask with a grin, seeing the token of our last *chat,* a large bruise and bump above his right eye.

'I owe you big time for this,' he growls, pointing to his bruises.

'We all do,' adds the third of their group, the short and dim-witted Jamie.

'Do you guys really want to do this again?' I ask as they circle me. 'I mean, all this time you have only had yourselves to blame.'

'We owe you,' Shane says, hands becoming fists.

'C'mon, lads,' I say with a broad, unwavering smile. 'Three on one, that's not exactly fair. You need more guys!'

'Enough talk!' Jamie roars, fist flying towards me.

Dropping the football, I block the first and second punch until Frazer joins the assault, kicking at me and catching me with a fist, grazing my cheek. I twist away, hammering a punch into Frazer's stomach and catching him under the jaw just as Jamie charges in. I step aside with ease, allowing Jamie to thunder past me with his momentum. I kick the back of his leg, pushing him as he falls straight into Frazer, both crashing to the ground.

'There's still me,' Shane utters, trying to grab me, to wrestle me down. I pull away, leaping up onto the nearby windowsill and propelling off and over Shane, kicking him into the wall. His head strikes brick and he tumbles on top of his cronies. All three are moaning in pain.

'See you next time, lads,' I say, leaving them all on the ground as I pick up the football and begin to walk away.

'What's going on here, boys?' asks a voice, stopping me in my tracks.

'Nothing, Sir,' I reply, turning to face Mr Beckett. He makes no effort of hiding his lighter and cigarettes, eyeing us coldly with contempt; me in particular.

'It doesn't look like nothing,' he says. 'Mr Hunter, is that Duncan Bowen's football in your hands?'

'This ball, Sir?' I reply with a voice as innocent as I can make it. 'No, Sir. Brand new this one is.'

'Funny. It looks exactly like the one I confiscated today,' he says with suspicion.

'Can't be, Sir,' I say, holding back a smile. 'Duncan's ball is locked in your desk, third drawer down, Sir. Next to your mostly empty bottle of whiskey.'

'How do you know...' he begins to ask, but I don't give him a chance.

'Got to go, Sir,' I say, hurrying away, leaving Mr Beckett, Shane, and his moronic thugs behind me.

Emerging onto the playing field, my friends cheer again as they see my success. I kick the football high into the air towards them.

'Thought you wouldn't manage it this time,' yells Duncan, a tall and broad boy, always the joker, and my best friend. Thick, dark hair, a nose broken many times playing sports and the typical looks that all the girls fall for. He likes to think of himself as the most popular guy in school; he's captain of the football and athletics teams. He's probably right. Despite all that, Duncan and I are good friends, best friends even, always up to some kind of trouble.

'I haven't let you guys down yet, have I?' I grin.

'We'll see,' he replies. 'You about tonight? Thought we could head over the green and see what we can stir up.'

'Wish I could, mate, but not tonight,' I reply, my mood quickly sinking. 'Busy with... family stuff.'

'Your mother?' he asks, jokey tone now turned serious.

'Yep,' I say, revealing little as always. 'Nothing to worry about.'

'Okay. You change your mind about tonight, give me a call, or if things are... bad. You can kip round mine again if you want.'

'Thanks, mate,' I say, trying to shake the bad feeling. Why did he have to ask about my mother?

'Here comes trouble,' Duncan says, pointing towards a group of girls walking towards us.

'I hope you haven't forgotten about me,' a voice calls from among them.

The girls chat and giggle, but I only look to the one at their lead. She has long blonde hair, green eyes, and I have to admit, quite a nice smile despite her high and mighty attitude. Just like the rest of the girls, she wears her most flattering clothes to impress. Her name is Sara Starr, and if Duncan is the most popular guy, then she is most certainly the most popular girl. Pretty and always confident, I have to admit I have thought about asking her out on a date a few times, not that she would ever say yes.

'You sure took your time,' she calls over to me.

'I never thought I'd need to break *into* college,' I reply. 'Always planned how I'd break out.'

'What happened to you? Walk into a wall?' she asks, seeing the graze at my cheek and the growing bruise.

'Something like that,' I say, explaining away my run-in with Shane and the others.

'Guessing you found what I wanted?' she asks, showing a little too much eagerness to know of my success.

'Maybe,' I tease her.

'You want your motorcycle keys back then?' she says, taking my unclear answer as a yes.

'Keep them,' I tell her, trying my luck. 'How about you go to the End of Year Ball with me instead?'

'Trying to bribe a date out of me,' Sara taunts, her friends laughing with her. 'Not a chance, loser!'

'It was worth a shot,' I reply with a grin.

'So do you have it or not?' she asks, twirling a set of keys – my set of keys – around a finger.

I pretend to search through my pockets, showing empty hands before turning one over, an apple resting in my fingers.

'Your cheap tricks don't impress me,' she mocks.

'If it doesn't impress you then why are you smiling?' My grin broadens before I take a bite of the apple. Speaking sideways out of a full mouth, I attempt to be smooth, like one of those bad-boy movie stars from a time ago. 'Besides, it's a Granny Smith apple, the best of them all. Hardly cheap.'

I lift my other hand towards Sara, turning it slowly. Across the palm lays the silver necklace and its rose pendant.

'Thank you,' she says, quickly taking the necklace and inspecting it closely, forcing the keys into my hand. 'I should've known better than to wear it here with the *no jewellery* rules. It was my grandmother's before she...'

Tears well in her eyes, startling me. I have never seen her like this - sincere. I have no idea what to do, always uncomfortable around emotional girls like any guy my age. She surprises me by reaching out and hugging me tightly. The others tease us but I don't care. Sara lets go quickly.

'That means nothing you know,' she says, hurriedly wiping her face of tears. 'You're still a loser.'

'I know,' I reply with a grin.

I sometimes catch her looking my way, a smile on her lips before hastily sticking out her tongue or raising a solitary finger my way. She is like me, rebellious in her own way; thinks for herself and cares little for what everyone else thinks – or at least that's the impression she likes to give. When Mr Beckett confiscated her necklace, I promised her I'd get it back for her. That was one of my biggest faults – making promises.

'Thank you, Adam,' she whispers to me when no one else is looking. 'This means more to me than you know.'

'Any time,' I say, always eager for a challenge and a chance to impress.

'MR HUNTER!' The screech echoes across the playing field.

'Yes, Sp... I mean, Mrs Rhodes!' I yell back in annoyance as Sara paces away, back towards her friends, Duncan and the others are laughing loudly at my near use of our teacher's nickname.

'You are needed in the staffroom!' she yells with a face turning redder by the moment.

'Now?' I dare to ask.

'Yes, now! Before I drag you and the rest of your delinquent friends into detention again!'

'If it's about the football and Mr Beckett's desk drawer, I

can tell you now I know nothing about any of that, honest!' I protest, unable to conceal a grin. Everyone is laughing around me.

'It is not about any of that,' Mrs Rhodes says. 'Although, I am sure Mr Beckett would like a word with you later. No. This is about your brother.'

3

ADAM—Richmond, London, England

I don't slow for cars or red lights, weaving my way home without ever releasing the throttle. The bike is a 250cc Honda military bike, all of it painted black; over fifty years old, yet still roaring like it has just been built. It belonged to my father, restored and repaired when he was my age. The helmet is black and emblazoned with a silver arrowhead. The faded grey biker jacket had been his, too.

Cutting across streets and down alleyways, no apology shouted to pedestrians I scare as I mount pavements, I am focussed only on getting home, not caring for my own safety as Spike's words echo in my head. *He's missing.*

Hurtling around the final corner, drawing a cry of anger from a startled pensioner, I reach my house and skid to a halt in the stony drive as near to the entrance as possible. Beside my mother's car, a beat up blue Ford Focus, is another vehicle in the drive, a spotless black BMW with darkened windows. Propping my bike against the wall of the garage – the stand broken weeks ago – I hurry in.

I hear her voice first before I see any of them. The anger I recognise all too well, usually directed my way though. Even for her, this sounds bad.

She stands in the doorway, dark hair showing signs of greying, wrinkles around her tired eyes, but still strong, still healthy and more than capable. Her face is redder than I have seen in weeks, the anger unleashed. There are tears in her eyes, but her fury is unending. She is Jane Hunter, my mother.

'Get out!' she yells. 'Get out! This is on you, Charles! Haven't you done enough to this family already?'

The targets of her rage stumble away, my mother slamming the door behind them. One is a young woman, only a year or two older than me at a guess. Brown hair tied back, slightly pale skin, wearing glasses, faded jeans and a t-shirt emblazoned with a slogan from some show or a reference I don't recognise. She looks on aghast, hands still clutching the cup of coffee my mother must have made her.

'Well, that went brilliantly,' her older companion mutters through his moustache. He hadn't seen me and is now painfully aware that he shouldn't have said that. He fidgets awkwardly for a moment with his walking cane. Dapper. Old school. As if to punctuate the whole unfortunate incident, he sighs heavily. He's disappointed in me already.

'You must be Adam,' he says, forcing a smile and offering a handshake, which I ignore.

'And you must be the people who have pissed off my mother,' I reply back with as forced a smile. 'Who are you?'

'My name is Charles Lovell, and this is my associate, Abbey,' he says.

'Hi,' she says, a slight Irish accent to her voice. She still holds the coffee cup and avoids my gaze, awkward and still embarrassed.

'We work for the British Museum,' Charles says, as if that explains everything.

'That's lovely,' I reply sarcastically. 'What are you doing here, and why are you upsetting my mother? That's usually my job.'

'We are here about Matthew,' Charles explains.

'Your brother,' Abbey adds, before blushing and looking away, realising how pointless her words were.

'When was the last time you saw or spoke with your brother?' Charles asks.

'How do you know Matt?' I ask, stubbornly ignoring his question.

'We worked... work with your brother,' Abbey explains, changing her words and avoiding my gaze.

'How? Matt works in some stuffy office in central London. Something to do with stocks or finances. I don't know. It was all very boring whenever he tried to explain it. Whatever it was, I really doubt it had anything to do with museums.'

'Well, that is where you are wrong,' Charles says with a smugness that I really don't like. 'Matthew actually worked for me – sort of incognito – hence the alter-ego.'

'Matt never spoke of any of this, nor of you two,' I reply, distrustful of the strange pair. 'Nor did he like being called *Matthew*.'

'You very much are brothers,' he replies, sighing heavily again. 'In looks and attitude. Matthew hid the truth for your own protection. Why you'd need protection is something I cannot explain at this moment.'

'Matt was a...' Abbey begins to explain, her voice uncertain before looking to Charles.

'A consultant for us,' he finishes. 'He has been in our employ for a little over two years now. Matthew travels to dig sites and excavations and makes acquisitions on behalf of the museum.'

'He's good at it, too,' Abbey abruptly adds, before blushing and then looking away into her empty cup. I see in that moment that Abbey is soft on him. Matt always did have a way with girls.

'So, where is he?' I ask, unable to make sense of it all. 'I assume you know he is missing?'

'Yes, we do,' Charles states. 'That is exactly why we are here.'

'Matt went north to Scotland,' Abbey explains. 'A chamber was uncovered in the Highlands that was of historical importance. We lost contact with him three days ago.'

'How did you *lose* contact with him?' I ask angrily. 'Surely he wasn't doing that kind of thing alone. He must have had a team with him? Back up?'

Abbey and Charles exchange a look that fills me with instant dread.

'Matt was on his own, wasn't he?' I realise. 'No wonder my mother was angry with you.'

'It was... *is* Matt's way, to travel alone when he can,' Abbey stutters.

'Despite my protests,' Charles adds.

I want to punch him in that moment. The old codger is already trying to wheedle his way out of his responsibility.

'And from the rest of the team,' Abbey adds.

'I thought you said there wasn't a team?' I ask, but my question is ignored.

Abbey looks up again at Charles, who now looks like he's chewing on a bee.

'Look,' he says, getting irritated with both Abbey and me. 'It wasn't an official project. Matt can be... impetuous."

I laugh. Yeah, I guess he does know my brother.

'He headed up to Scotland under his own steam and without proper authority.' Charles stiffens. He's an arrogant sod. Probably more pissed at Matt not asking him permission than actually concerned over him being missing. Met his kind before – like Spike. They're all the same.

Abbey hurriedly explains, 'We didn't know he was there until he made contact, three days ago, already descending into the caverns.'

'Why postpone what can be done today?' I murmur under my breath.

'That's what your brother always says,' Abbey replies with a brief smile.

'That's what our father always said,' I correct her. 'So what happened to Matt down in those caverns? What was he looking for?'

'I cannot divulge that information,' Charles says, receiving a brief look from Abbey. 'As to what happened to him in the caverns, we cannot say either, and not because we don't have authority, but because we don't know.'

'Communication was cut and we have been unable to reach him for days,' Abbey interjects. Charles sighs with irritation and flashes her a look that tells her to rein it in.

'But you are looking for him?' I ask.

This time, before she answers, she looks to Charles, who nods his approval. She begins, 'We have teams searching for him, but the series of caverns are a maze, a total honeycomb. There are hundreds of passages built upon a river network making many unstable and unsafe for use. Two members of the search parties have already been badly injured. It's a slow process and as of yet there is no way to tell which passages he took.'

'Have you told the police he is missing?' I ask. 'Surely they should be helping with the search?'

'All available and suitable resources have been mobilised to search for Matthew,' Charles informs me snottily. I really don't like this guy.

'He could still be down there, trapped, injured...' I yell at them. This pair are idiots. Matt hasn't got a hope.

'We will find him,' Abbey stops me, placing a hand upon my arm for a moment. I shake her off. Who does she think she is?

'We will find him,' Charles agrees, though his tone gives me no reassurance, as if this whole matter is of annoyance to him. 'With your help, we can find him.'

Abbey pulls a notebook from her bag. Its cover is scarred in hundreds of scribbles, markings, and sketches, and the pages are thick with notes. I recognise the tattered book instantly.

'Matt's journal!'

Matt is old-school, using a paper notebook instead of anything electronic. By his thinking, electronic journals and tablets are too easily damaged, the possibility of records being erased or hacked and stolen too great to risk. He used his own hand written journal all his life, the same cover used over the years as fresh pages were tied in.

Suspicion grows in my mind. Why would this man and

woman, strangers to me except for their word they work with Matt, have the one possession he always kept on him, no matter where he went? My doubts grow.

'He never went anywhere without it,' I say, unable to hide the suspicion from my voice.

Abbey nods her head. 'He always had it with him at work.'

'It was found at the entrance to the caverns, along with his rucksack,' Charles states. 'We came here to ask for help in deciphering his notes. Everything he has written in the journal is encrypted. We believe his notes might include clues on how to find him down there.'

'I've tried everything I know, every code breaking system,' Abbey explains. 'Nothing has worked.'

I can't help but smile – I'm weirdly proud of him. Cryptology, using codes and cyphers, communicating in secret, numbers, letters, and symbols encoded to mean something completely different, to keep the true meaning hidden. The Enigma machines used by the Germans in World War Two, the best example, ever changing encryptions for their coded messages, unbreakable by anyone until the British at Bletchley Park cracked the sequences.

Ever since we were little, Matt and I had spoken in codes, sending messages our parents could not read; plans, mischief and wind-ups all concealed in the combinations of letters, numbers, and symbols. The combinations always changed; that was what made the codes unique, just like the Enigma machines, but the patterns were there if you knew what to look for. No one had ever managed to decipher our codes except our father. He taught us the tricks in the first place.

'We have spoken with Kathryn Berry already but she was unable to help us.' Charles taps his cane against the stones, his irritation clear

Matt's girlfriend, Kat. I wonder if she knew what Matt's real job was. Unreasoned jealousy suddenly burns within.

'Your mother was unable to help us too,' Abbey says.

Before she threw you out, I add in my head.

'She has... issues,' I say defensively, finally taking the cup out of Abbey's hand and placing it on the ground. Abbey hands me Matt's journal and I flick through the pages. To the untrained eye, it would simply look like the scribbles of a mad-man or child. Not to me.

On the first page I see the large writing and symbols, as if they are a title. I know the symbols instantly and I am shocked. Δ23W.It means ADAM. I translate the line beneath just as quickly. All our childhood games flooding back like a second language.

Do not let this fall into the wrong hands.

'Can you translate it?' Charles asks with urgency, eyes staring intently into mine.

The wrong hands.

I shake my head and twist my lips as if it is a hard challenge. 'I'm not sure. Maybe. I'd need some time. What did you say Matt was looking for?' I ask, looking only to the journal.

'We cannot tell you that,' Charles says sternly. 'But you think you might be able to translate the journal?'

'And you work with Matt?' I ask, purposely ignoring the question.

'Yes,' he snaps. 'We have already been over this. Can you translate it?'

I pause, re-reading the warning over and over again.

Adam

Do not let this fall into the wrong hands.

'Can you translate it?' Charles asks again, more forcefully, beginning to shout as his face reddens. Abbey turns away, hands visibly trembling, eyes shutting, fearful.

I shrug. 'There's a possibility, but I'm really not sure.'

Charles startles me then by gripping my arms with surprisingly strong hands, leaving his cane to sway precariously until Abbey tries to snatch it in mid-air. All she succeeds in doing is knocking it away farther, and she scrambles after it.

'Your brother could be in serious danger!' Charles

shouts in my face. There is something in him that has shifted. The mask has fallen. 'So I suggest you make up your mind pretty damned quickly if you can read it or not, because if you are lying to me, it could cost his life – and many others!'

Do not let this fall into the wrong hands.

'Adam, get in the house!' my mother shouts from the doorway. 'I told you two to clear off! Leave now before I call the police! You've caused enough harm here!'

'You are not helping anyone, especially Matthew!' Charles yells back at her as he snatches the journal out of my hands as I'm distracted by the two of them. 'We are trying to save your son, your brother, but you're not helping, dammit!'

'Find my son, Charles,' my mother warns him. 'Find him or I swear to God, I will make you pay.' There is something in the way she says his name that makes me falter. She knows him.

'You'd better go,' I warn.

'Thank her for the coffee,' Abbey says sheepishly before hurrying towards the car.

'Fine,' says Charles, rage subsiding, though no apology offered. He tucks Matt's journal away inside his jacket, pulling a business card out and offering it to me.

'Here, take this. If you think of anything that could help in the search for Matthew call me.'

Do not let this fall into the wrong hands.

Without thinking, I act. I've been fighting my anger for too long now. Taking the business card, I grip the arm of his business suit, pulling Charles close, and not caring if I'm hurting him or not. I suspect not; the old guy is surprisingly strong.

'You ever speak to me or my mother like that again and you will be sorry,' I whisper with low menace. 'If anything happens to Matt, I will be coming to you for answers. I promise you that.'

He looks undaunted, glaring straight back at me, daring me to say more.

Distract and act – he doesn't suspect a thing.

'Goodbye, Mr Hunter,' he says stiffly, pulling away from me and walking towards his car. There seems absolutely no need for his walking cane; the guy is remarkably light on his feet. I watch as they leave, waiting until they are gone before taking a deep long breath to calm myself before going inside.

In the hallway, I pass piles of papers and school books for marking; my mother's job as a history lecturer at the University of London ensures she's always busy. I am glad of it. When she focuses on her work, she's less focused on me.

Farther down the hallway, a large framed picture hangs upon the wall. It is of a middle-aged man, blonde hair and the same blue eyes as me. He is smiling in front of a snow-topped mountain. He is bathed in sunlight. He was always a keen climber.

'Hey, Dad,' I always say, placing a hand on the wooden frame briefly.

On the wall are more framed photos; my mother and father happy on their wedding day, of me when I was a baby, of the whole family on a camping holiday, and many more memories. My eyes settle upon the last one, of me and my brother. The photo is from a few years ago. Matt is only a little older than I am now. He has the same blonde hair as our father but he has our mother's green eyes and a mischievous look about him that I know is my own, too. Over his scruffy blonde hair is the baseball cap he always wears – dark blue with a crimson stripe down the centre. He doesn't go anywhere without that hat on – drives our mother crazy.

Around the photos are trophies and awards, all Matt's; not a single one is mine. He is the perfect student, perfect athlete, perfect son. He is the golden boy. I was never quite good enough to get an award.

There are three years between us. Matt is nineteen now. The age difference has never been an issue between us, nor was his success and my lack of it. We were really close when he lived at home, but now he lives with his girl-friend, Kat, and he has a boring job and boring life – or so I'd thought. How wrong I was.

'Why did you lie to us?' I ask.

Looking at that photo makes me miss our old life; back then I felt we were truly brothers.

'What did he want?' my mother asks, storming towards me like a freight train.

'To give me this,' I say, still holding the business card.

'You don't need that,' she declares, snatching the card from my hand and tearing it to pieces. 'Don't trust him or any of them.'

I've already made up my mind on that.

It's then I see tears in her eyes but she looks away, trying to fight them back.

'It's okay,' I say, placing an arm around her. 'Matt's going to be okay.'

'How can you know that?' she snaps, knocking me away. The anger I know too well is beginning to rise. 'You cannot promise me he will be okay.'

Here we go again.

'He lied to us,' she says. 'He lied to me. I'd never have let him join...'

'The museum?' I ask. 'Why not?'

'Just listen to me for once,' she orders. 'Stay away from Charles Lovell – and the rest of them.'

'He knows something about Matt...'

'I don't care what he knows!' she yells. 'Just do as you're told. Why do you always have to be so difficult? Why do you always have to disappoint me?'

'I know why you are angry,' I say, unable to stop myself from snapping back. 'Your prized son, your pride and joy, he lied to you. He lied to both of us. He didn't tell us about the museum, his work, any of this. Now he's missing and I bet that you're just worried that you're going to be stuck with me. Oh, the disappointment!'

'What I am angry about is that you are still riding that bike!' She is yelling now, her rage unleashed. There's no going back now. 'It's illegal for you to ride that death trap!'

'Don't worry, maybe it'll prove to be a *death trap* as you keep calling it. Then you'll just be left with your perfect son! Oh, wait, he's missing too!'

'You're nearly seventeen years old! When are you going to stop being so childish and stu...'

'Stupid? Go on, say it. Call me stupid again. Well, I'm sorry I'm not as great and clever as Matt, but I'm not the one who has been lying to you and who has gotten himself lost.'

'Don't speak about your brother like that!'

'You're right. How dare I speak against Saint Matt. I've never been good enough, have I? Not worthy compared to Matt.'

'No, you haven't.' There is nothing but spite in her eyes.

I'm winded by her brutal honesty. I can barely speak. 'N...no mother should ever say that! You really are a bitch!' I blurt out, already disgusted by myself, but more angry that she should reduce me to this.

Her reaction is a raised hand, ready to strike.

'Go on,' I whisper. 'Do it again. It's been a while.'

Her hand trembles but holds still, the fire in her eyes still raging.

'If I was the one missing, would you even care?' I ask.

She doesn't answer.

'Thanks,' I simply say, unable to do anything else. Angry, hurt, torn up inside, I feel all of it.

I hurry up the stairs to my bedroom. Now I am the one who is fuming. I kick over the chair at my desk. I turn on the radio and crank up the volume, skipping through the stations quickly.

'...the city in Morocco has been evacuated with fire crews still tackling the inferno. Eye witnesses report of seeing strange blue flames... the weather will be mostly sunny... the seventh museum robbery this month across Europe, Roman artefacts the thieves targets including armour, coins and pottery including vases...'

Finally, I find a station with music; loud music. Rock, metal, drum and bass, the louder the better as long as it has a decent beat. I hear my mother shouting to turn it down, but in reply, I turn the volume as loud as it'll go. Standing there in the middle of my room, I clamp my eyes shut, hands clenched into fists. She is always like this, caring little for me and only ever praising Matt. She would never lift a hand towards him, not like she has with me. I will never be worthy.

As the anger passes, I open my eyes. Around me is my room, a cluttered mess of clothes, football gear, an upturned dismantled BMX bike, and scattered CDs. In the corner of the room is a bow, a recurve, scratched and marked that I have meant to repair for weeks. Trophies and awards from its use in competitions cover a small shelf nearby. Even those achievements were never good enough – not proper enough to grace the trophy wall downstairs. Apparently, 'Those awards don't count.'

On the wall behind the desk is a world map, a dozen pins denoting visited countries, and stuck to the sides of the map are hundreds of notes, plans for future travels. Every day I look at that map, every morning when I wake and night before I sleep. I long to see the world, all of it. It's those destinations my mind wanders to while I am supposed to be studying at college.

There are tears across the map, stuck back together by tape. That was another of her rants, telling me that I'd never make anything of myself and to give up my fantasies of seeing the world. That was when she turned on the map.

Map... location... Matt.

'The journal.'

Picking up the fallen chair, I quickly sit at my desk, taking the journal out from inside my jacket, taken when I threatened Charles Lovell. Distract and act, or another cheap trick as Sara would say. Stealing as others would call it. With Matt's encrypted warning, I had no choice but to act.

As I look through the pages, I focus initially on the words underlined, knowing these would be names of people or places. Very few of the scrambled combinations of letters, numbers, and symbols are people. The name 'Dave' features a few times. I have no idea who he is. Cuba, Morocco, Venice, Cairo, Mexico, Jamaica, Moscow are just some of the places listed in the journal. Each word would've taken an expert de-coder to unravel but not me, the youngest of the Hunter brothers. Matt has always been good with codes but we both know that I am better. For some reason, no matter how scrambled and encrypted the words and letters, my mind is able to unravel the mystery they hold. Strangely, I am awful at foreign languages.

On the last page, I see the name Scotland, followed by the words Loch Lomond. Pulling open my laptop, I search for a map of the area, seeing Loch Lomond lays thirty miles north-west of Glasgow, over four hundred miles from London. The loch itself is a large expanse of water on the Scottish mainland, an impossibly large area to search for one solitary cave. Reading through the final page again, I see one word jump out, not underlined but marked with the faintest of stars at its corner, an attempt to avoid drawing interest but highlight it. The word doesn't make sense for a long time until looking to the map on my laptop's screen again I see an unfamiliar place name, Inchlonaig, one of the dozen islands at the heart of the loch.

'That's where Matt is,' I say to the empty room.

My bedroom door flies open, crashing hard into the wall behind.

'TURN THAT BLOODY MUSIC DOWN!' my mother screams. She repeats it again and again until I finally lower the volume, quickly covering up Matt's journal in case she sees it and recognises it.

'I'm going to work,' she tells me. 'I need some peace and quiet.'

'What about Matt?' I dare to ask.

'He'll be okay,' she says with no certainty in her voice. 'I need to think this all over. He'll be okay. He's always okay. And don't even think about taking that bike out again,' she warns me. 'I've locked it up. I mean it this time!'

'So you didn't mean it all the other times?'

'You know what I mean, smart-ass,' she replies. 'You take the bike out again and I will sell it.'

'No you won't,' I say with certainty.

The bike belonged to her husband, and there is no chance that she will ever let go of that part of him. She has a faint smile on her lips sometimes, memories of him, I am certain, never truly gone, never forgotten by any of us. Sadly, I don't see that side of her very often.

'Just keep the music down!' my mother warns. 'And clean this room, it's a disgrace!' She slams the door shut behind her. Her heavy footsteps thunder through the house followed by the slamming of the front door.

'Bye,' I whisper in her wake.

Leaning back in my chair, eyes closed as a hundred thoughts run through my head, one comes to me clearer than the others. *He's missing.*

My brother's last known location was in a cave, presumably on that island in Scotland. Charles, and whoever it is he works with, are searching for my brother, but are they friend or foe? Would they help Matt? Or are they after him for another reason? They'll return soon once they realise the journal is missing. I have to decide what to do.

Rarely do my head and heart agree; for once, they are in unison.

I know I have to find him.

I print maps of the island, the loch, and surrounding areas, noting down the roads I will travel on my journey north. Alongside the journal, I pack a change of clothes, a pair of climbing gloves and a set of worn hiking boots. I place the maps and my laptop into the rucksack, which is as frayed and faded as my father's biker jacket. Into my pockets go my wallet –including all the money I have on me – a family credit card meant for emergencies, my pen-knife, a box of matches, and my mobile phone, along with a spare solar charging unit. Downstairs, in the kitchen, I take some packet soups, bread, cheese, a few apples, and a couple of bottles of water. I need to minimise my need to use the credit card as it could be easily tracked. From the understairs cupboard, I grab the old camping gas unit, the army cooking tin, and a flashlight – it's not much, but I have limited space, even with the bike paniers I've already recovered from the shed. From a drawer, I gather a smaller torch and plenty of spare batteries. Suddenly, it pops into my head to remember a black lightbulb, knowing Matt's methods of hiding things and communication. It's a long shot but I find one right at the back of the odds and sods kitchen drawer. Mum had kept us well stocked when we went through our spy stage when we were younger.

Lastly, I write a note for my mother. We argue all the time and she is always angry and disappointed in me, but I can't just leave without telling her. Especially not with Matt missing.

As I pack the last of the food, the home telephone begins to ring. I ignore it and the call goes through to the answering machine.

'Jane... Jane, it's Kathryn. It's about Matt. These people came to my house, said they worked with Matt, something about a museum. I don't understand it... none of it...' She breaks down in tears and I hurry to pick up the phone.

'Kat. Kat, it's Adam. It's going to be okay.'

'Adam, I don't know what's happening. They told me Matt works for their museum. He told me nothing about any of that. And now he's missing. I don't know what to do. I haven't heard from him in days. He always calls, always...'

'I promise you he'll be okay,' I tell her.

'Don't make promises you can't keep,' she warns me.

'I swear it. He's probably just gotten himself lost or stuck somewhere. Matt will be fine, you'll see.'

Her voice breaks down into tears again and I have no idea what to say.

'Adam... I'm pregnant.'

Okay, so that blows my mind for a moment. 'You're pregnant? Does Matt know?'

'No. I was going to tell him at the weekend. We were planning on going away.'

If my mind was not already made up before then it is now.

'I'll find him, Kat,' I tell her. 'I'll find Matt and I'll bring him home.'

'Adam, don't...'

'I'll find him,' I say one last time before hanging up.

Hoisting the rucksack over my shoulder and wrestling the biker jacket, helmet, and paniers, I head out of the house full of purpose. I'm stopped in my tracks when I see my father's old motorcycle. The wheels are wrapped in chains with the biggest padlocks I have seen yet.

'Well played,' I whisper with a grin.

Setting down my stuff, I pull out two thin metal rods from a pocket, one the width of a needle, and the other only slightly wider. Kneeling down in front of the bike, I begin my work, easing the rods into the locks, probing, applying pressure and turning until the gears inside click into place. The first three are easy and straightforward, but the last is trickier, a smaller lock needing to be released before the main mechanism can be reached. In my eagerness, the needle-sized rod snaps.

'Please don't be stuck, please don't be stuck, please don't be stuck,' I pray, thanking all manner of deities when the remnants of the rod comes away cleanly. Luckily, I always carry a spare, remembering another of my father's sayings. 'Always be prepared'.

It takes a total of four minutes and thirty-eight seconds to free the motorcycle, though I know I can do better. Using the locks, I wrap the chains around the statue of a naked woman in the centre of the garden, mounted above a fountain – I have always hated that statue – and make sure to place the chains and locks over its more embarrassing features.

'At least that's given you a bit more decency,' I say, imagining the look on my mother's face when she returns home. It would be priceless to see but I must go.

I turn my father's motorcycle and start the engine.

'Next stop, Scotland.'

4
_____

ADAM—Hadrian's Wall, England

It takes seven hours to travel from London to Inchlonaig by car. On a motorcycle, it's quicker, but more painful. I stop a couple of times, the last at a petrol station to refuel the bike and stretch my legs. The feeling of blood rushing through to my toes instantly gives me pins and needles.

Looking out across the horizon, the sun is beginning to set in the distance. I can see the remnants of Hadrian's Wall and I recall my history lessons; one of the few subjects I pay attention to... well, most of the time.

Ancient Rome, having seized control of most of Europe and parts of Africa, had invaded Britain and conquered much of it, only the north proved to offer significant resistance. The wall was built by the Romans by order of Emperor Hadrian to better defend the southern regions of

Britain from the aggressive Caledonians and barbarians of the north.

The wall was once an impressive fortification, so my teacher said. Now, very little remains, ruined and torn down by time, war, and nature. Most think the wall is the barrier between Scotland – known as Caledonia by the Romans back then – and England, but in reality, there are still a few miles to go before the border crossing. On one of our camping trips in the Highlands, when I was much younger, Matt and I walked across the top of a section of the wall near Birdoswald Fort. Our mother yelled at us to get down before we fell off, but our father laughed the whole time.

Thinking of my parents, I take out my mobile and turn it on. Sure enough, I quickly receive a dozen missed call notifications from my mother and a few from Kat, each leaving a voicemail. I don't need to listen to them as text messages arrive as well, all stating I should return home and not to do anything foolish. I scan through them for mention of my brother's sudden return, but this hope quickly vanishes. They do, however, mention that Matt's supposed co-workers want the journal back. I chuckle, imagining the look on Charles' moustached face when he realized it was gone.

Of all the notifications, it's Kat's last one that hits me hardest.

Thank you. x
Kat

Looking through the rest of my messages, I see a few from Duncan, asking me what Mrs Rhodes wanted, if I am available for football, and if I have finally asked Sara to the End of Year Ball. Reading on, it's clear he knows what is happening.

Your mother told me everything, in between her
interrogations to find out where you are. Good
luck in searching for Matt. Need anything, give
me a shout.
Duncan.

He has always been a good friend. Whenever I needed somewhere to stay, when things with my mother were too much, Duncan would always have me round. I spent a fair few nights with him and his family over the years. They were the perfect family, loving parents, happy and always welcoming; what a family should be like. No anger. No lies.

I send him a quick reply.

Thanks mate. I'll keep you updated. Keep my
mother calm. If anyone can it's probably you.

Perfect son, perfect student, perfect athlete, so of

course my mother thinks the world of Duncan too; another person I can't match up to. I don't begrudge him any of it though. We have been mates for too long for that.

> **P.S. Yes I asked Sara, she shot me down. Not all of us have your easy charm!**

He must be near his phone as he replies straight away.

> **Not all of us can be so lucky! ;) Take care of yourself mate. Find Matt. Bring him home.**
> **Duncan.**

I mean to turn off my mobile phone again, ready to set out on hopefully the last part of my journey, but before I can, I receive one more text message and from the most unlikely source.

> **Saw Duncan while out shopping for end of year dress. Got some awesome things, spent a fortune!! Duncan told me everything. Don't do anything stupid, like usual, you loser. x**
> **Sara S**

I can't help but laugh. More focussed on her dress shopping than my missing brother of course. At least she showed some concern, I think. I send a quick reply, unable to resist.

Stupid? Me? No idea what you mean.

Taking out my laptop and resting it upon the bike's seat, I log on to the service station's free Wi-Fi. I load up the previous search pages about my destination, Loch Lomond and the island of Inchlonaig. I search for anything about caves in the area or clues as to where Matt could've gone but see nothing of worth. There are mentions of findings in the loch, of armour and weaponry, possibly Briton and Roman in origin from some unknown and unrecorded battle. Apart from that, there is nothing of notable worth, meaning I will need to go through Matt's journal for any further clues or directions to the cave. I have no idea how long that will take, all depending on my brother's encryption. For now, all I have to go on is the name of the loch and the island.

There are monitors on the outside walls of the petrol station broadcasting the news, updates on the fires in Morocco before the breaking story of another reported museum robbery.

'There's never any good news, is there,' I mumble to myself. As if timed to perfection, my phone rings.

'More bad news,' I say to myself before answering the call. 'Hi, Mother.'

'Where the hell are you?' she screams down the phone at me.

'Didn't you see my note?' I reply, trying to keep calm.

'I told you not to be so stupid!'

'He's my brother,' I tell her firmly. 'I can't just do nothing. Those people from the British Museum...'

'I don't care about them!'

'But Matt's journal...?'

'I don't give a damn about that either! You need to come home now!'

'Listen to me, please...'

'No! You come home now!'

'I can't. No.'

'Why do you always have to be so stubborn?'

'Where do you think I get that from?'

'And the stupidity? The foolishness? Your brother certainly has none of that!'

'I'm just not good enough, am I?' I rant back. 'I'm not worthy of your support or anything else!'

In a rage, I throw the phone against the wall of the petrol station, drawing the attention of everyone nearby. Some laugh, some snigger, and the rest pretend I'm not there. Only one person stares right at me. Sat on her motorcycle, black helmet covering her face with long red and purple hair hanging loose, she looks only at me through her visor. I ignore the gaze, picking up my phone and inspecting the damage. The screen is cracked, case dented, but the phone still works well enough.

'Why does she always have to be like that?' I mutter.

Walking back to my bike, I hear others taunting and mocking me for my show of anger. I don't care. I look back towards the biker girl but she and her motorcycle are gone. Turning off the mobile, I tuck it into a pocket and start up the bike's engine.

'Onwards to Scotland,' I say to myself, pulling on the helmet and setting the bike back onto the motorway.

5

ADAM—Loch Lomond, Scotland

I reach my destination a few hours after nightfall, the loch as quiet as the roads and no light coming from the island at its centre. Looking out across the waters, I feel the fear threaten, rising within, hands beginning to sweat, knowing that dizziness and worse could follow. Past memories flood my mind; sheer dread, terrifying horror, water everywhere, choking, unable to breathe, and the coming unescapable fate. All of it hits me at once, my heart pounding, and I struggle to breathe as I look towards the waters.

All I can do is turn away, breathing deep until the fear passes. I curse myself. I knew I was heading for a loch, a mass of water. I should've prepared myself, knowing the fear would take hold, but in my haste to find Matt, I hadn't even considered it. I must cross the water to find him. It's my only choice. I urge the bike on towards the nearest house, a little cottage with lights on and smoke pouring skywards from the chimney. A sign hangs from the roof: *Lomond Boat Hire*.

All manner of boats are moored outside the cottage; ferries big enough to transport a handful of cars, to smaller day-hire craft secured to the small jetty. From the looks of them, damp and muddied, most of the boats have been in use today.

Leaning the bike against a large yew tree, old by the looks of it, I take off my helmet, resting it on the seat. The cold air hits me like a bucket of icy water, and any tiredness I felt disappears. My breath hangs in the air; winter is fast approaching. Standing feels good and the blood is keen to return to my feet.

I pull on my worn hiking boots just as the pins and needles set in again, and then I hurry towards the house, stumbling in the darkness. From inside, a woman's jovial voice sings. I knock but there is no answer. The music is drowning me out. I knock so hard it hurts my knuckles. The door opens quickly and an elderly man in overalls with thinning white hair and a thick Santa Claus beard greets me.

'Thank you so much, fella,' he says in a rolling brogue. I smile as he pulls foam plugs from his ears. 'The singing ne'r ends. Can't stand it myself but it keeps the wife happy.' He checks his watch, surprised by the time. 'Should ye be out this late, kiddo? I was about to go to bed myself, if she ever shuts up. I'll warn ye, if ye're selling, we ar'n buying and me wife detests salesmen. If you think her singing's bad, ye should see her angry.'

'Are you talking about me again?' I hear the man's wife and then she appears beside him, with an unending friendly smile.

'Good to meet ye, young man,' she greets me, wiping a strand of red hair from her ruddy face. 'I'm Gillian, and this old goat is me husband, Mike.'

'Adam,' I reply. She shakes my hand with vigour. Her husband just looks bemused. I am beginning to like this couple.

'Are ye here to learn more about our fair loch?' she asks me. 'The famous outlaw Rob Roy's cave to the north that he used as a hideout perhaps? Or the legends of this being the home to the Lady of the Lake, where King Arthur's sword Excalibur was drawn? The tree of Robert the Bruce, King of Scots, who won Scotland's independence from the tyranny of you English?' She jests me with the last point, smiling broadly and prodding me in the chest with a finger.

I am being dragged inside as she speaks. 'Or perhaps the monster of the loch itself? Aye, the bloodthirsty beast that has plagued us for centuries? Red eyes glowing in the darkest of nights across its waters, its roars making the very loch tremble.'

'Monster?' I ask with uncertainty, thinking of the water and the fear it instils in me without its own horror lurking beneath the waves.

'Enough, Gilly. Let the boy speak.' Mike quietens her. 'What are you here for, lad?'

'I'm looking to get over to Inchlonaig,' I say. 'I can pay for a ride or to hire a boat.'

'You want t' traverse the jewels of the crown? That's what we call the islands. Well, you'll have to wait until morning, I'm afraid. No boats on the water once the sun goes down.'

'I need to get over there as soon as possible.'

'You better start swimming then,' he jokes. Seeing the flash of frustration is enough to show him I don't find it funny.

'Sorry, but those are the rules,' he says, returning to the subject. 'You're not part of that big group that went over there a couple of days ago, are ye? If so, I'm sorry to say they're all gone, shipped out before sundown. Had all kinds of equipment, searching for something, I think. Left my boats in a helluva state, I tell you.'

'Who were they?'

'Damned if I know, but they paid bloody well to get all

their gear over there and to ask no questions. God knows what they did to the poor island.'

I think of Charles Lovell and Abbey. They said they had search teams looking for Matt, or perhaps they were only after whatever had drawn Matt to this island. If they were looking for my brother, then why did they stop? Why did they take all their equipment with them? Why did they give up?

Taking out my mobile, I turn it on and flick through my contacts until I reach Matt's and his bio photo.

'You haven't seen this guy in the past few days, have you?' I ask them. I'm now in the kitchen and Gillian is making tea.

'My memory is-neh what it was,' Mike says, peering at the image.

'Fading like the rest of you,' his wife mocks.

'Sorry, lad. Can't say I've seen him, but there's been a lot of folk passing through here in the past few days. All sorts of buzz about that island, but from what I've seen, everyone's returned empty-handed.'

'Any idea what it was all about?' I ask, taking an offered mug of tea with a silently mouthed *thank you*.

'Nope, neh a clue,' Mike says.

'Whole world's gone crazy if you ask me,' Gillian adds. 'Snowing in the Sahara, an entire city burning in Morocco, more shooting stars than ever seen before, the blood moon, and now all this fascination over one of our little islands.'

'Does anybody live on the island?'

'A few holiday homes, but at this time of year, they're all empty,' Mike says. 'With those teams returned there should be no one on the island.'

'And there's no way I can get across?'

'Not until dawn. Then I will be happy t' take yer over myself.'

'He's your brother, isn't he?' Gillian asks, looking at Matt's image and then to me. 'I see the resemblance.' She retrieves a Tupperware box from the side and flips it open to reveal a treasure trove of homemade shortbread. My stomach almost growls with the smell of buttery sweetness. I hadn't realised how hungry I was until this moment. She offers it out to me.

'Thank you,' I say, unashamedly selecting the biggest piece from the tub.

'He's been missing for three days,' I say. 'Four now with this one ending. His last known whereabouts was on that island.'

'Have you told the police?'

'Yes,' I lie, feeling immediately guilty. These are good people and lying to them seems wrong. 'But they've been no help.'

I bite into the shortbread and moan – it's the most amazing thing I have ever eaten.

'Good, eh?' Gillian laughs. 'Me mother's recipe, and hers before that.'

'Aye, our Gilly makes the best darn shortbread in Scotland!'

For a moment we are quiet. We are still strangers, events bringing us together. They exchange looks and shake their heads. 'There's certainly something strange 'bout it all, me lad.'

'I have to find him. He's my brother. Are you sure there's no way across tonight? I can offer money.' I say, scrabbling around in my pocket with the hope that actually seeing the money might tempt him.

'Mike, can't ye...' Gillian begins, sensing my distress.

'I'm sorry, but if I help yer across and folks around here got t' know, and they will, trust me, then I'll be in all kinds of trouble from the authorities. I've lost one boat already this week, pinched by some crooks – not that the police cared. Besides, it's just not safe in this light, what with the rocks scattered throughout the loch – especially with no clear moon to light our way.

'There's no way?'

'Sorry, son,' Mike says, shaking his head and standing. It's my signal it's time to leave. I follow him out and he stops me at the door. 'There's hotels further up the road where you can stay. Goodnight. I'll see you in the morning.'

I'm left standing outside, not knowing what my next

move should be. I could wait until morning, but Matt might need me if he is still trapped in those caverns beneath the island. He could be injured or dying of hunger and thirst after four days down there. My brother needs me. I could try another of the companies along the edge of the loch, but if Mike wouldn't do it, it's unlikely any of the others will. Swimming is out of the question; it wouldn't help Matt if I drowned.

Defeated, I begin to walk back towards my bike. I have vague plans of making some soup and building up my strength, but my attention is brought to the hills above where a strange light is shining. It remains for a few moments and I'm captivated – that is until the roar of a motorcycle engine echoes down the valley and diverts me.

A whistle comes from the house behind me. I turn back. Gillian is at the second floor window and she throws something to me; it's a set of keys with a note wrapped around them.

KEEP QUIET AND BRING IT BACK BY MORNING. IV27

Looking back to the window, I see she has a finger to her lips. Before I can ask her anything, she has disappeared inside and closed the window.

'Thanks, Gillian,' I whisper.

I look back towards the hills but the light and the sound of the motorcycle are gone.

'Doesn't matter,' I tell myself, keys in hand. I hurry towards the boats, trying to step as lightly as I can on the gravel and then onto the wooden boards of the jetty.

I search for IV27 across the side of each craft, knowing it must be an identifier. Across the hull of one of the smaller boats, I find it, the craft big enough for around ten people with a large outboard engine at the back. The sight of black sloshing water around the boat halts me. The dizziness threatens, and my heart hammers in my chest as the fear threatens to overwhelm me. *Think of Matt*, I tell myself. *He needs you.*

I untie the ropes, securing the boat to the jetty and then, summoning all the courage I have, jump on-board, cursing as I slip and bang my knee hard into the side. I stop and wait a few moments, ducking out of sight in case my crash-landing alerted anyone to my 'borrowing' of the craft. Peeking over the side, I see no signs of discovery, the door to Mike and Gillian's house unmoving.

The dashboard of the boat is, thankfully, vaguely familiar. My father, the great outdoors type, had taken Matt and I on regular fishing trips in a friend's boat. I put the keys into the outboard and shift the lever straight up into the neutral position, remembering all that my father taught me. That was back when my fear of water didn't exist, when I enjoyed swimming and diving. That was before I nearly died, and when my father was still alive.

The engine is cold so I pull the choke out first. It

doesn't make for the quietest exit. I check the house quickly for signs of movement and pop the choke back in. The engine is now running smoothly and I guide the boat away from the shore with the throttle arm.

With my free hand, I take out the larger flashlight from my rucksack, using its powerful beam to light the way. My printed map of the islands is now laid out over my lap. I instantly see why Mike was cautious of crossing the loch at night; masses of rocks rise out of the water unexpectedly with the tide, forcing me to veer the boat away several times. I should travel slowly but the need to find Matt overrules me and I urge the boat on as fast as it can go. I hear the hull grind against rock more times than I'd like, but no water floods into the boat and it's not sinking, yet.

To my left, I can only just make out a half dozen islands to the south, but my destination is northwards, at the very centre of the loch. I see it in the darkness, a land mass that grows with every moment. The island of Inchlonaig. Covered from shore to shore in trees. To the south, a few buildings are visible, cottages mostly which flank a small bay. I aim for the bay, seeing no other spot to moor up.

Taking hold of the bow line rope, I jump ashore. Gripping the tree tight until the fear passes again, I slowly back away onto the safety of dry land. I tie the boat to the tree trunk, keeping it in the water without grounding, not wanting to damage Mike and Gillian's vessel more than I already probably have. I will owe the couple for that, but hell, Matt can pay them, if I ever find him.

There are tracks from the machinery and equipment, and from the looks of it, the cottages have been occupied lately too. There are rubbish bags outside, and dry wood by the door. But it's abandoned now. I'm certain of that. You can just feel the emptiness. Following the tracks, I note they all lead in the same direction – towards the centre of the island.

Taking out Matt's journal, I flick to the page with Loch Lomond and Inchlonaig. I begin to decipher more of the page as I walk. It's difficult. My brother's encryptions were never easy to translate, especially in the gloom and when I'm trying to keep my footing. Amongst the letters, numbers, and symbols, I start to spot patterns. The words, HEART, BEEHIVE, WATER, and COIN rise from the maze. Seeing the word WATER sends a cold knot through my stomach and I dread to think what Matt meant by it.

The last word is different, a solitary symbol, a bird with outstretched wings. I've never seen that symbol before in Matt's writings, no clue as to what it means. Apart from that, there is little else; no clues as to the exact route or caverns Matt used. I will need to find him the old-fashioned way – by looking.

I hear the movement of branches in the darkness, something big forcing its way past trees and bushes. At first I think I was mistaken earlier, and it's part of the team

Mike helped transport to the island. I duck down behind a fallen tree trunk, listening intently. I sigh with relief when I hear the sniffing of an animal, but then I'm gripped by new fear, remembering Gillian's warning of the monster of the loch. A story that sounds childish in the cold light of day, but not now, not in the dark when you're all alone.

Backing away, it comes closer and at speed until it's almost on me. I draw back my flashlight, ready to use it as a make-shift weapon. Horns burst through the bushes and I fall back, yelling out in warning, trying in vain to scare off the terrible beast. Laughter escapes my lips as a rough tongue licks my face. The terrible horns were not horns at all but antlers. The monster was no terror, but a deer – a really friendly one at that. I stroke the animal's soft fur, surprised by the domesticity of the creature.

'Jeez, you gave me a fright!'

Our friendly moment is broken by the sound of an immense roar, horrific and bestial, from the far side of the island. The deer bolts, disappearing into the darkness as quick as it can run. I wait in silence, watching and listening. When I hear it again, I'm certain it's closer. I force myself up and run at full speed, following the tracks until I enter a clearing and almost fall down into the vast crater at its centre.

I am barely breathing. I listen intently but hear nothing. Calming, I begin to take in my surroundings, and the strange crater. The ground has been dug up to expose the entrance to the caverns below. Above the space are two entwined trees, the bulk of their branches wrapping together to form a heart shape. Maybe that's what Matt meant in his journal by the message, BENEATH THE HEART.

Around me, I see where men and machines have made their impact, clawing open the entrance to the caverns below and clearing the surrounding area. It looks ugly – hardly as if much archaeological care has been taken. There are hundreds of footprints, tyre marks and abandoned empty crates. Some of the equipment; ropes, helmets, and all manner of kits have been left behind too. Whoever those people were, they left in a hurry.

Peering over the edge and into the darkness of the cavern, the flashlight penetrates the gloom. I look over the discarded equipment and break open a crate marked CHEMSTICKS. Inside are dozens of translucent plastic tubes, filled with fluids that when mixed by the cracking of the tubes, creates glowing light. In short, they are large glowsticks, not much different to those used in bars and clubs, not that I am supposed to know about that at my age. I stuff a dozen into my rucksack and crack another handful, throwing them into the cavern.

Green, red, and blue lights shine from the tubes, giving the strange effect of a disco roughly a hundred feet down, the same as a ten storey building. It's alarmingly deep and I find no proper abseiling gear amongst the abandoned equipment, but the lengths of rope I discover should do the job well enough. I take out my climbing gloves, enjoying a moment of smug satisfaction at my own excellent planning, before making one last sweep of my surroundings with the flashlight. I see nothing and hear no more of the monstrous roars from before. Tucking the flashlight into a pouch on my rucksack, and gripping the rope with both hands, I run and jump down into the cavern.

The air whips past me, the sound deafening as I fall and my stomach lurching as the ground rapidly approaches. I can only pray that I haven't misjudged the length of the rope. Thankfully, fear of falling is not on my list of phobias. In fact, I have to admit, I enjoy the ride. I come to a sudden stop mere inches from the bottom. Mission Impossible indeed. I smile. *Reckless as always*, as others would tell me. *Anything to get the adrenaline pumping*, my reply.

I lower myself to the uneven rock floor and untie the rope from around my waist. The chemsticks bathe the cavern in their luminous light but they no longer look like a disco. They have taken on an ominous light, the reds making my surroundings demonic and hellish. All kinds of equipment is scattered around me. I have no idea what much of it is or what it might do, but it's more evidence that my predecessors left in a hurry.

Looking to the walls, it's clear now what Abbey meant

by honeycomb, and also the meaning of Matt's note, BEEHIVE. Across the walls are hundreds of tunnels, some barely wide enough for a rabbit to fit down, whereas many others a fully grown man could squeeze into. It's clear from the markings on the walls and the outlay of the remaining tools which of the tunnels have been searched, but there are many remaining.

Taking out Matt's journal, I scan the page again, focusing on the line that mentions BEEHIVE. The letters, symbols, and numbers give nothing else to me, no clues as to which route Matt used, just useless information about the structure of the cavern, the composition of the walls, moisture levels and such. None of it helps me find my brother.

'C'mon, Matt. I know you'd have left a sign,' I whisper. I peer into a few of the tunnels with the flashlight. 'Stop hiding from me. Hiding... a hidden message...'

I remember the black lightbulb and Matt's way of masking things in plain sight. Taking the bulb from my rucksack, I screw it into the flashlight.

'Show me the way, Matt,' I say, a grin growing across my face as I sweep the light across the cavern in the slowly dimming light of the chemsticks.

There it is, on the far side, glowing luminously, UV paint marking an X at the base of one of the tunnels.

'X marks the spot. Very cheesy, Matt.' I laugh. He knew I would come for him.

Using the tunnels below for footing, I climb up to the marked entrance. Unhooking the straps of the rucksack, I push it into the tunnel, knowing I can't fit inside with it on my back. I draw a smaller torch from the pack before heaving myself up and into the tunnel after it, the space tight but just big enough.

'I hope you haven't put on weight, Matt,' I say, struggling on.

It's slow going and my hands and knees hurt after only a few minutes of crawling in the stone tunnel. Pushing my rucksack before me is burning my arms. I'm already covered in cuts and scrapes where the harsh rock walls have caught my arms and legs. Spiders bigger than my fist scuttle across their broken webs.

After what I guess must have been an hour, which has nearly broken me, my rucksack suddenly falls away from my grasp. I leap forward, leaning over the sudden end of the tunnel, and grab onto one of the straps just before it's out of my reach and lost to the sudden cliff edge.

'Nearly,' I say, pulling the rucksack back to me. 'Woah!'

Beneath me there is an abrupt drop that ends roughly eighty feet down. At the bottom is a flowing river, cutting the vast cavern into two. My torch provides the only illumination and it falls on the far wall across the river. At the very back of the cavern, right in the centre, chiselled into the rock is an eagle, much like that from my brother's journal.

'MATT!' I call. My echo is the only reply. I shout a few more times but hear nothing except the running river. With no clear way across, my heartbeat begins to increase. All that crawling for nothing – and yet, Matt had found a way.

'One step at a time,' I tell myself, peering directly down to the rocks below me.

I look outside the tunnel for a foothold to begin my climb down but I am surprised to find to the right of me is a rope. It is secured to the wall by a piton hammered into the rock. Matt must have used it in his descent, but there is no sign of a harness. Cracking three more chemsticks, I drop them to the cavern floor below. At least I'll not have to wrestle a torch as I'm swinging from the rope.

'No worries,' I say to myself as I grip onto the rope tightly and swing my legs around so that I can place my boots against the wall. 'Matt would've hated this.'

We all have our demons. Mine is water and his is heights. How had he managed to climb down from the tunnel? My brother was supposed to have spent his days in a stuffy office, not abseiling down rock faces.

Loosening my grip, I begin to rappel down. My gloves quickly begin to heat up with the friction. Once down, I stretch out, glad to be free of the tunnel and on solid ground again. Above me, bats hang from the ceiling. Some are flying across the cave, swooping down before rising and returning to their perches.

The hidden cave, the bats... I can't help myself.

'I. Am. Batman,' I say loudly in a deep, menacing voice that echoes throughout the cavern. My dramatics disturb a few more of the bats.

Turning towards the eagle, I cross the rocks towards the river's edge, despite wanting to go anywhere but near the water. I struggle for footing; the rocks are slick with the river water which travels at a surprising speed. Taking deep breaths to try and banish the rising fear, I force my legs on, determined to get the ordeal over.

I run from rock to rock and leap across the river to the far bank, landing hard on the far side and rolling with my momentum. I stop, teetering at the edge of a crevice. I didn't see it before, and if I'd rolled another metre, I would've fallen into the dark water below.

Dusting myself down, I stand, peering over the edge and feeling my hands tremor and heartbeat quicken as I see the water crash into the rocks beneath me. Across the chasm is the only way to reach the eagle wall. The gap is almost ten feet wide.

'Matt, you had better be in here!' I shout before whispering to all the deities that might be listening. 'Please don't let me fall.'

I back up as far as I can then break into a sprint, yelling as I leap. I'm flying, but not enough – I reach out frantically as I start to fall. My fingers grasp the far edge and it's only thanks to the resistance of my gloves that I am able to cling on. The ledge begins to crumble away and my grip threatens to go with it.

'Noooooo!' I'm slipping towards the rushing water. If I don't act now, I'm going to end up dead. With one last effort, I reach out and pull as hard as I can, dragging myself, struggling for purchase on the wall with my boots. I heave myself up and roll forward, lying there, arms aching, panting for breath, my whole body tired.

'No worries,' I mutter to myself, closing my eyes for a moment to thank all the gods I can remember.

I rise to stand before the eagle. Taking out the flashlight with the black bulb, I shine it over the walls; sure enough, there is another X marking the spot, right across the wall. It has to be some sort of door; there is no other way to go on.

I step forward and the ground beneath my foot suddenly shifts. Without warning, a spear rises from the stone floor. I'm only just quick enough to avoid it, the iron tip ripping through the edge of my boot. It is sharp, deadly. Recoiling, another spear rises, then another, one tearing the flesh of my left arm, and another catching my rucksack. It pierces something inside and I hear damaged metal and glass but can't worry about that in this moment. Diving away from the wall, the spears only stop when I am at the edge of the crevice again.

'Somebody didn't want intruders,' I tell myself, feeling

blood run down my arm and to my fingertips. 'Thanks for the warning, Matt!'

I pull off my jacket, more annoyed that it has been torn than by the injury. I am always disappointed when something of my father's is damaged. A crimson patch has already grown around the spear's puncture, but there is nothing I can do about that now. Tearing off the sleeve of my shirt, I tie the material tightly around the wound at my arm. The cut is deep but doesn't hinder my movement. The make-shift bandage stems the flow of escaping blood. I scrutinise the ground and see dozens of small circles, which have been revealed by my footsteps moving the dust-covered ground. Pressure triggers and spear traps.

'Matt, how can you possibly be mixed up in all this?'

Looking closer at the spears, I see they are ancient, the spearheads rusted but still sharp and deadly.

'Great. I'm going to need another tetanus shot,' I say, looking at the rusted iron and then to my wounded arm. 'Matt, if you're in here somewhere, I'm warning you, I'm not happy!'

No reply. It's then I notice other prints in the thick dust; a different tread to my own.

'Matt's route.'

With the utmost care, I step into his prints. Some are very close to the triggers, others too close to the water's edge for my comfort. Backing away from the crevice, I accidently catch one of the triggers with the toes of my boot, a spear rising and stabbing into the air an inch from my face. Too close. Far too close.

Pushing on, I narrowly avoid two more of the traps before I reach Matt's final steps. Face to face with the eagle, its intricate carving becomes more apparent. Below its wings, faded with time, are the letters SPQR.

'Roman,' I remember from some distant part of my memory, initials for a Latin phrase. *'The Senate and People of Rome.'*

There are no further footprints. I push against the wall but it does nothing. I inspect the wall carefully, looking for another way through, but my eyes are again drawn to the lettering beneath the eagle. SPQR. The centre of the Q is deeper than the rest of the carving. I place my fingers inside, feeling for a mechanism of some kind.

'C'mon. Matt managed to figure this out,' I taunt myself.

I look around, inspecting everything, even the floor and its triggers again. Then I spot something, a single, circular piece of metal not dissimilar to a coin. Leaning over, I stupidly reach down and pick it up. A spear rises from the floor, which narrowly misses my outstretched hand.

'Nearly needed a change of underwear.'

I run my fingers over the deep notches along its edging. Not a coin but a key. On one side, an eagle, an exact duplicate of the one on the wall. On the other, a faded stamp,

'Property of the British Museum'. My hand trembles with excitement as I place the coin into the hole of the Q. It locks into place. Turning it causes the entire wall to shudder. It's a door; I was right. I'd move back if I could but any step would set off more of the spears. The mechanism churns, ancient levers and cogs still working. I advance cautiously, the door still rising behind me. My sore arm is a warning not to be too foolhardy.

I shout out my brother's name, swinging the torch from side to side over the chamber. It is full of stone caskets; on top of each one is armour, weaponry, and coins, which I recognise as Roman. The caskets are not big enough to store bodies, more like large urns to contain ashes and possessions. Across the summit of each casket, chiselled into the stone, are Latin words and phrases; names and titles by my guess. Across every single one is the large carving of IX, the Roman numerals for nine.

'My God, this isn't a cave, it's a tomb!'

I can't understand it. The Romans never travelled this far from Hadrian's Wall for fear of the northern Britons... except – no that was just a legend. I look at the caskets again and I have to wonder, are the legends true? On each is the inscription LXXVIII, the number seventy-eight, the year the men fell in battle? Maybe the number of their legion?

Torches hang from both sides of the chamber, the old kind, the ones that require fire rather than batteries. I ignite the nearest on both sides with the matches, which have squirrelled their way down to the bottom of my rucksack. The whole chamber is illuminated. There are carvings on the floor and my mind flips back to the entrance around the stone door behind me. From my pocket, I take one of the apples and roll it down the chamber into the darkness at the far side. My caution is rewarded – spears rise from the floor and arrows soar out of niches in the walls.

'Defending their dead,' I say respectfully, knowing only their brothers, the soldiers who fought beside those who perished, could've created such a burial guard like this. I don't blame them. I'd want to do the same for my family and friends, to honour and protect their remains.

The triggers on the floor are more spread out than the others, making it easier to travel down the chamber, as long as I take care with my footing. I light the next torch on the wall and pull it from its fixings, saving the battery power of those I brought with me. I count the caskets. Twenty, fifty, a hundred. There are other chambers adjacent, housing even more of the fallen. More armaments are stacked against the caskets, the typical Roman tower shield, helmet, and gladius sword easily distinguishable despite the decay of age. This is greater than any museum collection of Roman artefacts I have ever seen. Hell, it's bigger than any museum I have ever seen. I can't believe it.

'This is why you were down here, Matt.'

Arrows are scattered across the cavern floor. My brother has been the possible target of those traps. Amongst the remains of arrows, several objects are spread; a spent flare, a torch, and a pair of glasses, all out of place amongst the honoured Roman dead. The torch particularly worries me as blood covers much of its heavily damaged casing. Then there's the glasses, too. One lens broken and the other streaked with more blood. Matt doesn't wear glasses, or perhaps that was just another thing about him I don't know. I pick up the glasses and tuck them into a pocket on the chance that maybe Matt will want them back when I find him – if I find him. I call out for him again but there is still no reply.

A rumble sounds out from the far side of the chamber, but the farther I walk, the more certain I am that it's the sound of rushing water. I am proven right as I see the cavern ends in a waterfall, which cuts through the chamber from ceiling to floor, feeding the river from the loch above into the wider cavern beyond the eagle engraved door. There is a gap in the floor to allow the water to flow through of about a metre; easily jumpable.

Remarkably, there is a small doorway concealed beyond the falling water. I thank heavens it hasn't been heavier rain or I would have missed it entirely had the water been faster flowing. Taking care to not step on any of the triggers or disturb the graves of the Roman soldiers, I approach the waterfall, and with a deep breath, I force myself to leap across the gap in the chamber, through the falling water that utterly soaks me. Above the doorway, two words are chiselled into the stone. TANTUM DIGNOS. I have no idea what it can mean, but I don't have a good feeling.

6

OPTIO MARCUS AURELIUS—76Ad Caledonia, Britannia

'Hold the lines!' I shout. My men can barely hear me over the chaos of battle. 'Force them back!'

Our shield wall falters as each Roman brother falls. The gaps close swiftly on the barked orders from the remaining optios and centurions. The Britons throw themselves at us. They bear spear, blade, even teeth and nails at us; barbarians – the rumours are true. It is not just men, but women too; thousands of them encircling us on this hilltop, cutting down our legion with an unending hatred.

'Fight for the empire!' yells Legatus Thadian. He is leading from among the lines as a commander should. 'Fight for the legion! Fight for your brothers!'

I take up the cry, 'Fight for your brothers!' The men

around me roar back in encouragement. Barely two hundred of us still draw breath, but each and every Roman will fight to the last.

I stand on the blood-soaked ground. I am sixteen years of age, two of those years spent at war. The dead are all around me; crazed Britons and our honoured fallen. We marched north into Caledonia numbering close to four thousand; support had been pledged by dozens of the tribes on route. Almost all of them have turned on us; tens of thousands storming our lines since dawn. The sun is now beginning to set and the dark will bring more slaughter.

Our wounded crawl behind us. Those who can still stand, fight. If they don't, they will die. One man, blinded in action, kneels, praying to the gods for salvation. His prayers are silenced by arrows.

One brute, taller than all others, thunders his blood-coated axe into my shield, screaming an ungodly battle-cry. I hammer the shield into him, stabbing my gladius deep into his chest with swift, controlled thrusts. Another blade swipes down from the man at my left, tearing through flesh and silencing the crazed Briton. But he is replaced by two others, eager for our blood.

'Close shields!' I yell.

The men fall in beside me, our shields interlocking before spears, clubs, and all manner of weapons pound against them. Amongst the agony and terror, I hear a cry of pain above all the others. Antonius Thadian, our legatus, staggers back and falls to the ground, weapon lost as his hands clutch the wound just below his neck. It pulses with crimson blood.

'Close shields!' I yell, stepping out of the line. My men obey, and I hurry to our commander.

'Marcus,' he says as I kneel at his side. Blood dribbles from his lips. His face is pale. 'My boy, has aid arrived yet?'

'No, Legatus. No sign of the promised reinforcements,' I inform him.

Our legion stands alone, surrounded by enemies, facing oblivion.

'Betrayed by our own,' he curses. 'Marcus, this is my fault. It is my pride that led us to this! The Britons cannot be ruled! Fight to the death! Don't surrender! They'll do God knows what to our men if they are captured. Fight!'

I see his eyes wander, struggling to find something.

'The Eagle!' His voice is barely more than a whisper now. 'My boy, don't let me die with it fallen!'

I find the standard not far behind us, its bearer impaled by two spears through the chest and an arrow in an eye. Another body has fallen on top of him, but I drag the standard clear. The bronze, outstretched wings of the Eagle are coated in the blood of the dead. I force it into the hands of my commander, the Eagle rising above him.

'One last time,' our legatus says as the dimming

sunlight strikes the bronze. Tears run from his eyes – not for his own impending death, but for the death of his men.

The remaining line begins to buckle; Britons pour through any gap they can. I cut two down before they can reach us. They are thundering towards the shining Eagle, our standard, the most prized of trophies.

'Fight for your legatus!' I command. The men roar back ferociously as Thadian draws his final breath.

From the mass of fiends, one rises to face me. The severed heads of Roman soldiers hang over his shoulders, and their blood coats his face. He is clearly a chieftain of his people. He towers over me, spear and club in hands. I turn, thrusting the tip of my gladius towards his stomach, but I meet only air.

He laughs manically, slamming his club down on my arm. My grip on my blade fails just as he stabs his spear towards me. Swinging my shield round, I smash it across his face, causing teeth to fly free. For a brief moment, the brute is stunned. It's all I need. I charge the fiend, drawing my dagger and forcing him to the ground. He lashes out; his fists strike my head, casting stars before my eyes and causing bleeding lips and nose. I stab my dagger down, the blade pushing through his flesh until he no longer moves.

I stagger to my feet, dazed and spitting blood, but managing to recover my shield and gladius – always the soldier. The lines are breaking; they'll be overrun at any moment. As five of our foe charge me, I know my end is coming. The afterlife is waiting for me.

'Goodbye, Lucilla,' I whisper to my young wife, half the world away, readying myself for a final stand.

'FOR ROME!' Thadian screams with his last breath.

Everything is engulfed in light and flame. Momentarily, I am blinded, but when my sight returns, I swear I see Thadian standing at my side again, along with thousands of my fallen brothers. They charge as one.

7

ADAM—Loch Lomond, Scotland

I emerge from the waterfall, shaking myself like a dog in a vain effort to dry myself. My flame torch is extinguished, soaked like the rest of me, so I discard it. Fortunately, someone from the past had thought this through, and dry torches are handily positioned on the wall beside me – now I just have to hope my matches are dry enough. The box is a write off, but the matches are dry enough that one quick strike against the wall and they sputter into life.

Once illuminated, I see the rounded chamber houses, only one solitary casket at its centre. The name Legatus Antonius Thadian is chiselled into its stone above Legio IX Hispana. The chamber was for their commander; the highest place of honour given to the man the soldiers followed into battle. Beneath the inscribed name of the legatus are his helmet and sword, still in its ornate red and gold sheath. Around the casket are piles of weapons and trophies. They are unlike the Roman artefacts; these are more barbaric and archaic – they belong to the Britons. Staring at the IX that marks this grave just like all the others, a trigger in my memory goes off.

The disappearing legion. The Ninth Legion famed for their battles in the north, and then – its complete disappearance.

Nothing had been heard of them since; no remains found, no trace. It was as if they were nothing but a legend – until now. Now I am standing in the burial chambers of its men and commander, undisturbed for hundreds of years until my brother found it.

Carved into the casket is the inscription LXXVIII again, the number seventy-six. It's the year the legatus marched them north, 76 AD. It's the year the legion fought its final battle. It's the year that the legatus and his soldiers were entombed within these caverns, and became immortalised in myth.

'I can't believe it, Matt,' I say to myself in amazement, unable to contain my smile. 'You found it. You found the lost legion.'

There are no more doors or passages. This chamber for the legion's legatus is the end of the tomb. Chiselled into the rock walls, I notice words for the first time. They are places. Eboracum: York. Camulodunum: Colchester, and many, many more. To the son of a history teacher, this kind of knowledge is the equivalent of knowing how to tie your shoelaces, or button your coat. And to be fair, the Roman invasion had always interested me. Something about it had captured most of my childhood imagination – war, battle, death, and destruction is how you get young boys to remember things. These place names are where the legion was victorious; a testament to their heroism, remembered for all eternity.

There are more words, more inscriptions, but most I can't translate. One I do recognise though. TANTUM DIGNOS, the same as at the tomb's entrance under the waterfall. I take out my mobile and use the camera to photograph as much as I can; the walls, the casket, everything.

I look for signs and my heart leaps at what I find. I've been blinded by the discovery of the tomb, but now all I can see are the scattered flares, the claw marks, and the blood-stained stone at my feet.

A roar echoes through the caverns, making adrenalin crash through my system.

'It can't be,' I whisper. 'The monster of the loch?' Fear roots me to the spot. The roar grows louder as it nears, until I can hear claws on rock and the waterfall erupts before me. The beast emerges from the water, roaring. Red demonic eyes scan the room, searching for its prey. It's the largest wolf I have ever seen. It roars its giant mouth at me again. I reach for the legatus's sword, drawing the gladius from its sheath; it's my only protection. The blade still shines with sharpness even after all this time.

The wolf doesn't move; it's waiting in front of the waterfall, blocking my escape. All at once, the waters erupt and two men emerge. They are carrying the latest climbing equipment, their harnesses still tied about them, and their flashlights attached to the shoulders of their packs. The wolf doesn't stir at their appearance, looking only at me with those demonic red eyes.

'Wow, that'll wake you up!' The shorter of the two laughs loudly in a broad Australian accent as he wipes water from the biker goggles over his eyes. Seeing me, his smile grows. 'I told you there was someone down here. Pay up, bro.'

'Fine,' the other man says, pulling out a ten dollar note from his pocket and waving it in front of his partner with a heavily scarred arm. Throughout this transaction, the towering brute's eyes never leave me. 'What's he doing all the way down here? Who are you?'

'Just a local lad,' I say in my best, but terrible Scottish accent, hoping they won't know a true accent from these parts. 'Thought I'd go for a wee bit of a wander...'

'And you ended up down here?' the big guy laughs, his own accent unmistakeably American. 'That's one helluva wander, don't you think, Leon?'

'Unbelievable,' the shorter one – who I've now clocked as Leon – says. He is eyeing me suspiciously.

'Yeah, I guess,' I hurriedly reply, lowering the blade in my hands as I try to cover for myself. 'I saw all the crews and equipment coming over here and had to have a look.'

'And see what you can steal more like,' the American snarks.

'A guy's got to live...' I begin to say but it's hard to keep up the act when a wolf is growling at you. It takes a step towards me, his red eyes glowing with evil.

'Don't worry about him,' Leon mockingly reassures me before the beast howls madly.

'He can tell when something's wrong,' Bishop says. 'Like when a punk is somewhere they shouldn't be, or when they're hiding something. Leon, I think he's lying to us.'

The wolf takes another step closer. My arm raises the gladius instinctively.

'My bro Bishop here thinks you're lying to us. Are you lying?' Leon asks.

'What does it matter to you what I'm doing?' I ask, dropping the accent entirely. 'And more to the point, what are you both doing here? What's with the beast?'

'We're the ones asking questions.' Leon's grin grows across his lips. His eyes are nearly as crazed as the wolf's. 'I've got to say, it's impressive. We're seasoned climbers. Everest, Kilimanjaro, Aconcagua, you name it, we've conquered it. Spelunking pros too. That's cave exploring to you. I know aces who couldn't get down here, and that's before you get to the old traps the Romans set up. Yet you got past it all, with hardly any equipment. How?'

'Luck,' I simply say, giving nothing away. They both fix me with hard stares, waiting for me to elaborate but I will say no more.

'We've been down here a few times,' Leon says as the big American continues to try and psych me out.

'You stole Mike's boat,' I accuse them without thinking. 'You're nothing but low-life grave robbers!'

'Yep, no point in denying it, although less of the low-life, thanks.' Leon smirks. 'Anything for a big fat cheque. Quite the find this place, isn't it?'

'The world should know about this,' I say.

'The mystery of the Roman Ninth and its disappear-ance solved,' he agrees. He is prowling around the casket, closing in on me. 'You're right, it should be known to the world, but not yet. Something's missing. Something that should be with every legion.'

'Something very important to us,' Bishop adds, taking a step closer, crushing a flare beneath his boots.

'What?' I ask, backing away so Leon can't circle behind me. 'What are you after?'

'You see, I don't think you simply found your way down here. No one could simply end up down here by luck. I think you're part of that team. I think you're something to do with the guy we found the first time we came down here.'

Bishop reaches into his pockets and draws a baseball cap, which he pulls onto his head. The cap is frayed, a hole torn through its side near the top. It is dark blue with a crimson stripe. I have seen that cap a hundred times before.

'Where's Matt? What have you done with my brother?' I yell at them, threatening him with the blade.

'So you're here for him!' Leon laughs, hands raised in mock surrender. 'And here we were thinking you were searching for the Eagle.'

I think of Matt's journal inside my rucksack, the eagle emblem on the page with the other encrypted messages. My expression betrays me.

'You know something!' Leon laughs.

Bishop leaps forward in an act of aggression. 'Your brother told you something. Left something with you? What is it? What do you know?'

'No messing about, punk. Give us what Matt left you. Tell us where the Eagle is!'

In the dim light of the torches and flashlights I see the barrel of a handgun in Bishop's hands.

'Where is my brother?' I yell back at him, trying my hardest to ignore the weapon.

'He's with us,' Bishop says with a grin of uncontained glee.

'He's back at our camp,' Bishop states, petting the wolf as it continues to growl. 'And no, it's not here on this island or anywhere nearby.'

'Why have you taken him?'

'Who says he didn't come willingly?' Leon asks. 'Who's to say he isn't working with us?'

'Drop the blade, punk.'

I don't say anything, and I don't lower the gladius as the men and wolf edge nearer.

'Do the smart thing, punk. Drop it,' urges Bishop, gun still pointed straight at my head.

'This isn't worth someone getting hurt over,' Leon adds. 'Come with us. Tell us where the Eagle is and you can both go home. Matt and you.'

'I don't know anything about an Eagle,' I tell them.

'Why is it I don't believe you?' Leon asks.

'Drop the blade,' orders Bishop.

Without warning, I throw the blade down, its tip tearing into a flare at Bishop's feet and igniting it in a blaze of red light, blinding us all. The red smoke becomes a thick fog, filling the tomb, but through it I see the wolf's eyes glow brighter still. Even though I can barely see, I take my one and only chance, jumping onto the legatus's casket and leaping past the wolf's snapping jaws. I'm moving by instinct.

I land on the cavern floor and roll, ducking beneath Bishop's swinging arm. The gladius is at my feet and I grab it, circling round, ready to defend myself, but they can't see me amongst the sparks and smoke.

'Grab him!'

But I'm already gone, emerging from the billowing smoke as I charge through the waterfall.

Tucking the gladius into my belt, I run, taking all the care I can to avoid the traps but needing to escape the caverns as fast as possible. Arrows fly from the walls as I catch their triggers across the floor but I am moving far too quickly for them to hit me. I feel one impact into my rucksack but I am undeterred.

I hear the wolf roar as it thunders towards me. Grabbing the nearest Roman tower shield as I feel the beast's breath on my back, I turn, the fiend slamming into the ancient iron, clawing and snarling at me. It takes all my strength to hold it back, the relic bending under the pressure but holding the beast at bay.

My sight falls on the floor, seeing a trigger directly beneath me, between my boots. A quick glance behind, sweat running down my face from the effort to hold off the wolf, and I see my chance. Leaping back with the shield still raised, I let the predator advance, jaws snapping as it tries to bite flesh. It never sees the trigger or the spear rise up, ripping across its face and ruining an eye. I slam the shield into the beast one more time before turning and running, the wolf howling in pain behind me, its pursuit ended. A curse from Bishop tells me his and Leon's is not.

Nearing the great stone door, I grab a handful of Roman coins, throwing them over the massed triggers across its entrance. Dozens of spears rise up in front of me and I dart between them, much easier to avoid when already activated than carefully treading around them. My pace grows as I clear the entrance and, taking a run up, I leap across the great chasm and over the river below without thinking of the water or the fear.

I never make it; a hand grabs me by the shoulder, holding me over the rushing water.

'Do not struggle, Adam.'

I turn. It's neither Leon nor Bishop holding me, but another man, tall and thin, face twisted by his manic smile. He is otherworldly – skin so pale that his veins are almost as pronounced as the tattoos that stretch out across his body in the pattern of sharp twisting thorns. His black staring eyes are half concealed by his raggedy black hair. I'm terrified.

'I sense it inside you. Fear,' he croons. 'I know where your dear brother is, but there's a price – the Eagle.'

'Where is he?' I struggle to ask.

'The Eagle?'

'I don't know...' I begin to protest.

Without warning, blue flames erupt from the man's hand and over my torso, wracking me with excruciating pain. I scream but he doesn't release me. The flames engulf us both.

'With the rise of the blood moon, I shall find it,' he whispers to me, pulling me close. 'The Eagle shall be mine.'

The flames vanish in an instant. My skin is somehow unharmed yet steam still rises from me.

'Give my greetings to the afterlife,' he whispers, before lifting me high and throwing me down towards the river.

Somehow, I miss the rocks below, but a worse fate claims me. The waters swallow my body and drag me under the current. I struggle to rise up, to breathe, but the river pulls relentlessly.

I'm pulled deeper. Kicking with all my strength, I'm finally able to surface and fill my lungs with precious air, but it's not enough. I know it's not enough. I lived this death before, and every night since. I know this is the end. I have cheated death once, but this time I can't. This is it. My head is in agony. No air, no breath. All I see is stars scattered across the dark of the swirling water.

My body strikes a rock and I reach out to grip it, not knowing whether I am saved or not.

My vision returns and I see trees around me. The loch is beyond them, and beyond that, mainland. Rising in the distance, ushering in the dawn, is the sun. My body shakes uncontrollably, not from the cold but in terror. I have barely escaped.

.　.　.

The boat remains moored where I left it. I jump aboard and sever the mooring rope with the gladius, the blade still with me somehow despite my fall into the water. Thankfully, the outboard engine roars into life on first attempt to start and I guide the boat away as fast as it'll go. I head towards Mike and Gillian's, where my motorcycle is waiting. An argument is growing in my thoughts. Those men have Matt, and I should have played them better, but they had a gun, and they would've killed me long before I ever saw my brother. I should've tried though. In the end, I reason I need to read more of his journal. I need to find out the secret of the Eagle and why they want it so desperately. Then I will rescue Matt.

Risking a look back over my shoulder, I see another boat, much bigger than mine and quickly gaining on me. Matt's captors; the goons from the cavern. Without slowing down, I beach the boat, the hull grinding on the rocks and stones, insurmountable damage done.

'Hey, you nicked my boat!' I hear Mike yell as he and Gillian emerge from their home. 'What the hell have you done to it?' His face is red with anger – and I don't blame him.

'Sorry!' I yell as I run for the bike. 'I'll pay for the damages! Just get inside and call the police.'

'Too bloody right I'm calling the police! You stole me boat!'

I reach the motorcycle, dropping my keys in the haste to start up the bike.

'I'm sorry, Mike. I swear I'll pay you back. I promise.'

Mike is distracted by the sight of his other stolen boat, heading at speed towards the dock.

'Ruddy hell!' Mike curses.

I'm trying to start up the engine, failing twice. 'C'mon! C'mon!' I shout at the bike, praying for it to start.

Just in time, the engine roars into life. 'Yes!' I cry in triumph. Pulling on the helmet and turning the bike, I hurtle away along winding roads through the Highlands, over hills and around lochs. My mind races with a thousand options of what to do. All I know for certain is I must escape the area, vanish until I can read Matt's journal and decide my next steps.

The growing thunder of an engine and blaring horn behind warns me I am not yet free. In the bike's mirror, I see a beaten up, filthy four-by-four rapidly gaining on me.

'Come get me then,' I taunt, increasing the throttle on the bike and heading towards the motorway in the distance. The early morning traffic is already building up ahead. I'll be able to weave it, but it will slow those goons down.

I accelerate until my speed is reckless, even for me. Suddenly, cutting across from the fast lane, the familiar four-by-four swerves, hitting my back wheel. All control is lost and I veer towards the hard-shoulder, the bike disappearing from beneath me. The world spins in noise and pain and I land on the grass verge, my body rolling down towards the ditch.

I look up, not knowing how long I have been unconscious. My helmet's visor is cracked and all of me hurts. I try to get up but a figure is rushing towards me. I know their urgency has nothing to do with their desire to help me. My rucksack, straps torn, lies just out of reach, Matt's journal is inside. It is that which they are coming to rescue.

'No...' I struggle to say. My body is failing. Darkness is claiming me.

8

OPTIO MARCUS AURELIUS—Caledonia, Britannia

In the sky we see Luna, bright and crimson like blood, bathing the night sky red. The gods honour the dead as we now do. As the fires of the funeral pyres die, I turn to the last remaining brothers untouched by death. I have seen thousands of them laid to rest this day, but this pyre is the one I have dreaded most of all.

'Sir,' Legionary Ocullus, one of the few survivors of my cohorts, calls to me. 'It should be you, Sir,' he says, offering me the flame, 'He would be honoured.' I look to Centurion Decimo, the highest ranked survivor and my superior. He nods in approval.

'And so we honour him,' I say, pacing towards the pyre. The eyes of all those who remain of our legion are on me. One hundred and seventeen of us from what was four thousand. We are no longer an army, barely a single cohort. We were betrayed, by both Romans and Britons, torn apart.

'My brothers,' I call to all those who remain. I am the youngest on the field yet must speak to them as a brother, a leader. I swallow any fear and doubt, forcing it from my mind as I honour the fallen. 'The Legio IX Hispana will forever live on in us who still draw breath and in the memory of all of Rome, our enemies slain and scattered, our victories and valour legend.' My words do little to cheer the men, but nor do they jest or mock. They are silent.

'We have honoured our fallen brothers this day, but there is one last man we must bid farewell to. He will live on forever in the Elysian Fields – our legatus, Antonius Thadian.'

Though he marched us north to this barren land where all we found was death, no man speaks against him, nor betrays his memory. Their loyalty is true and fast.

'For seven years he has led the legion, never once forsaking us, fighting beside us, giving blood and sweat in our struggles. He was a righteous man. An honourable man. He gave all for this legion.'

I do not mention his final acts, nor his words of self-blame. Instead, I lower the torch to his pyre and let the men's final memory of the legatus be untainted. He lies with his armour and weaponry removed. Coins have been placed upon his eyes to pay the ferryman for safe passage to the afterlife across the River Styx. The wood beneath him catches flame; the legatus's final journey has begun.

It is because of him that I stand upon these foreign shores. My father fought in the legions, a friend of the legatus for many years. When my father died, I was left penniless and alone in the city of Rome. Barely fourteen years of age, I was inducted into the legion and raised to the rank of optio as favour by the legatus. I struggled to earn the respect of the men, small and feeble to many I outranked. It was only thanks to the training and instruction of the legatus over almost three years that I truly earned place as soldier. Now he is gone.

The men are striking sword and spear upon shield. The beat continues until the flames are at their highest and our once commander is engulfed in the blaze. It lifts my heart to see the men united, especially after all we have endured. None of us can understand what we saw. It is beyond a mortal's mind. Only the gods can conceive such a thing and return the dead to fight amongst the living.

I stand at Centurion Decimo's side and he hands me a flask of wine. The taste is rancid and sour, but it matters not; it numbs the pain and memories.

'What will you do next?' he asks in a hushed tone so as to be unheard by the men. He is the eldest of us all, a veteran of wars long before I was even born.

'What do you mean, Sir?' I reply, confused. I thought

our course was set; return to the garrisons south and report what happened here.

'Only you and I, and a handful of others, are true Romans,' Decimo informs me. 'The rest of our brothers were taken from lands and homes far from here. We took farmers and merchants and made them soldiers.'

'So now what do you propose? Let them go? Disband? One legion rebelling against all of Rome, our home.'

'You are still young, Marcus. Look around you. The legion is no more. We are barely a cohort and half of us are injured, unable to ever march or fight again. What I am saying, and most of the men are too, is that we should stay here. Let the legion die, with our brothers. We can live on. Those under the dragon banner, Uther's tribe, they stood and bled with us when all others turned and drove daggers in our backs. They are here now, honouring us and our dead. They will need protection if those who betrayed us return. It's the least we can do and they have offered us shelter and food. We can have new lives here.'

'And what of the garrisons, Sir?'

'They betrayed us as well! Rome betrayed us! We were promised reinforcements, three additional legions, but none came. We were sent here to die and so our brothers and our legatus burn. The men we led were taken from their homes and forced to fight for an empire they have never known. Their leaders are gone...'

'We are their leaders.' I insist. I do not like this dangerous talk.

'We are barely more than they; risen from the gutter and given purpose,' Decimo rants at me, heard by all who still draw breath upon the fields. 'Do not be the foolish boy. No titles or land await me when I return, nor do they for you now your guardian is gone.'

I ignore the jibe about our legatus. 'We are men of Rome.'

'Rome abandoned us. By the gods will you not see sense or reason?'

My loyalty will not waver. 'We swore oaths, sacramentum before the gods to forever serve Rome.'

'Our oaths were fulfilled the moment we were abandoned. You saw what the gods did! They cast down their might, blinding our foes. They opened the gates to the afterlife and let our fallen brothers stand and fight beside us one last time. They did that because they knew we were wronged. We were saved for a reason.'

Decimo gestures towards the hilltop where our standard still stands, marked by blood, battle, and the gods own touch; the bronze shines in the light of the burning pyres. The Eagle, raised by the legatus one last time, called the gods to our aid. A magical totem. A light surged down, blinding our enemies yet we were unharmed. Our brothers and legatus swept over the battlefield, striking down all in their path, all who sought to destroy our legion, all who claimed their lives. Once the battle was over, our fallen brothers were gone.

'Unlike you and the men you have turned, I am a true Roman,' I tell him. 'I have a wife in Rome who I must return to.'

'Wife?' he scoffs. 'You held her for a single night before departing with the legion? How old are you, boy? You'll soon learn that one night with a woman and some words from a priest doesn't make her your wife – thank the gods!' He tries to goad me, but I will not bite.

'I cannot forsake her nor my orders. I have made oaths in front of the gods.' I turn my gaze to the pyre of the legatus. 'It is what he would have wanted.'

Some of the fire in his belly is waning. 'I know,' he states, nodding his head and letting out a smile of regret. 'I knew you would be like this. That is why I raise you to the rank of centurion. Return to Rome, Centurion Marcus Aurelius. Return with what remains of the legion. The men respect you, and those who choose to, will follow you home – especially after how you fought this day.'

The rank of centurion, it is honour and rank I never thought I would survive to see. It is bitter-sweet. I did not wish to gain it as a consequence of the legion being all but destroyed.

'I will stay here,' Decimo declares, 'along with any who wish to remain. We will lay our brothers to rest and see that they are never disturbed or desecrated. We will

protect them. As far as Rome knows, we are dead alongside them. Do you understand?'

I know for certain no words I say will change his mind.
His path is set, unchanging despite all argument. Though I
do not like it, I have no choice but to accept his plans.

'I will leave at first light,' I say, drinking deep from the
flask.

'To the garrisons south? I do not think that the best
course.'

'Agreed,' I reply; their betrayal is raw. 'We shall travel
west and then follow the coast south. There we will find a
ship, cross the ocean, and tell Rome what happened here,
of the honour gained and the sacrifice given. I will tell
them you perished here with our brothers and if it is the
gods will then hopefully you will be left in peace.'

'That is all I ask,' Decimo says. 'Take the legatus's mark
and what coin and jewels he carries to buy passage to
Rome. He won't need either anymore.'

'What of the Eagle?' I ask, dreading both the question
and the answer.

Both of us turn our gaze to the hilltop, where our last
stand was fought. It stands there still on the hill, not one
man daring to approach it.

9

ADAM—No idea, but in agony

The pain comes in waves, as does my consciousness. I can't make sense of where I am or what is happening. The hum of a vehicle's engine and distant rock music is my first grasp of the real world. My eyes flicker open and I begin to understand that I am in a car. It looks like the four-by-four that was chasing me, but I don't see Leon or Bishop. I try to move but my body is like lead, weighted despite all effort, strength and energy gone.

'Em, you clear?' The gruff male voice alerts me to his presence beside me.

'Just about,' she replies from somewhere. It doesn't sound like it's from within the car - maybe over a phone or radio, I'm not sure where. 'They've given up the chase anyway,' she adds.

'You okay?' he asks, his accent unmistakeably northern.

'Ask me on another day,' she replies. Car horns blare in the distance, making me wince. 'What about him? How is he?'

'Still alive, I think. Took a helluva tumble.'

'He's not bleeding all over your Jeep is he?' She laughs.

'Nah, he's just a bit bruised and beaten up.'

'Heard anything from Delta Team yet?' she asks.

'Yeah.' He doesn't sound too happy.

'That bad, huh? I'll see you at the rally point.'

The conversation terminates. Delta Team? Lovell? The museum?

'It's okay, kid,' the man says, placing a hand on my shoulder briefly. 'You're safe now. I'll patch you back together.'

I see stubble and tattoos on his arms; a hard man. I see military clothing and a gun. He's a soldier and I am his prisoner.

'Adam Hunter,' I mumble, barely able to keep my eyes open. 'Student. Six six six.'

'Very funny, kid,' the man replies, though he doesn't smile. 'Name, rank, and serial number. That's good. I ain't your captor though.'

'Matt? Where's Matt?' I manage to ask before the darkness takes me again.

10

CENTURION MARCUS AURELIUS—Oceanus

It is thirty-three days since the hilltop battle that we near the southern coast. We have been ever cautious of discovery by patrol and legion during our march. Twenty-eight of my brothers march with me; some through loyalty, some through not knowing what else to do, others just wanting to abandon this accursed ever-cold, ever-wet land where we witnessed enough blood and death for a life-time. I march for all of it and more, knowing that the only family I have left in the world await me in Rome.

It is thirty-three days of marching before my command is questioned.

'Marcus, are you sure we're headed in the right direction?' Legionary Molenus murmurs. He is a wretch of a man; scarred face, foul stench, rotten teeth and always eager to moan and complain when opportunity arises.

'That's Centurion Aurelius to you,' Optio Acer Xarox replies gruffly.

Acer is the eldest of the survivors; brutish, taller and stronger than all the rest. At the legatus's orders he trained me in combat, hardened me into a soldier that could stand with the rest of the legion. It is thanks to him I now have the respect of the men, and more importantly, I still draw breath. I raised him to the rank of optio, second in command, not one man daring to question or rebel against his orders. He is loyal to a fault and I am grateful he stands at my side.

'*Centurion* Aurelius,' Molenus replies, contempt in his tone. 'Are you sure we're marching the right way?'

'Do you usually question your commander?' I say without looking back to the man. 'Yes, we are still marching south. Another day or two and we will reach the coast.'

'And then where?' he speaks out again.

'Molenus,' Acer growls.

'Seriously, where to then?' the legionary continues. 'This boy going to march us all the way back to Rome?'

'He is your Centurion...' Acer begins to shout back at the man, before I call a halt to our march.

Though I feel a nervous fear clench tight within me, I must cease his dissent before it spreads through the rest of the men. This is the first challenge to my command with no superior to assert their influence. I cannot let Acer deal with the man as that would just show cowardice to some. I must do this alone.

I pace back through my command until I face him, looking Molenus straight in the eyes.

'And what do you propose, Legionary?' I demand in as firm a voice as I can muster.

'We sail for Sardinia or Sicilia,' he says, eyeing me coldly and without respect. 'Plenty of fertile lands – and women, if you get my meaning?' He lowers his voice so only I can hear, 'Perhaps being so young, you don't, virgin!'

'Sardinia or Sicilia?' I question, ignoring his taunt. 'With you at command I suppose?'

'Better than a jumped up boy,' he sneers. I feel it then, fear fading, fire in its place.

'You...' Acer rages, stepping forward to attack the man.

'Stand firm, Optio,' I order, ceasing his approach before he can reach Molenus. My eyes do not look away from my challenger. 'Call me boy again,' I say, the fire within growing, raging free.

'Bo...'

He never finishes the word. My fist strikes below his jaw, sending the wretch crashing to the ground. I strike him twice more as he tries to rise, stopping only when the man is spitting his own teeth to the dirt. Not a single brother of the legion steps forward to support Molenus and I feel their eyes watching me in awe.

'You men,' I address them all, fists glistening with the blood of Molenus. 'You soldiers of Rome. You swore oaths, sacramentum. You could have stayed with Decimo and the others but you followed me. You are still legionnaires. The legion still lives as long as we draw breath. We will return to Rome and honour our fallen, our brothers who fought and died so that we may live on. Our brothers, who came back from the afterlife to ensure the survival of this legion.'

I wait a few moments, giving chance for the words to sink in.

'Do any of you, like this man here, disagree?'

Not a word is spoken by anyone.

'And what of you, Molenus?' I ask, looking down on him.

'No, Centurion Aurelius,' Molenus replies. He staggers to stand, wiping blood from his mouth. In his gaze I do not see anger or contempt. His eyes are forward and steady. In a way, he is reassured – almost pleased that I have put him in his place. He spits blood to the ground and grins at me once before standing at attention, the rest of the men ready to march.

'Legion, forward!' Acer orders.

As the optio passes me, I see the hint of a smile on his lips; possibly pride. I look to the rest of the men and see the same on all their faces, even Molenus now.

I wait until they all march beyond me before raising my bloodied hands from behind my back. Out of sight of the rest I see how they tremble. The tremors only cease when I form them into fists.

I am Centurion now.

Two days later, we are at sea. I detest being at sea. On the voyage across to Britannia, I spent most of it vomiting my guts up over the side, wishing the oceans would swallow me up just to cease the nightmare. This time, though, I am able to hold my stomach, despite rough seas and endless storms.

At the southern coast, we found supply ships at moor, providing food, weaponry, and reinforcements to the other legions. With the legatus's gold, I bartered passage for all of us across the waters, back towards the ports of Rome. It took more coin than I'd hoped, and it was only thanks to the legatus's mark that we were not branded deserters and traitors for fleeing our legion. Cursed threats and a waving blade added to convincing the ship's captain, especially when he did not believe I stand as Centurion – too young in years by his thoughts.

On board the ship, the men struggle, the waves churn their stomachs; the water is unnatural for soldiers who have spent their lifetimes marching and fighting upon earth. Thankfully, it is not difficult to keep order among

them in such cramped conditions, even without the legatus's command. There has been no more resistance to my
command. Even Molenus has stayed silent, although the
missing teeth might be the cause of that – that and his
injured pride. All they want is to be off the ship.

The men mostly sleep; they are still recovering, some
still struggling with wounds received in battle. The thing
that makes them most uneasy, even more so than the
punishing storms, is the sight of the Eagle, bound in rags
for concealment. No one risks approaching it. No other
would carry it and so it was left to me – though I do not
dare to place a hand upon it.

No one has, not since the incident – the one that none
of the men have spoken of since. Some fool took hold of it,
lifting it high in attempt to command the gods. No holy
might was bestowed on him except for fire. His ashes
joined those of our brothers. Perhaps he was not worthy of
such power – only our late legatus was worthy to
commune with the gods.

'How long will the march be from port, Sir?' Optio
Acer asks.

'Depends where we make land in Gallia,' I reply
wearily. My own wounds are still healing from the battle,
and our long march has taken its toll. 'If the gods be with
us then we will be able to gain passage to Rome by horse
or cart.'

'Anything to save marching again.' He laughs heavily. 'When was the last time you saw your wife?'

'Too long ago. I left her on the steps of the senate before we marched in honour to begin our campaign.' I linger on the memory, remembering her beauty and her voice as it called out to me.

Lucilla and I had loved each other since we were children, but we married just the day before I swore my oaths to the legion and set out for Britannia. Memories of her tears cut me sharper than any blade, but I had no choice. Without a coin to my name, we had no promise of a life for us together if I did not leave. She said she understood, but in those last looks, I saw her pain – part of her thought I was leaving her forever.

'I long to see what Rome has to offer,' Acer says cheerily. 'I have heard much. I'm eager to savour its many pleasures.'

'Wine and women!' one eavesdropper cheerfully offers. 'You'll find plenty of both true enough.' He is a merchant, given the amount of jewellery he wears. He is sweating profusely through his colourful robes. He lets out a belly laugh and wags his finger 'Be careful though. The city is its own beast.'

'As any city is!' I bark back at him with annoyance. I take an immediate dislike to the man.

'You misunderstand me, Centurion,' he says. My curiosity is piqued by the slightest trace of fear in his voice.

'I speak of the lawlessness; the abandonment of its people. It is hell infected by a plague of villainy.'

'That is Rome, you fool,' one of my men mocks him. 'It took us from our homes, dragged us halfway round the world to fight, to claim land and glories in honour of the great empire.'

The man quietens as my gaze falls upon him. 'What villainy do you speak of?' I ask the merchant. His disloyalty has angered me.

The merchant snorts. He is not intimidated by me. He is firm in his convictions. 'The villainy of the state. Her people are without food, the waters polluted, the drinking wells run dry. Soldiers steal whatever they want – daughters and wives included. Beggars and cripples are kicked into the gutter. The senate has abandoned all; the emperor focuses his power on conquering the lands of all the world, but he isn't able to care for the people under his care. Blood and riches are all he seeks. The whole of Rome is monument to his vanity.'

'Hush your tongue, fool,' Optio Acer curses the man, 'or I will remove it from you.' He pushes the merchant hard into the far wall of the vast cabin. 'Do not speak of Emperor Vespasian as such. 'The gods strike you down for your heresy.'

The merchant retreats. He is shaken.

I wait as the voices calm, the men returning to slumber, dice, and disgruntled words again. They unearth a small cask of wine from somewhere in their provisions, raising it high and drinking deep. Anything to forget the voyage.

'To Emperor Vespasian!' they cry in cheers, looking to provoke the merchant, but he says nothing from his corner.

'To our centurion!' commands Acer. 'Who we'd follow to the gates of hell if he commanded!'

The men roar in agreement but I ignore them. At least their spirits are raised. It does not take long for the cask to empty, and then they sleep.

I approach the merchant, who now dares not sleep for the rest of the voyage for fear of being murdered in his sleep. 'Calm yourself,' I say, seeing fear still grips him.

'Apologies,' he mumbles. 'I did not mean to draw your men's anger,' he says with quivering lips.

'The Emperor Vespasian? You truly see him as tyrant?'

'How long since you were last home, Centurion?'

'It must be near three years by now. Honestly, I have lost track of the days.'

'The emperor and Rome are not what they once were. I fled not just from the fear, or the riots from the poor and hungry, but the emperor himself. Men, women, and even children are crucified; not just errant slaves but citizens – and not for terrible crimes, but for the slightest misdeed. Now, please, I can speak no more of it. I have said too much already.'

As the merchant takes his leave, climbing up towards

the deck of the ship, my eyes wander to the far corner of the cabin. There the Eagle stands. I cannot help but wonder whether returning it to the emperor's hands would be a curse upon us all. He was, after all, the man who murdered his predecessor.

11

ADAM—Still no idea. SOMEWHERE WITH STUPIDLY bright lights.

I wake, almost blinded by a pounding head. At first, I fear it is car headlights, but as my senses return I realise I'm far from the road and the cars that chased me. A heart monitor beeps steadily near my head. The room is white and sterile. Empty except for me. Most of what I see looks like a hospital, but there's something wrong; there are no doctors, nurses, or other patients anywhere to be seen - just four white walls and a door. My left arm is in a sling and there are bandages wrapped around my forehead. My mouth is dry. I've never been so thirsty.

'Hello,' I call out with a hoarse voice, but there is no reply. 'Hello!'

A security camera hangs in the corner of the room,

silent and unmoving, its lens focussed on me. It doesn't have a light and it doesn't move. In my right arm is an intravenous drip secured just below the crease of my elbow. I almost vomit at just the thought of it, let alone the sight of it. I hate needles.

I scan the room again. My clothes are missing but worse still, my rucksack, which contains Matt's journal, is nowhere to be seen.

Pulling the intravenous drip from my arm, purposely looking away as I do it, I swing my legs off the bed. The floor is surprisingly cold. Then the crash comes back.

I've been captured and brought here, wherever here is. Torture and interrogation await me, I am sure.

'Matt's here,' I whisper.

Pulling on a set of doctors' scrubs I find in a cabinet during my search for anything to use as a weapon, I then try the door and am surprised when it is unlocked. Opening it leads to a long corridor and more rooms like the ones I woke in. They are all empty, filled with medical equipment but nothing more. They are all dimly lit as there are no windows.

'Where do you think you're going?' a voice echoes through the corridors, a faint Irish accent in her tone. The voice stops me, but when I search for the source of it, there is no one to be seen.

'Who are you?' I ask, but there's no reply.

I walk on until I come to a window that reveals a gym

with full assault course; beams, obstacles, cargo nets, things that would all look more at home on a military training base. I'm quickly coming to believe that this isn't a hospital – not in the usual sense. Everywhere is deserted, but that doesn't mean I am alone – eyes are on me, I'm certain. At the end of the corridor is a door, which leads onto a stairwell.

'I wouldn't go there if I were you,' the voice returns to taunt. This time I see the source. Just below the security camera, positioned up in the far corner of the hallway, is a speaker. I see no microphone on the camera, so I give it a one-fingered salute.

'That wasn't very nice,' the voice says, imitating hurt feelings. 'Such gratitude after all the medical attention and care we've given you.'

I repeat the gesture.

The door to the stairwell is locked shut, and without my picks, I resort to striking the lock five times with a fire extinguisher hanging nearby.

'Don't hurt yourself.' The voice laughs. This camera follows my movements. After another dozen strikes, she speaks again. 'Look, if you want to get to the stairs that bad, I'll open the door. All you had to do was ask.'

An electronic hum sounds and the door opens, revealing the stairwell beyond. Inside there are signs leading up to the ground floor several levels above, and down for operations and numerous containment &

storage levels. This facility, whatever it is, is underground.

I have to look for Matt. I can't leave if there is a chance that he could be here. I walk down towards containment, guessing Matt might be imprisoned there.

'Closer,' the female voice encourages me from cameras on the walls of the stairwell. 'Closer.'

We're playing a game, but I'm not in the mood.

As I pass the operations floor, she speaks again. 'Close, but not close enough. You definitely shouldn't go any further. I'd turn back now if I was you.'

'Not a chance,' I say as I reach the containment & storage floors.

The door unlocks before I can touch it. I open the door, fully expecting to find iron bars and jail cells. Instead, I find myself in a dark room, surrounded by glass cabinets.

'You shouldn't be in here, kid,' a northern accent admonishes from across the room.

Unable to see the man and expecting it to be another speaker, I reply, 'Who says?'

I'm startled when I'm suddenly grabbed. 'I do,' he says.

'I tried to warn you,' the disembodied woman's voice is laced with laughter.

Instincts kick in. I twist away from the man's grasp and strike his arm at the elbow, loosening his grip and then kicking him away.

'You shouldn't have done that,' a woman says,

approaching me. Without warning, she lunges her deceptively slight form towards me; she is fast and agile. Too fast. Two, three, four times she strikes me with her fists and kicks before I can react, and I stagger back in a daze.

'C'mon, give me a challenge,' she goads. She is enjoying this.

'Enough! Where am I? Where is my brother?'

She doesn't answer; she's still looking for a fight, but this time I am ready. I charge forwards, catching her unexpectedly and slamming her into the far wall.

'That's more like it,' she says before twisting her way free from my grasp. She kicks out the back of my knee and I lose balance. She lands hard on top of me and pins me down, resting the sharp tip of a blade on my throat.

'Enough, Emma! Abbey, get the lights!'

'Sure thing, Mr Lovell.'

I let out a groan. Charles Lovell – it had to be him!

Blinding white lights flicker on through the room. The first thing I see is her eyes, the left one green and the right one blue.

'Hi there,' she says, with a smile on her lips.

She is roughly my age, or at most a year or two older, and her purple and red hair is instantly recognisable. She is the girl on the bike. The one who I now understand has been following me.

'Emma, please let our guest stand.'

She does as instructed but can't resist blowing me a mocking kiss.

It takes me a moment or two to take my eyes from her – I don't trust she won't come back and lump me, but when I do, I see that the area around me is far bigger than I first thought. Transparent panels separate sections of what looks more like a vast warehouse. There are glass cabinets as far as the eye can see.

'Most people prefer the tour but, as we know, the Hunter brothers are not like most people.'

'Where is my brother?' I stand and dust myself off.

'Mr Hunter, I promise you we had nothing to do with Matthew's disappearance,' Charles says, pacing towards me with his walking cane. 'We spent days searching for him before you reached the loch.'

'Then why did you pull the search teams out?' I demand.

'To see how you performed in the caverns,' he says. 'I was curious to see what your next actions would be. Did you really think you managed to steal Matthew's journal without me noticing?'

'Damn,' I whisper, disappointed.

'We did not expect you to run into... company down there. You proved us all wrong in finding the tombs.'

'How do you know I found the tombs?'

'The gladius. You certainly are Matthew's brother,' Charles says.

I snort derisively.

'Will you stop for a moment and hear me out,' Charles asks. 'If you do not like what I tell you, then you are free to leave.'

'Fine.'

Charles looks back over his shoulder and summons, 'Dave.'

My initial attacker steps forward, grinning. 'Dave Conway,' he says, reaching out a hand. 'We've already met.'

I recognise him. He's the man who took me from the crash. Dave, that was the name mentioned in Matt's journal.

'You knocked me off my bike,' I accuse.

'No, kid. That was whoever took Matt,' he says. 'They chased you from the tombs and ran you off the road.'

My attention turns to the girl with the crazy hair. 'You were there on that motorcycle. I saw you at the petrol station near Hadrian's Wall! You've been following me!'

'And at the loch, the night before you stole that boat,' she says, taunting me.

'Borrowed,' I correct her. 'Why were you following me? Why did you bring me here?'

'For the same reason those men chased you from the tombs,' Charles says. 'Matthew's journal.'

'Where is it?' I ask. 'The journal, where is it?'

'We'll show you,' Charles says. 'We just need you to listen to us. Help us and we'll find Matthew.'

'Where am I?' I ask.

'H.Q. The place your brother worked as part of our team,' he says proudly.

'That doesn't answer my question. Where am I?'

'Take a look around you. Where do you think you are?'

I cast my eyes around the vast room again, finally getting a proper look at the glass cabinets. Those nearest contain full sets of medieval armour, dinosaur bones, Ming dynasty pieces, and even mummies, perfectly preserved within their sarcophaguses. Past them are dozens of vehicles of all different ages; planes, tanks, cars, and motorcycles, even a rocket or two. Most prominent among them is the ship, vast sails, wooden hull, a dozen cannons on each side with a skull and crossbones flag at its rear. I can barely believe my eyes. It's an actual pirate ship. Beyond that is another ship, smaller, but just as impressive, a Viking longship with its dragon head mounted on the bow.

'I thought this was a training camp, military or something from the other floors but this... this looks more like a museum.'

'The museum,' Charles corrects me. 'The British Museum, London. These are the hidden archives. This is just the tip of the iceberg.'

A curious smile grows across my lips.

12

CENTURION MARCUS AURELIUS—Rome

It takes more days than I can remember to cross Gallia and more still until we finally see Rome on the horizon. We travel by foot, cart, and horse. The coin of the legatus barely covers the expense but it is far quicker than if we march the entire journey. Two men are lost, one to fever and the other to drink, falling in a river as the world spun around him one night. To our credit, not one man deserts, despite the hardships.

Finally, after so much toil, my home is in sight, the distance between Lucilla and me the shortest it has been for many years. She is in the village just beyond the city, less than half day's march. I would see it shorter still, but duty first.

The Campus Martius is our destination, just outside the city itself, close to the waters of the Tiber. Named after Mars God of War, the camp is the training ground, where new legions are forged and boys turned into soldiers. It is where I trained under the tutelage of Acer and the legatus before our campaigns began in Gaul and the cursed lands of Britannia.

As we, the battered last of the Legio IX Hispana, approach, we see within the grounds hundreds of enlisted recruits training with spear, gladius, and shield; lifting weapons far heavier than those they would carry into battle to build strength in their weak arms. They wrestle, swim, and march, their doctore trainers barking orders every waking moment in preparation for when they will march from Rome as legion under their Eagle. I see dozens of standards, one for every legion, planted before the command buildings. Eagles shine brightly in the sun.

'Clear off, boy, I can't be dealing with you lot today,' a gruff sentry of advanced years mutters as we approach the gates.

'Is that any way to address a centurion, Legionary?' I ask, tone dead serious.

'You? Centurion? You're nothing but a whelp,' he sneers in annoyance.

'Centurion Marcus Aurelius of the Legio IX Hispana, reporting to the commanders of Campus Martius,' I state.

My men draw down their arms and stand with backs straight at attention in perfect ranks. We may appear as beggars but we are Roman soldiers at heart and soul.

'We had heard the Legio IX Hispana was utterly destroyed in Britannia,' the sentry says with disbelief.

'Not all of us,' I state, raising my forearm to his gaze; the brand of H IX clear. It's branded into the arm of the entire legion.

'By the gods,' he says aghast before hurriedly calling for the legatus to be summoned. 'Apologies. Apologies.'

We are guided to the command buildings, and within moments of arrival, not one but four legatus stand around me, each demanding explanation as to what happened to the Legio IX Hispana. I answer all I can but that does not stop them from asking me the same questions again and again. My men are dismissed, all seeking food, wine and rest, except Optio Acer, who stands loyally at my side.

At noon we are presented with nourishment before another flurry of activity engulfs us. Acer and I are given fresh clothes, armour, weapons, and scented oils to cover the stench of travel – there's been no time to bathe as horses are summoned and we are escorted towards the city by armed praetorian guards; the emperor's own body-guard. There is a knot of fear in my stomach. There is a sense that we are somehow guilty of a crime.

As night falls, we enter the city of Rome. The streets

stink of excrement and there's not one soul to be seen but those of the emperor's guard. We see dozens of crosses bearing ruined remains of men and women, their chests mutilated and scarred by the V of Vespasian. Our escort does not talk until we reach the very steps of the senate. There we dismount and are stripped of our weapons.

'You are not permitted to carry them in his presence,' we are told. Acer offers a natural resistance until I order him to relinquish his blade. I hand mine over and feel strange, as if I am parted from a limb.

'Bow in his presence and do not rise until given permission,' the praetorian prefect, orders. He is tall, strong with hardened face, scarred by war. His armour is perfectly polished, without a single blemish or mark, his gaze and commanding voice enough to draw respect and fear from many. I care neither for his words nor his damning eyes, eager to get this over with and seek out my wife.

'Do not speak unless questioned, and say nothing that will anger him unless you wish to have your head parted from your neck, or to join those upon the crosses.'

'As ordered, Sir,' I manage to say. Acer repeats my words but with a voice less steady. The prefect fixes me with one last judging stare before guiding us on.

We are taken into the marbled halls of the Curia Julia, the house of the senate, where senators, consuls and praetors gather, where the rulers of Rome preside. Praetorian guards wait studiously. The hall is lit by the flame of torches. In the very centre, waiting patiently on his throne, is the power of the empire. Acer and I bow before him, my heart thundering in my chest.

'You are granted audience with Flavius Caesar Vespasian,' the voice of the praetorian prefect booms. 'I present Centurion Marcus Aurelius and Optio Acer Xarox of the Legio IX Hispana.'

'Heroes of Rome,' Emperor Vespasian announces, rising from his seat and clapping three times. 'Rise and stand before me so as I can judge you as such.'

Slowly, we rise to stand and I see for the very first time the Emperor of Rome, gold laurel wreath upon head. There is strength to him carved in the features of life spent as soldier before ruler. Two scars line his face; tokens of battles fought and won. There is no weakness, despite an advance of years and thinning, white hair. There is intensity to his eyes as they narrow upon us. He is judging our worth.

'I see the spirit of the legion within you,' he says, inspecting Acer. 'And you, Centurion Aurelius – for one so young to hold such rank. Tell me, how many years of age are you?'

'Sixteen,' I stumble my reply.

'Centurion and hero of the empire already,' he says

proudly. 'Word reaches me that you have returned from Britannia. I too served on those isles when I was but legatus with the Legio II Augusta. I fear you have a tale to tell that far outshines mine. Tell it and fill my ears and soul with your glories.'

Acer merely looks to me, struck dumb in the face of the highest authority in the world. It is not his place to speak anyway; it is mine. I take a deep breath, calming before speaking.

'As were your orders, Emperor, the Legio IX Hispana, under the command of Legatus Antonius Thadian, marched north into Caledonia in pursuit of the tribes that were harassing our garrisons. Many loyal tribes allied their strength with ours in the march. Three other legions were ordered to support but never appeared.'

'Heads will be severed for such treacherous dereliction of duty. Orders were written by my own hand, and yet you report they were ignored. It pleases me to know that at least one of my legions acted with honour. I assume this is why you did not report to the garrisons in Britannia and instead chose to return to Rome?'

'It is, Emperor,' I state, utterly uncertain of how he will react to this. 'Apologies if this action is unacceptable.'

'No, Centurion. You acted as I would,' he says, patting me roughly on the shoulder of my armour. 'Continue your tale. Tell me of when you clashed swords with those barbarous northern Britons.'

'When battle started, all but two of the tribes we thought our allies, turned on us, stabbing blades into our backs. Many of our brothers fell in those first hellish moments. We were surrounded and vastly outnumbered.'

'How many of the enemy faced the legion?'

'Fifteen thousand, maybe twenty thousand,' I pause. I'm flustered. I don't want to lie by error and upset the emperor. I shake my head. 'Apologies. It was difficult to tell, such was the chaos and confusion.'

'Take your time, Centurion. Explain it all as thoroughly as you can.'

'Our lines were formed, impenetrable but for those who betrayed us. Order was lost, but not through fault of the legatus. He stood and fought to the last, giving his life in honour of Rome.'

'I am sure he did.' His tone is too cold for my liking, but I continue.

'We slew hundreds, thousands, but the enemy was endless. Onwards they came, like demons spawned of hell. Savage and ghastly, even women among their number, hacking and slashing with minds lost to madness; they were crazed fiends.'

'And as ferocious as the men,' the emperor agrees. 'I remember the horrors of Britannia well. Continue.'

'We fought and died on that hilltop. When there were but a few hundred of us left, we fell back into order, ready for one final stand in honour of Rome and those who had fallen. Surrender was never a choice.'

'It makes my heart swell to hear such. What miracle transpired to deliver you both to safety?'

That word, miracle. He knows. I can see it in his eyes. There is a certainty and expectation unlike any I have seen before. I feel Acer's eyes on me, both of us dreading this moment, just as we had when telling the tale to the commanders of Campus Martius.

He is the emperor. I must trust him.

'Legatus Thadian was struck down and then ...' I say, struggling with my words, the memory of my commander's death, and what followed is still haunting me.

'And then *what*?' the emperor barks. 'THEN WHAT?'

'He called for the Eagle, the Aquila...' I say, remembering the formal name rarely used by men in the ranks.

'And? AND?'

'With his dying breath he raised it high...'

'AND THEN WHAT? DAMN YOU!' he screams at me, face crimson, hands trembling.

'The clouds above parted, piercing light striking down from the heavens to engulf the Eagle.'

'The gods reached out to you,' he whispers as he breathes heavily, a smile growing across his lips. 'What of our enemies?'

'Blinded,' I state. I'm still in disbelief, despite seeing it for myself. 'Their eyes were burned from their skulls, and yet not one single Roman was harmed, nor those few Britons who remained loyal. When the light ceased, all who sought to destroy us were blind. Then we saw the legatus and all our dead standing with us. Their souls had returned to that hilltop to save the legion. In frenzy, we slaughtered our foes'.

'The gods and your fallen brothers saved you, young centurion,' the emperor states proudly. 'Tell me, how many of the Legio IX Hispana still march?'

'Twenty-six,' I reply quickly. My words are not a complete lie.

'Chosen by the gods and saved,' he says, smile growing larger still. 'You are chosen, you few of so many who perished. I stand in awe of you, heroes of Rome. You shall be decorated and triumph held in your honour.'

'And all who fell,' I add, though instantly regret my words as he turns on me with sharp fury that thankfully breaks down into an almost sincere smile.

'Of course, to the legatus and all the brave warriors of Legio IX Hispana who gave their lives defeating Rome's enemies. All of you have done us a great honour. I will see you both elevated to ranks more befitting of such noble warriors. But first, before we call an end to this night, I must ask to see this bird touched by the gods themselves. Present me the Aquila. Give me the Legio IX Hispana's Eagle.'

'Apologies, Emperor. I do not have it.'

'You do not have it?' he asks in a mocking tone before shouting, 'YOU DO NOT HAVE IT!'

I see it then, the vileness and evil behind it all. I was warned, on the ship from Britannia, on the roads through Gallia, and at the very gates of Rome itself. Our emperor is truly a tyrant.

'WHERE IS THE DAMNED EAGLE?' he screams.

The praetorian guard is advancing on us with their swords drawn.

'WHERE IS THE POWER OF THE GODS? WITH IT I CAN PURGE THE MUCK AND FILTH OF THIS ONCE GREAT EMPIRE UNTIL ONLY PURITY REMAINS!' He is so angry that spit is foaming on his lips. He is mad. Mad and dangerous.

'It was lost on the battlefield,' I hurry to say. 'It was destroyed.' I feel Acer's eyes. He is alarmed at the lies but I have no choice. I cannot let the Eagle fall into the hands of this madman.

'You lost a gift bestowed from the gods?' he asks, voice low, barely more than a whisper. 'WHERE IS THE EAGLE?' he yells again.

'Destroyed by the very gods that saved us, shattered into a thousand pieces,' Acer attests, speaking his first words in attempt to stem the emperor's wrath.

'No! I do not believe it.' His fury continues to rage. 'You lost the Eagle and your honour. The Legio IX Hispana's shame survives only through those who yet live, and as such, I shall see it torn from sight, existence, and memory. The Legio IX Hispana shall be struck from the lists, eradicated from history, its honour and glories lost, forever forgotten – just as you will be. You are no one now.'

'No, Emperor. It was not so. You're mistaken...'

He strikes me hard across the face with a speed and strength I did not credit him with possessing. The taste of blood is quickly on my lips.

'You dare speak to me as such! I will see you crucified, boy!'

'Emperor, please...' I try to stop him but it is too late; the praetorians are already closing in.

'No!' Emperor Vespasian yells at me, stepping back to let the guards pass him and face us. 'You men are all that remains of your shame. You abandoned your legion and the garrison in Britannia. You will be an example to all foolish enough to think of deserting their posts. The rest of your men, those at Campus Martius, will be crucified as deserters, traitors, and cowards.'

Hiding the Eagle was the only right choice in all of this madness, even if it has damned my brothers and me to the afterlife.

Acer roars in defiance and throws himself towards the emperor, despite having no weapon to hand. A praetorian blade tears at his flesh but it does not stop him. Two guards fall onto the polished marble floor as others rise to face him. I am there beside him, felling one guard before firmly striking the prefect across the jaw and disarming him. With a flurry of death and blood, the emperor's finest are defeated by a lowly centurion and his friend.

'No!' I yell as a spear stabs through Acer's armour and into his chest, but the brute does not slow. Acer tears the weapon from his bloody wound and uses it to vanquish more guards. He spits blood but fights on. He is a true warrior.

As I face the last guard in my path before I reach the emperor, my vision suddenly turns dark. Agony tears at the back of my skull as I fall to my knees. My sword is wrenched from my grasp.

'Stop!' The emperor's voice rings through the chime of a thousand bells in my head.

Five blades are poised, ready to pierce my flesh and end my life. The fury in their eyes is as wild as the man who commands them. Acer lies before me, his eyes open and staring into the distance. Pools of blood spread across the floor.

'You are a true Roman warrior,' the emperor declares, standing before me. 'Crucifixion would not be honourable enough for you – it is for the scum that plague our empire. Death would not be lasting or agonising enough for you. You are noble – to a fault –and so your life will be spared, but it is not your own. You are now my war-slave, and your true punishment is to witness the death of your remaining legion, with them knowing you have been spared. Know this, in the last moments, they will hate you.'

'No...' is all I can utter before the darkness claims me.

13

ADAM—The British Museum, London, England

I am given fresh clothes – jeans and a t-shirt – before I am led up to the operations floor. We use the lift instead of the utility staircase I apparently broke into.

'How far underground are we?' I ask as the lift passes floor after floor of artefact storage.

'Far enough to house castles and pyramids,' Emma replies with a smirk. I can't tell if she is being serious or not.

'Really?' I can't help but ask.

'Yep,' Dave replies. 'All without a single window to the outside world. Hope you don't get claustrophobic, kid.'

As we exit the lift with Charles at the lead, I see the operations rooms are a hive of activity. Small teams of people, all wearing headsets, are working at stations that link into vast screens, which cover the entire walls.

'Each room denotes a different team,' Charles tells me as we walk past them. 'Echo, Delta, Charlie, Bravo, and Alpha. Charlie Team, headed by a husband and wife team, and Delta Team, led by famed Professor Helena Lainson, are on active hunts as we speak.'

The screens in Charlie show lands with dense tropical jungle. Ruins of long lost civilisations nestle between the verdant foliage. The screens for Delta show a very different scene. There are flames everywhere. A city on fire. From what I can work out, the teams in these rooms radio in instructions to the ground team using information gained from the drones and satellite images.

'Bravo team is...' His words falter as we pass the Bravo room. The lights are out and it is occupied by one single man. He is buried in his chair, coat wrapped over him as he sleeps. His feet are up on the console, which also houses an empty bottle of whiskey.

'Well, you can judge for yourself what Bravo team is like,' Charles says before speaking to Dave. 'Remind me to have words with Gabriel.'

Dave nods.

'We also have in support Chief Physician Dr Scott Wallace who helped see to your wounds, and our lead technician, Tristram Hill.'

'What of the Alpha and Echo teams?' I ask.

'Alpha is stood down for the foreseeable future,' Charles explains after a brief pause.

'A long story, apparently,' Dave adds to end the subject. Beyond him I can see the Alpha room lights off and long since occupied.

'And as for Echo Team,' Charles says as we reach the doors. 'You can see for yourself.'

Inside, the screens all show maps and satellite images of Loch Lomond, the island of Inchlonaig, and the tombs of the Legio IX Hispana. One smaller set of monitors is the camera feeds showing the medical rooms, the corridors, and stairwells I walked and the containment & storage floors of the British Museum. In the centre of the room is the young woman who seemed so nervous when I first met her outside my house. Here, surrounded by all these monitors and maps, she seems completely at home.

'I suppose you remember Abbey,' Charles says as we walk into the room.

'I thought I recognised that voice,' I say.

'Sorry, couldn't resist,' she says with a big grin, high-fiving Emma as she perches against her desk.

'So, what does this have to do with Matt?'

'Echo Team was assembled two years ago when the previous team disbanded,' Charles explains. 'I recruited the brightest and best of the new generation; Matt, Abbey, and Emma, with Dave as support. They trained for six months before they were sent into the field.'

'For what reason?' I ask. 'What was the point in these teams?'

'Each team down here is focussed on the acquisition of items of historical importance...'

'Grave robbers,' I interrupt.

'Far from it – we're guardians,' Emma disagrees. 'We act to keep relics out of the hands of thieves and tyrants. Each team has at least one or two specialists that are dispatched into the field,' she continues.

'Operatives is the correct term,' Charles corrects her.

'Hunters are what I call them,' she says, ignoring both Charles and Dave as they sigh with annoyance.

'Good choice of name!' I quip drily.

'Matt and Emma are Echo Team's hunters,' Abbey explains, bringing up an image of the team – Matt is at its centre.

'The best of the best,' she adds, drawing a brief smile from Emma who fixes me with a hard stare. I struggle to ignore it and focus, her green and blue eyes almost mesmerising.

'So my brother was a relic hunter?' I ask, barely able to believe what I was hearing. 'This all sounds ridiculous. Did he wear a fedora too?'

'A baseball cap,' Charles says without humour. Abbey is unable to contain a small laugh.

'So you recruited the best and brightest?' I ask.

Charles nods with pride.

'Yeah, that sounds like the golden boy.'

'Is that jealousy I hear?' Emma teases.

'Yep,' I admit, 'but not in the way you think.'

'Anyway,' Charles says, thankfully ignoring my last remarks, 'Matthew has been very successful. He has acquired many items of historical prominence, preventing them from falling into the wrong hands. We protect them here, below the main museum.'

'How do you fund all this?' I ask, looking between the monitors and thinking of the other teams all over the world. 'Somehow I can't imagine the museum donations quite cover it.'

'We're a branch of the British government. The British Museum is our storefront, so to speak,' Charles explains. 'We link with aspects of MI-5, MI-6, and occasionally, other units that deal with things... stranger. Our division has been in place since before the creation of the museum above in 1753. Some of our funding comes from the government, but not nearly enough. The rest we find through the sale of some of our acquisitions to private collectors, or as we call them, custodians.'

'Meaning you pawn off some of what you find?' I remark.

'Pretty much,' Abbey whispers to me.

'This all sounds crazy,' I say. 'The museum was built to cover your facility beneath it?'

'Exactly,' Charles replies. 'Fortunately, the museum

doubles as a site where we can display the objects of lesser interest to us. Others, like what your brother went to Loch Lomond to search for, are too dangerous to house anywhere else.'

'What was my brother after?' I ask. 'I assume it was more than just the legion's tomb.'

'You found the coin down there, right?' Abbey asks.

'Yes,' I say, remembering the edged coin, the imprint of an eagle on one side and the Property of the British Museum stamp on the other.

'That coin was of the Roman era,' Abbey says. 'From 27BC to 476AD, the Roman Empire ruled much of the known world. Roads, bridges, aqueducts, baths, theatres and arenas; the Romans built them all. They had the best army in the world, setting many of the standards that are still in place in armed forces. Julius Caesar, Mark Antony, Augustus, Vespasian, Titus... the list goes on of rulers and emperors, names that are still well known by most.'

'So, about the coin,' I say, lost in Abbey's history lesson. 'It opened the stone doorway into the tombs below the loch.'

'As Matt thought it would,' she says with a smile. 'That coin was found in northern Scotland on a dig five years ago; the Eagle emblazoned on one side and, very faintly on the other, the words Legio IX Hispana. You know the tales of the legion, right?'

'It marched north into Scotland and was never seen again.'

'Until now. Your brother heard talk of a cave system found on the island of Inchlonaig. Another Roman coin, almost identical, was found at the scene. Matt took our coin from the vaults and set out without word to any of us. Always impulsive.'

'It runs in the family,' Charles added, looking to me.

'He only got in touch with us when he was already inside the tombs,' Abbey adds.

'Why is that legion of so much interest?' I ask. 'I mean, sure it vanished without a trace and it's inspired many books and films ...'

'Channing Tatum...' Abbey whispers, in a daze.

'On track, Abbey,' Dave says.

She rolls her eyes at him and I see then just how close their team is. I'm strangely jealous that Matt is part of this world. Abbey is tapping something out on her computer screen and talking over her shoulder, as if all of this is the most perfectly normal thing in the world.

'The disappearance of the legion isn't the end of the story.' Excitement grows in her voice. 'Do you know what a legion's Eagle is?

'Like a regiment's flag?'

'Exactly,' Abbey responds. 'In the Roman army, the legion's standard was the most sacred possession, touched by the hand of the emperor himself. Men fought and died for their Eagle. It was the greatest dishonour for the Eagle to be captured by the enemy. It's a tradition that continued on into the armies of French emperor, Napoleon Bonaparte, his brigades carrying Eagle standards too. Even the British armies under the Duke of Wellington marched beneath their colours, their regimental and national flags.'

'Back to the Ninth Legion, Abbey,' Charles instructs.

'Yes, so you see, in 76 AD, the Legio IX Hispana, known commonly as the Ninth Legion, was stationed in Britannia as part of Emperor Vespasian's invasion. They marched north to deal with barbarian hordes in the north of Britain, aiding one tribe in particular under the dragon banner, its leader being Uther.'

'You mean *the* Uther, Uther Pendragon, as in King Arthur's father?' I ask in surprise. 'You're kidding, right?'

'That's off track, Abbey,' Charles intercedes. 'A story for another day.'

'Right,' she says, taking off her glasses and rubbing them clean. 'So the Ninth Legion marched north with a dozen tribes in pursuit of one. Except when battle came, it wasn't just one tribe they faced. All but a few of the tribes they called an ally turned on them and the legion was massacred.'

'So far so Hollywood film,' I say.

'Until we come to the end,' Abbey says, her eyes alive and the speed of her words rapid, which, along with her broad Irish accent, was making her increasingly hard to follow. 'When they were down to a handful of men, the legion commander took the standard, their bronze Eagle, and with his dying breath, raised it to the heavens. The heavens replied, a beam of light striking down and blinding all those who faced the Romans. Victory was seized from certain defeat. Whether it was a bolt of lightning striking the Earth, the gods answering a dying man's prayers, or something else, nobody can be sure. It had long been thought of as a rumour, an old wives' tale told generation to generation,'

'A myth, you mean,' Dave mutters.

'That's not the end of the story,' Abbey says. 'Once their foes were blinded, the Romans found they were not alone on that hilltop. The souls of their fallen brothers supposedly rose up to save the legion. Their fallen never truly stopped protecting their own.'

'It's a ghost story, then,' I say, enthralled by her tale. 'How do you know it isn't anything more than a myth?'

'We don't, not truly,' Charles says, 'but that coin was the only proof in existence that we had relating to the Eagle and the legion. That and the vase.'

'Vase?' I ask.

With three taps on her computer, Abbey brings up a rotating image of a chipped and faded vase on the main screen. There are pale images on the vase, but time had not ravaged them beyond recognition. Roman soldiers with raised Eagle, holy light shining down, and deformed demons falling to the ground. It was an impressive sight, depicting what Abbey described perfectly, except the demonic Britons. My eyes settle on the Eagle.

'The vase was found in a dig just south of modern day Glasgow,' Abbey states, 'along with a small amount of Roman armour, coin, and weaponry.'

'Where is the vase now?' I ask.

'One of our rivals has it,' Charles states coldly, anger simmering within. 'There has been a spate of robberies on museums across Europe in the past three months by two men, an Australian and an American.'

'Leon and Bishop,' I say under my breath.

'This vase is recorded as currently missing,' Charles continues.

'Until you and Matt found the tombs, the coin and vase were the only proof of the legion.' Abbey indicates to the main screens on the wall as she displays the live feeds of survey teams heading into the caves of Inchlonaig.

'Your own token of the crypt,' Dave says, placing the Roman gladius blade upon a table in the centre of the room. 'I believe it now belongs to you. Fortunate you didn't land on it when your bike crashed. I found the blade a few yards away from where you landed.'

For the first time, I get a proper look at the gladius in good light. Engraved across the blade is the name of its last owner, Thadian, and on the pommel of the ivory hilt are the letters H IX, Legio IX Hispana.

'It really is a beautiful place,' Abbey says, looking up to the live feeds of the island and surrounding loch.'

Looking up to the monitors, I see the teams making their way through the caves, following the route I took. 'Make sure to warn them of the traps down there,' I say, instinctively feeling the bandages at my arm.

'The support teams are aware,' Charles replies.

'How are you feeling, anyway?' Abbey asks, showing some genuine concern.

'Better than I look, that's for certain,' I say. 'Injuries aren't that bad, although I don't remember the one to my head.'

'That was from your tumble off the bike,' Emma says. 'You need to be more careful.'

'Dave patched you up before bringing you here for further medical attention,' Charles explains. 'He is a former combat medic, among other things, formerly of the Royal Marines Commandos and the Special Air Service.'

'In a past life,' he mutters gruffly. 'Best forgotten, believe me.'

'Thank you,' I say but he says nothing back. 'How long have I been here?'

'Two days recuperating,' Charles explains. 'We kept you sedated so your body would have time to recover. It proved difficult as you kept waking up, despite the sedation.'

'Probably something to do with being hyperactive,' I

say. 'My mother always says that, as a boy, I ran before I crawled.'

'Yes, well we notified your mother that you are here and safe,' Charles says. 'She was exceedingly pleased to hear you are not harmed. We told her you are helping us with the search for Matthew. To be truthful, we were concerned about your head injury but it was not nearly as serious as we first feared. She wasn't happy though ...'

'Wouldn't be her if she was happy,' I say.

'She wants you home as soon as possible,' he adds.

'Why does she dislike you so much, Charles?' I ask, ignoring his last comment.

'I lost her son.' His voice is distant. 'I lost someone she loves.'

'What of the guys who ran me off the road and nearly killed me?' I ask, changing the uncomfortable subject. 'Leon and Bishop?'

'Jack Bishop and Leon Bransby,' Dave says. 'They call themselves climbers and explorers but they are more like hired mercenaries. I've faced them once or twice before.'

'And put a bullet in one of them,' Emma adds with a wink.

'Anyway,' Dave continues, undeterred, 'they wouldn't be in Scotland without being on the payroll of someone.'

'There was someone else down there with us,' I say. 'Covered in tattoos, black hair, black eyes. He... he used fire on me, blue flames.'

I see Charles and Abbey share a knowing glance, before Dave speaks. 'Sounds like you were hallucinating down there. Fear can do strange things to the mind.'

'He engulfed me in flames. It burned me, yet when it was gone there wasn't a mark on my body. I'm sure that he has Matt – there was something about him.'

'We have alerted MI-5 and MI-6 and they are aiding us in every way they can to track them and your brother down,' Dave explains.

'They wanted the Eagle,' I say. I'm coming to understand that my brother is no closer to returning home to his family.

'And I'm guessing it was not in the tombs?' Charles asks.

'Not that I saw,' I reply.

'And not that your camera did either,' Abbey says. With a few button clicks, the main screens change to the photos I took with my phone, showing the tombs, caskets, and Roman armour.

'How did you get these?' I ask.

'Your phone and laptop were utterly ruined in the crash,' she explains, 'but I was able to recover the data files from the remains and your SIM card. A lot of text messages came through as well. Who is Sara? I'm guessing she's the pretty girl who takes up most of your phone memory.'

'On track, Abbey,' Charles says. I'm grinning with a mix of embarrassment and pride.

'From the photos of the legatus's tomb, I was able to transcribe some of the Latin inscriptions on the walls,' she says.

'You can read Latin?' I ask in surprise, thinking it a dead language.

'Everybody needs a hobby.' She shrugs. 'Anyway, most of the inscriptions on the walls are names of battles and the legion's past glories. Colchester was one of them. I wonder if they fought Boudicca... Anyway, there is mention of the Eagle but the photos are not clear enough to make out the rest. When our teams breach the tombs they will send me further images.'

'How does this help us find Matt?' I ask.

'Until we know where they have taken Matthew, all we can do is pick up his trail,' Charles says. 'If they took Matthew to find the Eagle, they will likely be on the same path. We don't know where Matthew or his captors are, but we know what they are after. Find the Eagle and we will likely find your brother.'

'You hope,' I say doubtfully, but Charles doesn't reply.

'We need only one thing from you,' Charles says. 'The journal.'

'You already have it and the rest of my belongings,' I say, not quite able to hide the irritation from my voice.

'It will be given to you in due time. But Matthew's journal... can you decipher his encryptions?'

'You already know the answer to that,' I reply.

'Unless Matthew told you directly, there was no other way you could have known to travel to Inchlonaig and how to enter the tombs,' Charles says, waiting for my reaction. 'In the pages of his journal it said exactly where he was going.'

'And it also says for me not to trust *anyone* with his journal.'

'Does it have any mention of the Eagle or where it might have been hidden?' Abbey asks.

'I have seen some information on the legion, mentions of it, and the Eagle,' I lie. I have been beaten once already by Matt's captors. If I help Charles then he and the rest of them may help me in finding my brother.

'Translate it for us and we will do the rest.' Charles is doing his best to be coaxing and friendly, but I'll not make it that easy for him.

'No.'

'What do you mean, no?' Charles says, a flash of anger rising. 'Why the hell not? If you want out, if you want your brother to suffer and die at the hands of those madmen, then go ahead, leave. You know where the stairs are.'

I turn, about to leave. I can't trust them, not completely. I don't need them and I will find Matt on my own.

'Wait,' Charles says, stopping me. 'Abbey, bring up Delta's live feeds onto the screens.'

It shows a city burning.

'This was Tatunkech, a thriving city in Morocco,' he explains. 'Seven days ago, I sent Charlie team in to recover a chalice rumoured to gift healing powers to the drinker. They were not the first to reach the city in search of the chalice, but were the first to find it. Their rival brought entire buildings down to stop my team, destroying the chalice in the process. He burned the entire city, starting the fires with blue flames.'

Blue flames. The man in the tombs.

'Did your team get out?' I ask.

'Yes but not without injury,' Charles says, his sadness laced with anger. 'That city still burns. Thankfully, we were able to conduct a full-scale evacuation, but lives were lost. We failed. I will not let that happen again. I will not lose Matthew.'

'Who is he?' I ask. 'The man with the blue flames?'

Charles indicates for Abbey to flick up the screen. There he is; the same twisted tattoos, the same terrifying black eyes. Despite his clothes changing, one thing remains in each image: a chain hanging from his neck from which a black crystal pendant hangs.

'His name is Vladimir Makov,' Charles says. 'The British Museum has encountered Mr Makov many times over the years. He is judged as a highly dangerous individual, for more than a few reasons.'

The images on the monitors change to show more photos of the man, going back several years based on the quality of the images.

'We can't be sure of his true origin, his age, or even if Makov is his real name, but what we can say is, he has been sighted many times over the years around the world.'

A map appears on another screen, dots appearing to denote his locations, covering hundreds of countries.

'He has many rumoured *talents*,' Charles says. 'Conjuring and manipulation of blue flames is one, as well as control of certain beasts and some form of telepathy...'

'Utter rubbish,' Dave moans. 'Children's stories.'

'...but his most profound ability is proven by these images,' Charles finishes.

I look at the many photos, the images going back decades until finally, they are in black and white. In every single one he appears exactly the same, those haunting black eyes, the dark veins and twisted thorn tattoos – the man shows no sign of aging.

'He doesn't age.' A knot is pulling tight in my stomach. I shiver at the memory of his touch – his ice-cold touch – like the hand of death himself, and of course, the flames.

'Exactly.' Charles sighs heavily. 'The earliest sightings we have of him are these photographs from 1916 at the outbreak of the First World War.'

'Over a hundred years old but still looks in his late thirties,' Abbey says. 'His sightings include many events that have shaped history, crossing paths with world leaders, revolutionaries, and inventors.'

On the images Abbey shows on the monitors, I spot Makov's face behind possibly the most famous band in the world.

'Is that him with...'

'Yep,' Abbey replies. 'All this and he is even rumoured to be a necromancer.'

'There's no such thing,' Dave says with unmasked laughter.

'He can summon and control the dead?' I ask in disbelief.

'I am impressed,' Abbey says.

'It is only a rumour,' Charles intersects. 'How he gained any of these so called *talents* is unknown to us.'

'A deal with the devil,' Abbey adds, nodding sagely. Emma rolls her eyes but Abbey is not deterred. 'There are other beliefs, such as the crystal pendant he carries is the source of his power and...'

'What we do know for certain,' Charles continues, 'is that he is highly dangerous and cares little for loss of life.'

'He mentioned a blood moon,' I say, remembering his taunts before he threw me into the river.

'A blood moon is the term for a totally eclipsed moon, where it has a reddish shade,' Abbey explains. 'There are many prophecies associated with it, some stating a blood moon will usher in the end of the world. The Book of Joel of the Hebrew Bible states, '*The sun will turn into darkness, and the moon into blood, before the great and terrible day of the Lord comes.*''

'That's not foreboding at all,' Emma says sarcastically. 'Perhaps that is what Makov wants. To usher in the end of days.'

'What is interesting,' Abbey says, 'is in many of the stories about the Ninth Legion and the Eagle, it is reported that there was a blood moon on the night of the battle.'

'Whoever... whatever Makov is, necromancer, fraudster, or gangster, he has Matt and I need to find him,' I say.

'Wait a second...' Dave begins to argue but I stop him before he can say more.

'Thank you for patching me up, really, but this is something I have to do. In Matt's journal he warns me not to let it fall into the wrong hands. Until I can trust you people completely, I can't let you have his secrets.'

'You're not the only one who wants to find Matt!' Emma bites, showing her anger for the first time. 'Why don't you grow up and help us?'

'He's my brother.' I look her straight in the eyes. 'If anyone will find him, it will be me.'

'You're just like your brother,' Charles says with resignation. 'He's always bloody difficult too. There's only one way I will allow this and that is if you take the trials, just like every single one of our operatives.'

'Trials?' I ask.

'Tests of your physical and mental capabilities,' Abbey explains. 'They're designed to train and better our hunters...'

'Operatives,' Charles corrects her.

'...and as a proving ground for those seeking to join their ranks.'

'I don't have time for your games, trials, whatever you call them,' I say. 'I need to find Matt.'

'With our current information, we do not know where Matthew is or where Makov has taken him,' Charles says. 'With no clues, where should we look? Tell us because we are all eager to hear. We need you to decipher his journal for us, but you're an outsider and you're still behaving like one. If we're going to work together, then you need to join the team, and to do that, you need to pass the trials.'

'You can't be serious,' Dave blurts out. He's risen from his seat and is looking at me hard. 'Look, kid, no offense, I've seen you in action and I can tell you have potential, but there's no way we can send him out there as one of ours. He's barely recovered from the crash or the injuries sustained in the tomb.' He pauses. 'How old are you, anyway?'

Charles steps forward, his voice low and soft. 'Although he's far too arrogant to admit it, Adam needs our help, and if we're honest, we need his. Our end goal is the same, but I'm not prepared to give unofficial personnel access to our resources or to operate under our protection. Think about it,' he says, placing a hand on my arm. 'You need us as much as we need you, and you've already demonstrated such a similarity with your brother that I know we're all going to get along just famously.'

Dave tuts and sighs, but backs off.

I do think about it. As much as it pains me to admit it, Charles is right – and this could all work in my favour. Exploit the exploiter – what's that saying about keeping your friends close but your enemies closer? I still don't know which these people are, not yet.

'Fine, I'll do your damned tests,' I say.

'If he thinks he can handle them.' Emma chuckles in disbelief.

'I'll prove myself.'

'Sure you will, hero,' Abbey says. Dave throws his hands in the air in exasperation. 'Aw, come on, Dave. What's the worst that can happen?'

'You do remember what happened to Tristram...' Dave begins to say before Abbey hushes him to stop.

'He wasn't that bad,' she says quietly in his defence, cheeks blushing.

'Good luck,' Emma says to me as she heads off towards the door. 'You're really gonna need it!'

'This is a load of...' Dave begins to protest.

'You can coach him and see him through them your-self,' Charles orders the former soldier.

'Babysitting duty, fantastic,' Dave mutters.

'First things first,' I say. 'Where is my bike, my clothes, my rucksack, and Matt's journal?'

'About the bike,' Abbey replies with a pained expression, sending dread coursing through me.

'What about my bike?'

14

MARCUS AURELIUS—Rome

Buckets of water rouse me from the darkness. An unknown hand drags my head up. As my eyes clear, I see my men dying upon crosses throughout the Campus Martius. Acer is amongst them, the eyes of his lifeless body finding me. I led my brothers to this end; to this terrible death.

'No...' I try to stand; there is fight still in me, but the fists of the bruised and bloodied praetorian prefect force me to the ground. Again, I'm beaten before being stripped naked and dragged into the open square of the camp before hundreds of recruits. As my hands are tied about a post, the prefect speaks to all gathered.

'This man and all who followed him are traitors of Rome. Their oaths forsaken, the sacramentum sworn to the gods broken and abandoned. Emperor Vespasian commands they be put to death, the Legio IX Hispana struck from the lists of honourable legions, and this man, this centurion, be condemned as a slave to spend the last of his days fighting for his very survival.'

The prefect approaches me with a glowing iron heated in fiery coals.

'Upon the arm of all who fight, is the mark of their legion. This man... this boy,' he corrects, adding to my humiliation, 'is not worthy of such honour.'

The iron is lowered to my skin and searing pain wracks my arm as my flesh burns, filling my nostrils with its wretched stench until the mark of H IX is stricken through. Then the flagellum strikes, the whip tearing the skin and flesh of my back apart until the darkness seizes me again. The last thing I feel is the blood running down my legs. One word passes my lips before I fall. 'Lucilla...'

15

ADAM—The British Museum, London, England

After seeing my first attempts at the assault course, they allow me to watch them in action. 'An example of how it's done,' they tell me. I must admit, I'm impressed. Abbey gives clear direction and instructions efficiently like a commander from base, and seeing Emma and Dave in action is a sight to behold. Dave is like an action hero of old; all military, all testosterone and strength. He shows no weakness, never slowing or admitting defeat, powering through the course.

Emma is something else. Lithe and agile, strong when needed, and with a pace I have never seen before. She roars in triumph as she beats Dave's recorded time. The girls I know from home are only interested in their beauty, clothes, and shopping, but this one, Emma... she is different. Sweat drips down her muddy face, arms marked with cuts and scars of old, punching the air in success. I can't take my eyes off her, and the memory stays with me as I prepare for my next attempt, despite her attitude towards me.

'Go! Go! Go!' roars Dave, urging me on, trying to snap sense into me.

Sweat drips from my face as I run, finishing the last of the three mile course before hurling myself at the cargo net. I clamber up as fast as my legs and hands can move. At its top, I grasp the high wires and shimmy along them like a trapeze artist. At the far side is a zip wire and I fly down it, all the while being judged, timed, and ranked. A vast clock ticks above me as Dave and Abbey watch on from the control tower, monitoring the very environment around me and selecting the trials I will face next.

As I near the ground, hurtling down the zip wire, a climbing wall rises before me, emerging at Abbey and Dave's command. On landing, I leap to the wall, finding the grips quickly and pulling myself up and onwards. At the summit is a rope bridge and rows of monkey bars. I swing across the course, my arms bearing all my weight and carrying me from bar to bar. After that, finally, the end is in sight. I drop down onto the final stretch, a one mile sprint.

An alarm sounds to signal the trial's completion and I

fall to the ground, shirt soaked through with sweat, panting for breath.

'How...did...I...do?' I gasp.

'Sorry, Adam,' Abbey apologises. My time flashes on a large screen over the tower window and then the required time. Three seconds short.

'Run it again,' I demand.

'This will be the fourth time,' Dave says.

'Why put off what can be done today?' The family motto.

Three seconds, three measly seconds.

My time flickers away and I see Dave standing in the tower, looking down on me with arms crossed.

'Your speed and agility are not good enough,' he judges. 'Though I disagree with him, Charles has ordered me to train you. It's my job to help you to survive out there. If you want to join in the search for your brother, you must pass these trials. This is only the first trial too. There are more you must face. More physical and mental challenges that will test your intellect beyond any exam you took in school. Very few people succeed and even less become operatives. Your brother was fortunate, the youngest to pass the trials at the age of eighteen. I'm not going easy on you just because you are now the youngest to take these tests, and the fact Matt is your brother.'

'Well, it doesn't help with you keep changing the

course,' I protest, though I know expressing that frustration was stupid of me.

'The outside world will not be predictable,' Dave states in a voice from the army ranks. 'There are dangers you will face and serious threats to your life, as you did in the tombs in Scotland. It's a miracle you survived. We will only allow you out there to find your brother if I deem you ready. Abbey, bring up the listing.'

'Yes, Sir,' she replies in her own army voice.

On the tower's window are a list of names and times which appear under the heading, Trial Leaders. Matt's name is on there, thirty-eight seconds faster than me. At the top of the list is the name Gabriel, his time a whole three and a half minutes faster than my last attempt.

'These are all people who earned their place among the operatives,' Dave states.

'Hunters,' Abbey tries to correct.

'There are plaques in the operations rooms of each team, dedicated to the fallen,' Dave explains. 'Walls of Honour, we call them. Operatives, analysts, technicians, they all died for what they believed in. I don't want Matt joining the names on those plaques – or yours by association.'

'Run the tests again,' I order.

16

SLAVE—Capua

For days, I slip between life and death. I am in terrible agony. It is only the skill of the medicus that ensures I live and heal in body, if not in mind. My head is full of my wife's touch and haunting voice, the legion's roar of laughter and cheers of battle won, the screams of Lucilla's fear, the agonised cries of my dying brothers.

I wake to a dank cell, with blood-stained walls and a dirt floor for my bed. My hands are bound in chains. The only clothing is the subligaculum, which covers my loins. There is still searing pain from my mutilated flesh.

'Another weak fool soon to die,' mocks a voice from the darkness.

'Feeble boy won't survive to see the arena.'

'Nor another sunrise unless the gods show favour.'

'He bears the legion's mark. Damned deserter.'

'Coward by my bet.'

'The boy's corpse will feed the dogs.'

Their cruel mockery continues until sleep takes hold again.

By morning, I am roused and dragged from my cell, forced into line with boys and men also newly enslaved. Around us, others scorn and jeer, each one appearing strong and marked from conflict. They are warriors: gladiators. In ludus I now stand.

'Be ready and show honour to your Dominus,' a voice shouts.

Whips crack to gather our order as our master approaches. His skin is darkened and aged by the sun. He is an elder by any other reckoning.

'My name is Albinius Hader, but to you, I am Dominus,' he introduces himself as he walks up and down our line. 'I purchased each and every one of you. You belong to me. I am your master. Your very existence belongs to me. I gift you the food you eat, the water you drink, the very air you breathe because it is my will.'

'Damn this,' mutters one of the youngest in the line, not old enough to grow a beard. Our Dominus does not miss the boy's sneers and responds swiftly by slamming a fist into his stomach. It is a display of strength that none of us fail to doubt.

'Speak out of turn or disrespect me again and you will be feed for the dogs – whilst alive!'

Hader turns to the rest of us, calming after his quick show of anger.

'You stand in my ludus, the training ground for warriors of great renown. Around you stand heroes of the arena, the blood of the gods runs through their veins! They are gladiators of the House of Hader!'

The men roar and cheer, chanting the name Hader in honour of their Dominus.

'All have shed blood. All have claimed victories and glory for the House of Hader. Train and prove yourselves worthy to be among their number. Join them and as gladiators seize glory upon the sands – and then, one day, maybe you will earn your freedom. Swear your oath to me! Fight for me! Spill blood for me! Claim victory in the name of the House of Hader!'

It is the recruits' turn to cheer, but I do not. It does not go unnoticed.

'We have one not swayed by my words,' Hader proclaims as he faces me. 'And of course it is the one who cost me the most coin and arrived in the worst condition. This rotting boy of the legions.'

'Why make purchase then?' I dare to ask, unconcerned for my fate.

His fist slams into my stomach, and although my knee

buckles, I stumble but still stand, unlike the foolish boy who spoke out before who remains on the ground still.

'So there is some life in the corpse yet,' he sneers. 'You see this boy?' he addresses the rest in line. 'He is branded a deserter from the legions. He abandoned his brothers.'

'I am centurion of the...'

My words are ended by lash and fist until I lay on the ground, beaten but not broken. When the attack stops, though bleeding and aching, I rise and revert to the ways of raw recruit of the legion, eyes straight forward, not meeting the Dominus's gaze. My tongue is still. Success in war is as much about intelligence as it is strength. Timing is everything.

'This goes for all of you,' Hader states to every man before him. 'I do not care what you did in your life before entering the walls of this ludus. Glories or sins, it matters not to me. The men you were no longer exist. You are mine and you will be forged anew. Join my gladiators or die and be feed for the dogs.'

As all around me cheer, eager for blood, eager for glory, I realise I have escaped one life of war and bitter struggle for survival and entered another, where the cheers of the crowd will decide life or coming death.

17

ADAM—The British Museum, London, England

Standing there, sweat covering me, I face Dave. His hardened glare is settled on me, an anger bubbling under the surface.

'You may have beaten my assault course, barely reaching the needed time,' he tells me through gritted teeth, 'but you will not pass what is next. Survive for one minute. That is all you need to do.'

'What is the test?' I ask.

'Unarmed combat,' he tells me. 'Leon Bransby, Jack Bishop, even Vladimir Makov, they are but three of many rivals you may face out there and they will stop at nothing to claim power and riches beyond understanding. It's our job to stop them and I need to know that you can protect yourself.'

There are no weapons or objects with which to make use of in our fight, just our bodies and the clock.

'This should be fun,' Emma says from her perch above us on a climbing wall. I don't know if I should be pleased or nervous that she is watching.

'There will be no cheap shots this time,' Dave warns. 'Abbey, start the clock on my order. NOW!'

He charges at me, fists flying, and though I dodge the first punches, I don't see his boot rising, kicking me in the chest and driving me to the floor,

'Reset the clock,' Dave says, barely short of breath from his sudden attack.

'Yes, Sir,' Abbey says from the control tower as Emma giggles.

I stand but he gives me no time to recover.

'Again!' Dave yells. The clock is restarted and his assault renewed.

I last longer this time but he makes use of my wounds, grabbing my arm where the spear had cut. I weaken but fight on until his shoulder catches me, then an elbow to the ribs and finally a sweep of the legs that sends me tumbling.

'This is not good enough, Adam!' Dave yells at me as I struggle to stand. 'When we fought in the containment & storage floor you showed something close to skill and determination. Now I see nothing. What has happened?

Don't you want to find your brother? Don't you want to prove your worth?'

With those last words, I snap. I charge at him, barging him over. He's like a wall – and now he's angry – properly angry.

'Clock restarted!' Abbey cries over the loudspeaker, but I ignore her. My only focus is on Dave.

'Here we go,' Emma says, but I ignore her too.

His punches and strikes come thick and fast, but mine do as well. I twist and turn around him, landing a few of my own upon him with little effect. Ducking beneath a coming fist, I kick down on the back of his knee and strike him across the head. It dazes him for a precious few seconds before he attacks again.

'Thirty   seconds!'   Abbey   declares   over   the loudspeakers.

I draw him in, hands raised like a boxer's guard, before ducking down and rising with his fist under his jaw. It connects, but his only reaction is to wrap both arms around me, trapping my body against his.

'Now what, kid?' he taunts, before the temple of my head connects with his, reopening the stitches at my forehead, but releasing Dave's grasp.

We both stagger back, seeing stars but still standing, and we charge again, exchanging blows relentlessly.

'Enough!' Abbey orders.

We part, and I know I have passed but not without injury.

'Very good, kid,' Dave says, glare breaking down briefly into a smile before disappearing. 'Where was that fire before?'

'I just needed the right encouragement,' I say, panting for breath as I lean on one of the rocks of the assault course.

'Where did you learn to fight?' Emma asks, swinging down and approaching me, inspecting the reopened wound at my head.

'Why? Are you impressed?'

'Hardly,' she replies.

'Loundwell High School,' I tell her. 'There were a fair number of bullies around. Guys who would keep pushing you until you learned to stand up for yourself. My brother taught me that. They quickly learned it's much harder to bully people with a broken nose.'

18

SLAVE—Capua

My new *brothers'* words are unending.

'He still won't last to see the arena.'

'He's survived this far.'

'I hear our *centurion* has a wife.'

'Liar. Bet he's never touched...'

'Swear to the gods, he has a wife.'

'Bet she's a lovely little thing, if you know what I mean.'

'Better than you've ever been with, you fool.'

'He won't see her again. He's going to die here!'

'He won't speak. Hasn't since Dominus's introduction.'

'A boy and a coward. He wasn't centurion. He won't be a gladiator.'

'He will die, and his woman...well, his woman...'

I remain silent despite all the curses and taunts of those within the ludis. It is thoughts of Lucilla that will ensure I survive.

19

ADAM—The British Museum, London, England

'Tristram Hill,' the tech advisor greets me, shaking my hand enthusiastically with a broad grin. 'Congratulations on passing the first levels of the trials. It was good to see Dave face a real opponent for once.'

'You were watching?' I ask, placing a hand lightly to the re-sewn stitches at my head.

'Yep. Keeping Abbey company in the control tower,' he tells me, his tone happy and cheerful.

'I'm sure you were,' I say quietly to myself, already having suspicions of the pair after Abbey's blushing at the mere mention of his name earlier.

Tristram is a few years older than me; thick stubble across his jaw, an eyebrow pierced. He wears glasses, a short beanie hat covering his hair, and a Guns N' Roses t-shirt marked with oil stains. The smell of cigarettes is about him like an aftershave. I can hazard a pretty good guess at why he failed the trials.

'I'm here to talk you through your equipment,' he tells me, still smiling as he sweeps his arms across the table before him and all the kit laid out.

Water canteen, knife, versatile waterproof jacket, a one-man tent, torches, rations, lighter, flares, a large first aid kit, all manner of climbing gear, a compass, maps and journals, and a rucksack to carry it all in, flashlights connected to the shoulder straps. Above it all, my eyes are drawn to what I can only call a uniform or jumpsuit, dark grey trousers and long sleeved top with light blue lining cross both.

'You go out in these?' I ask.

'Lightweight but sturdy, similar to Kevlar but not as strong,' Tristram explains as I step behind a screen and pull on the clothes. 'It won't stop a bullet but it's tough, waterproof, and will keep you warm in colder climates and cool in the warmer places you may find yourself.'

'I look like I'm out of Tron,' I say, stepping back out.

'Don't knock it, it could save your life.'

'Yet no parachute or fancy gadgets?' I joke.

'You've been watching too many films,' Tristram replies with a smirk. 'But we have a few items that may be of interest to you. Abbey, can you bring up the electronics and countermeasures?'

'Sure thing, Tri,' she says via the loudspeakers; her voice is notably softer when speaking to Tristram.

A section of the flooring near to us parts and cabinets rise from below. Tristram inputs combinations into a keypad and then a palm and eye scan before the doors swing open. Within the cabinets are dozens of items, none of which I have any idea about what they are or what they can possibly do.

'Flash bangs, smoke grenades, bolas, infra-red cameras and visors, thermo clothing and equipment for the arctic or the depths of a volcano, EMP devices, knock-out gas...'

He goes on and on, using words I have never heard before let alone understand. As he speaks, he enthusiastically shows me the use of a few, the smoke and flash bangs in particular, hurling them across the room to show their effects. The bolas interest me more; wire cords weighted at both ends that, when thrown, wrap around a person, trapping and incapacitating them. I practice a few times with these on dummies raised into the room by Abbey.

'We do have one more neat toy,' Tristram tells me, taking a small case from the cabinet.

Inputting a combination into the case, he takes out a set of glasses; thin with clear lenses and silver frames. The tips hook around the ears, earpieces at their ends. Tristram places them onto me, extending and shortening so that they fit and the earpieces are secure.

'I've seen these before,' I say, recognising the design.

'You recovered Matt's pair from the crypt,' Tristram agrees. 'Thank you for returning them. We should be able to repair that set, for a small-fortune.'

'Silver?' I ask, unsure of the colour of the frames.

'I call it gun-metal grey,' Tristram replies quickly.

'And this is for...' I begin to ask before an all too familiar Irish voice speaks to me through the earpieces.

'The cameras in the frames feed directly back to us,' Abbey explains. 'I see whatever you see. This way we can stay in touch and I can advise you.'

'Creep me out and nag me you mean?'

'Exactly.' She chuckles. 'With this headset, I can upload any information and display it directly to you.'

As she says this, images and information appears across the lenses of the glasses before my eyes.

'And the range of these?'

'We have uplinks to and control of a hundred satellites around the world meaning the range is pretty much limitless,' she says cheerfully. 'They work on any bandwidth and are nearly impossible to block, meaning even in the depths of crypts miles beneath the surface, I can reach you.'

'How much did these cost?' I ask with disbelief, carrying what is easily the most technologically advanced item I have ever seen in person.

'There are only five sets of them in Europe,' Abbey explains. 'Three are in our hands and we only got them through doing Japan some favours with certain ancient artefacts we recovered. Let's just say, finding blades of the samurai nobility was very important to them. Even then it was only thanks to a friend of a friend of a millionaire's son that we have them. Their cost – let's just say, don't drop them.'

'You wanted to go out there?' I ask. 'Into the field, as they say.'

'Yep,' he replies, looking away in annoyance. 'You've got to pass the trials to go into the field though.'

'What happened?'

'It was a complete embarrassment. Anyway, here comes your drill sergeant.'

'Are you fully equipped?' Dave asks gruffly as he approaches. A bruise or two and at least one fresh cut grace his face from our combat. I can't help but feel a little smug about having roughed up his handsome face. 'Your next trial begins in three minutes.'

'Yep, I look like an idiot,' I say, pointing to the uniform and picking up the rucksack and equipment. 'Why do I need all this for the next level of the trials?'

'The next level of testing requires you to carry all the equipment you would into the field,' Dave states. 'That way, it's realistic with the endurance required of you. It's the same way the army trains.'

'And that's where you got the assault course from? Your army days?' I ask, to which he simply nods.

'Suit up, Mr Hunter,' Charles says as he enters the vast training complex. Again, as I take it in, I can't believe that it is all underground and all beneath one of London's biggest attractions.

'Come to see him fail?' Dave mocks me, but I don't react.

'I have come to go over Mr Hunter's file,' Charles states as he flicks through several pages of a report. 'I pulled up his records and it makes for interesting reading.'

'I'd ignore what you see in there,' I say as I pull on the waterproof jacket.

'High grades in sports and modest grades in all other subjects,' Charles surmises. 'You complete coursework and assignments in days rather than the weeks and months given. This is not because of intelligence, but simple drive.'

'Hang on, where does it say that?' I ask, no answer given.

'Matches my evaluation so far,' Dave adds. 'Brakes are broken but the accelerator works just fine.'

'Meaning what?' I ask as I pack the rucksack.

'I think you put it best with that saying of your family's,' replies Charles. 'Why put off what can be done today. It also says you are quite combative, getting into many fights at school and college.'

'For the record, I started none of them,' I say in my defence.

'Ended them though,' Charles concludes, to which I simply shrug.

'Three nights spent in police cells,' Abbey says over the loudspeakers from the control tower. 'Multiple counts of breaking and entering.'

'I never stole anything that I didn't return to the rightful owners,' I reply.

'A regular Robin Hood indeed,' Abbey says.

'A thief you mean,' Dave mutters.

'He should fit in well here then,' announces a voice as another man staggers into the facility. He looks dishevelled, in his early thirties, thick stubble, a couple of scars and dark rings under his eyes. His clothes are creased, dirty, and torn. He looks like a beggar.

'Not all of your record is for honourable deeds,' Abbey says, ignoring the newcomer.

'I can explain the one you mean,' I quickly say.

'Let me guess,' the beggar says, rubbing his eyes. 'It was all for a girl. It's always a girl.'

'I stole the headmaster's car,' I reply a little too defensively. 'Okay... it was to impress a girl.'

'Thought as much,' the man replies with a smug grin. 'Recruiting straight out of high school now, are we, Charles? My how desperate your little quest has become.'

'Adam Hunter, meet Gabriel Quinn, operative and sole member of Bravo Team,' Charles says, making the introductions.

'You work alone?' I ask as Gabriel slumps back against a wall.

'Safer that way,' he replies, taking a hipflask from his pocket and drinking deeply. 'For everyone, trust me.' He laughs.

I can't be sure if the laughter is from the alcohol I can smell or from his quiet lunacy.

'Why aren't you helping to find Matt?' I ask.

'Your brother's a big boy. He can take care of himself,' he says without sign of concern. 'Don't tell me you worry like that old woman,' he says with laughter, pointing to Dave, who replies with a middle-finger salute.

'I wanted to speak with you in private,' Charles says to Gabriel sternly. 'But since you have no shame, I might as well say it now. If I find you in the operations rooms with a woman again...'

'Please, Charles, we both know it was more than one woman.' He grins broadly, winking at me. 'She brought friends.'

'If I find you have broken the rules again, I will have you posted to the wastelands,' Charles warns.

'Even there, I'm sure Gabriel would find... how is it you put it? Wine, women, and song' Abbey says from the control tower.

'Indeed.' He nods in agreement, flashing a grin in her direction.

'This is your third and final warning,' Charles says to Gabriel.

'Third?' Tristram laughs quietly. 'Try twentieth.'

'And you, Mr Hill.' Charles turns on Tristram. 'Don't think I haven't noticed you smoking on the museum's grounds. If you must feed your filthy habit, you are to do so far from here. The last thing we need is for you to start a fire.'

'Yes, Sir,' Tristram says, turning away in annoyance.

'Here to see our latest recruit then?' Dave mutters to Gabriel sarcastically.

'Curious to see what Matt's brother is capable of,' he replies. 'Besides, the bar doesn't open for another hour.'

'I bet you want to see if he can break your records too,' says Abbey over the loudspeaker.

'It's about time someone did,' Charles adds, to which Gabriel simply raises a hipflask in mock salute before drinking deep.

'I bet he manages it,' Abbey announces.

'I don't,' Emma adds over the loudspeaker, revealing she is watching alongside Abbey in the control tower.

'Hundred pounds says he doesn't,' Gabriel replies with a laugh, offering the hipflask to Dave.

'Deal,' Abbey eagerly replies.

'No pressure, kid,' Dave whispers to me as he helps tighten the straps of my kit. 'Ignore them. Just focus on the damn trial.'

'No worries,' I reply with little confidence in my voice. The kit I carry is extra weight that will slow and hamper my movements, but it doesn't matter. If I have to prove myself to these people, then so be it. I have to find Matt.

'You're all set,' Tristram tells me. 'Good luck.'

'He's gonna need it,' mocks Gabriel.

Charles, Tristram, and Gabriel stand at the back of the vast training complex behind a sheet of reinforced glass as Dave returns to the control tower, his military voice booming out over the loudspeakers.

'This trial will feature three essential parts,' he instructs. 'The first is the firing range.'

A wall covered in weaponry and ammunition racked from top to bottom rises from the ground. There are rifles, handguns, shotguns, and even bows; a range from military and policing forces around the world.

'Why all the weapons?' I ask.

'Were the men you faced in the Roman tomb not armed?' Dave asks. 'Jack Bishop and Leon Bransby are far from the worst we have faced.'

I choose the bow, a recurve just like mine at home. Testing the string, I find it tight and ready for purpose, a quiver of silver-tipped arrows nearby. Feeling the bow, my mind drifts to home, to some of my earliest memories and my father teaching me archery in the back garden. It was originally just to calm me, to focus my hyper and erratic mind on a single task. *When technology and computers fail us, this will remain handy*, he had told me. Remembering him brings a smile to my face.

Dave issues orders from the side. 'Strike down both the stationary and moving targets.

'Just like in the military,' Tristram adds, unable to contain his excitement as he watches with eyes wide in expectation.

'No worries,' I simply say, readying myself. I check the glasses one last time and align an arrow upon the bow.

'Ready?' Abbey asks through my headset.

I take a deep breath, calming myself.

'Yeah. Do it.'

'GO!'

The targets rise from the ground and I strike each one down in turn, loosing arrows with speed and urgency. Then there are mobile targets, moving in all directions and growing more difficult to strike. They appear behind obstacles and walls, and I fear I will run out of arrows.

'One more and you will hit the required score,' Abbey encourages me through the headset. I hit the next target dead in its centre.

The range lowers into the ground to be replaced by the running track I have endured before.

'Four mile track, go!' Abbey yells and I throw the bow behind me and drop the quiver as I begin the run. The gradient increases with each mile until sweat is streaming down my face, my legs aching already.

'Cargo net next,' she says, the netting rising up, and I jump straight into it, clambering up and on.

Climbing walls, balance beams, more running, more jumping, high wires, monkey bars, and rope climbs. I endure it all, pushing on, thinking only of Matt and forcing the pain and tiredness in my body to the back of my mind. The added weight of the equipment slows me down as expected but I force myself on until suddenly posts rise in front of me and to my sides, loaded crossbows at their tops.

'What the hell are they?' I ask in shock.

'What do you think?' Abbey replies, unable to contain a laugh through my headset. 'Expect the unexpected. Did you not face similar traps in the Roman crypts of all places?'

'Fair point,' I mumble, ducking and diving to avoid the bolts of the crossbows. Hurling myself past many, I evade all but one that catches in my fully loaded rucksack.

'A little close, don't you think?' Abbey asks as I run on.

'Not close enough,' I say as I roll away from another bolt soaring towards me, pushing myself up and into a sprint. I have to duck again though as a wall of flame rises and soars towards me. Dropping flat to the ground, the flames pass over me, and I feel the sheer heat on every inch of my skin until it is behind me.

'You're making good progress, Adam,' Abbey tells me

as I force myself up again. 'You've even got Gabriel worried you'll beat his times.'

The running track returns and I follow a winding course littered with rocks and other obstacles, pushing on into a sprint as I near the end.

'Nearly there,' Abbey tells me. 'Next is a water dive into a tunnel. You swim a hundred metres and then go under the water until you emerge on the far side of the tunnel.'

I don't hear half her words, skidding to a halt as the water opens up before me. The fear tears into me, hands shaking, stomach churning, head spinning.

'Adam, what are you doing?'

'I...I can't...' I stammer, barely able to get out the words. I take a step back, unable to do it.

'Adam, you must go into the water to complete the trial,' Dave orders over the loudspeaker.

I don't move or speak. I can't, rooted to the spot.

'Dive into the water, Adam!' Dave yells at me.

'NO!' I scream back at them, stepping away from the water's edge. I throw off the rucksack, sending it crashing against the control tower as I storm away, angry and humiliated.

'What's wrong?' Abbey asks, but I pull off the glasses and throw them to Charles without a word.

'Well, that was mightily disappointing,' Gabriel mutters. 'What a waste of time.'

'Return to the hole you crawled out of, Gabriel,' Abbey yells at him over the loudspeaker.

'Gladly.' He smirks. 'Seek me out when you have work for me, or when you have more school kids to embarrass.'

I ignore him and all the others, thundering past them.

'Mr Hunter, if you want to find your brother, you must complete the trials,' Charles yells after me.

'I can't,' is all I can say. I'm furious with myself for my weakness.

20

SLAVE—Capua

We train day and night. In endless heat and pouring rains.
The crack of the doctores' lash drives us on. Three of our
number die within the first days. One falls in training,
throat torn open in an unwise manoeuvre against an opponent far more skilled. Another fades in the heat, body and
soul too weak to survive. The last caught in attempt to
escape the ludus.

His body hangs from the walls, hands nailed to the
stone, disembowelled and left to bleed to death as a
warning to others. There is no escape except for death.

Hader warns us that there will never be another Spartacus, King of Escaped Slaves. I still remember my father's
tales of the Thracian's exploits and the punishment given
to all who followed him; crucifixions lining the Appian

Way from Rome to Capua. The slave revolt began in the very city I now stand a slave.

The training is hard, even for a centurion of the legion. The recruits learn to fight by the Doctores' instructions, gladiators retired from the arena and now giving instruction to those who would fight upon the sands. Punishment by the lash is frequent, even for those already skilled in the use of sword and shield and bloodied on the sands of the arenas.

Though Hader urges us to forget our past lives, it is impossible for me. The betrayal of my men and the desecration of my legion haunts me, the still healing scars on my back and arm are a constant reminder. Worse still, is the fear for my wife. If my name was remembered, Vespasian could easily hunt Lucilla down as further punishment to me. I would send word by messenger to her, as I know those standing as gladiators do to their loved ones, but I cannot until I earn coin from victories in the arenas.

No matter the dreams that rob me of sleep, I must rise each day to train. Heavy wooden weaponry is provided to build strength, much as the legion trains newly enlisted recruits. Death awaits any who do not make progress, such is the severity of life in the ludus. If we do not earn our master coin then we are worthless to him and will provide feed to the dogs as he often warns. For many days, I simply do what is ordered, lacking effort and focus, body still healing and mind wracked with guilt. It is when the boy who spoke out of turn on his first day, Garus, falls for the fifth time that day that I speak. He gives the missio, two fingers raised in surrender as a plea for mercy. It makes my blood boil. Surrender on the battlefield, as in the arena, will likely mean death.

'Keep your shield raised, you fool,' I yell at him, forcing Garus up and facing him myself. 'Protect flank or see yourself fall in your first fight.'

I show Garus what I mean, ordering him to attack and blocking his pitiful assault with ease.

'Now you,' I command as I lunge forward, his shield barely blocking the lunges of my wooden blade.

We repeat again and again until both of us are sweating from our efforts.

'Gratitude,' Garus thanks me. 'Your lessons are well received.'

'Well, you've learnt enough times how to fall on your arse. About time you learnt other skills.'

He is not the last I instruct that day on how to stand and defend against oncoming attacks. I follow the style of Optio Acer from when he taught me, which now feels a lifetime ago. In a way, it feels like I am honouring my fallen brother by passing on his lessons. It isn't long before I attract the attention of the established gladiators as well as the Dominus.

'Doctore!' our Dominus barks from the villa's balcony

above. His finger is pointed down towards me. 'I would have words with that man!'

With weaponry removed and hands bound in chains, I am led up from the ludus to the villa above, always four guards with me to ensure obedience. The villa is much different to the dark dredges of the ludus below; there are feasts of food and wine on every table, and dozens of slaves devoted to the whim of every nobleman and woman. Statues to the gods stand in every room, watching. It is heaven above the hells where I train and slumber.

'I knew from first purchase you would be different – and difficult,' Hader greets as I enter his chamber. There are books piled high on the table and floor, parchments and maps held down with coins. 'Others warned me against it, my own wife among them. They said you were an abomination. Living but dead – cursed.'

'Yet you made purchase anyway?' I ask, breaking slave laws by talking without permission. I do not care for their rules.

Hader does not scorn, instead there is a wry smile on his lips.

'You are new to your slave bonds,' he says. 'That is clear from your loose tongue. Slave, you are already proving your worth upon the sands below. The men, your future brothers, they name you *Centurion* for lack of name. To me you were sold as a deserter. Not a name to strike fear into an opponent.'

He's waiting for a response but I remain sullen. He is mocking me, and there's no point putting up a fight.

'Now I see you take it upon yourself to train my men – as any Doctore would,' Hader continues, pouring himself wine. 'They look to you, the best among my latest recruits, despite your age. And fine Doctore I think you will make if you live long enough. Plenty of years upon the sands for you still to come, but is this your wish for future days, to train rather than seize glory in the arena?'

'I desire neither,' I state, wary of betraying my heart's true wish. He finds it anyway, without further words from me.

'Freedom then?'

Though my face be as iron he sees it, and nods his head sagely.

'I see it. Freedom is what you seek. Maybe you think me not so wise, for all men in your circumstance would surely desire the same – but you'd be surprised. Most men here, no matter what they say, just want to die.' He drinks deep from his gold goblet, never breaking his look from my face. 'But you, you're not going to die. I can see that. There are only two reasons a fire like that burns – revenge, or love.'

'Yes,' is all I can say.

'Which is it?'

I remain silent, but he is not deterred. 'When was the last time you laid eyes on one another?'

'Three years, before the legion set out upon campaign. It is long since I last had word.'

'And you would do anything to be reunited with your woman again?'

'I would fight the gods.'

'Good,' he says with a smile growing wider. 'Fight for me. Join the brotherhood of the House of Hader. Make us both rich men, Centurion. As one of my warriors, victories will be rewarded with coin, and with enough, you shall gain your freedom. Live, fight, and win, and you will not only see your wife again but you will be a wealthy man.'

'I fought alongside brothers before and they were slain for uncommitted crimes,' I state boldly. 'Their honour and memory were desecrated by a madman's whim.'

'I am not our Emperor Vespasian,' Hader says. 'Here you have a choice. Win or lose; which shall it be?'

'I have but one request,' I say, stepping too far again.

'Slaves do not make requests of their Dominus!' he says. 'You have guts, Centurion. Perhaps that is why I am beginning to like you. Because of that, I would hear your demand, though do not expect it to be fulfilled.'

'The other men, your warriors, they have messages sent to loved ones for exchange of coin. I possess none but would send word to my wife.'

'So, you would have coin from my own pocket, too?' Hader bellows with laughter. 'I knew you to be different,

Centurion. No other slave under my command would be so brazen.'

'I do not desire coin, just favour to lift my heart and give me purpose.' The pleading in my voice betrays me.

'Prove yourself worthy in the arena in the next games. Win for me and I will see a messenger sent to your wife. You have my word.'

'I will not lose. Gratitude, Dominus.'

21

ADAM—The British Museum, London, England

I walk aimlessly at first, my head a storm of anger and embarrassment until I find myself in the main garage used by the teams of the museum. There are a dozen vehicles of all manner, including Dave's, motorcycles and quad bikes. Amongst them, I find something that snaps me to focus.

Standing before me is a copper red convertible. It's Matt's car, his most prized possession, shining bright and spotless. It's as much a part of Matt as his journal. Now it's here, cold, empty, waiting for its owner to return.

Next to it is my father's bike, his pride and joy. Now it's a wreck, body smashed, exhaust missing, wheels more square than round. It's a wonder I emerged from the crash in as good a condition as I did looking at the ruin of my father's bike. Seeing the battered bike and Matt's convertible abandoned suddenly spikes emotion.

'I'm sorry, Matt. I've failed.'

Quickly, anger replaces sorrow. I pick up the nearest object, a chair, and slam it into the wall behind me, smashing it to pieces of splintered wood. My head swims with rage. I jump into the driver's seat of Matt's car and slam my hands into the steering wheel.

'There you are,' Emma's voice calls out across the garage. Her face is red with anger. 'What the hell happened to you?'

I don't answer.

'Are you deaf as well as stupid?' she demands, storming towards me. When she sees my face, she slows.

'Do you want me to leave you alone?' Emma asks.

'No,' I mutter with a shake of my head, opening the passenger's door for her.

'Here,' she says, throwing Matt's journal over to me. 'It's pointless us keeping hold of it if we can't read it. You need to talk, or perhaps we could contact your mother?

I laugh. 'She is the last person I want to speak to.'

'How come?' she asks, flopping into the seat beside me.

'Let's just say, we don't get along,' I say. 'She's an angry lady - especially when it comes to me. We barely speak.'

'All families argue.'

'Not like this,' I say. 'In her case, her bark and bite are as bad as each other.'

'Why do you argue?' Emma asks. 'Matt never mentioned any problems.'

'No matter what I do, it isn't good enough. I am never worthy in her eyes, not even close, especially compared to the golden boy.'

'Jealous of Matt?' she guesses.

'Not at all,' I say. 'He was the only one who understood. He protected me when he could and offered me a place to stay when needed.'

I fall silent again at the memory of Matt. Failing the trials meant I'd failed him.

'I'm sorry about what happened to your bike,' she says, trying to take my mind off the trials. 'You think you can fix it?'

I look to the wreckage, shaking my head again.

'It would need a lot of work and more spare parts than exist in the world for such an old model. I don't know.'

I briefly look to her and see she is trying, saddened for me, the anger now gone.

'Is Abbey angry I cost her the bet?' I ask her.

'She'll be fine,' Emma says. 'I doubt Gabriel would ever collect anyway. Beneath all the booze and everything else, he's actually alright; a little damaged, but who isn't in some way?'

She flashes me the briefest of smiles, but I see she wants to ask a question, dying to know why I would not go into the water. I thank her silently for not asking, but I know I must speak with someone about it, so it might as well be Emma.

'When I was ten years old, Matt and I were playing near a river. Our parents warned us so many times to be careful, but of course, we never listened. On the banks, I lost my footing, falling into the water. Swimming was never a problem but the current was too strong. No matter how hard I kicked and fought, I couldn't surface. Water filled my lungs, the current pulled me farther and deeper. All I saw was darkness. My chest burned as I gasped for air and swallowed only more of the river.'

I stop, body shaking as I relive it. Closing my eyes, I can remember it all so vividly, a haunting nightmare I can never shake. The rushing water, the burning in my lungs, the choking of the foul water, the reeds tangling around my legs and the cuts to my body from the rocks below the surface. Every night, the memory returns to me in my sleep. Every time I see a river or sea, the fear threatens to overwhelm me.

Emma places a hand on my arm, calming me for a moment.

'It's okay,' she whispers.

'I woke up in the hospital five days later. They had to restart my heart twice. Matt dragged me out of the river, nearly dying himself in the attempt. Matt saved my life.'

I breathe deeply, whistling as I exhale.

'The fear has had a hold of me ever since. No matter

how hard I fight it, it always wins. I barely survived the tombs in Loch Lomond because of it, and I failed the trials...'

Stopping again, I calm myself.

'I'm sorry,' she tells me. 'If I'd known, I wouldn't have let Dave feature water in the tests.'

I say nothing, falling silent for a long time.

'Fire,' Emma then says, breaking the silence.

'What of it?' I ask.

'I'm terrified of it,' she utters, gaze fixed on the far side of the garage where a mechanic wields a blow-torch. 'Can't go near it, can barely look at it. I even hated seeing it in your trials. Ever since I was young, when they...'

She says no more, unable to.

'So I guess I'm not on the team then?' I ask, changing the subject. 'I doubt you'll let me be one of your hunters if I can't face water.'

'No,' she simply says, unable to think of any other way to reply, still distant, lost in her own thoughts, her own horrors.

'It doesn't matter,' I say. 'I failed. I just... I just can't, not water.'

Emma doesn't have the words to reply. The data-pad in her pocket beeps, signalling a received message.

'A-ha,' she says, excitement now in her voice. 'Abbey has received the rest of the images from our excavation teams at Inchlonaig. They include the carvings on the walls of the legatus's burial chamber.'

She shows me the data-pad, the darkened tomb and the Latin inscriptions in the stone.

'What does it mean?' I ask her.

'Abbey has translated,' she says, taps on the screen increasing the resolution and definition of the images.

'Here laid to rest are the ashes of our noble Legatus Antonius Thadian. He and our brothers died honourably in battle, our Eagle returned to Rome by Centurion Marcus Aurelius.'

'The Eagle was never in the tomb,' I say, laughing at the futility of it all. Matt was taken for something that was never even there.

'If it was to be returned to Rome, it should have gone to the emperor,' Emma explains, fingers working the data-pad, searching information and known records. 'Usually, a legion returns to the city in triumph and there is a celebration of their victories. The Eagle is then given to the emperor as a sign of honour. Many were recorded, accounts mentioning those of dozens of legions but there are no mentions of the Legio IX Hispana – of its return or the Eagle. We would have seen them before if there were mentions of this but there simply aren't any. I don't understand it. Something must have happened.'

The data-pad beeps, a new message received.

'The inscription outside the legatus's tomb,' Emma says.

'Tantum Dignos,' I remember.

'Only the worthy,' she replies.

'Only the worthy,' I repeat.

'I'm sorry, but I have to go and run this through our central database,' she says as she exits the car, all focus on the data-pad in her hand. Just as Emma begins to depart, she hurries back and fumbles in her pockets, pulling free a mobile phone.

'Sorry, I forgot to give you this. It's a replacement for your destroyed one. I've already uploaded your old SIM card. You should reply to your friend Sara. She seems worried about you, despite repeatedly calling you a loser!'

'Nosey,' I taunt her, knowing she has read all my messages.

'Just curious,' she replies. 'Besides, Abbey had first look. You should reply to your mother, too.'

I look at the phone and cycle through the messages, new to my eyes but already opened by Emma and Abbey. I look over the words but can't take any in. Something at the back of my mind is calling to me.

'Wait,' I call out to Emma, stopping her before she has vacated the garage.

'What is it?' she asks, puzzled.

Something she said. A name. Matt's journal. Searching the pages, I find it.

'That's it,' I exclaim, laughing in shock as I decode more. 'In Matt's own words. CENTURION. GLADIATOR. COLOSSEUM. LEGIO IX HISPANA. POSSIBLE EAGLE LOCATION.'

'It's a thin lead,' Emma says, looking to the pages of Matt's journal but seeing only symbols and scribbles.

'Are there any records or documentation of previous gladiators?' I ask, heart pounding, a lead at last. 'If it is the centurion, this Marcus Aurelius who returned the Eagle, following his path, his history, may lead us to it.'

'There are few records of gladiators' names,' she says, tapping away at her data-pad again. 'None matching the name of our centurion. There is one depository of records that may have mention of him, if any would.'

'Where is it?'

'In the very place your brother mentions and tried to gain access to more times than I can count. The Colosseum in Rome.'

'Wait, anybody can go into the Colosseum? There are tourist trips through it every day,' I reply.

'Not in the lower depths,' she explains. 'Within chambers below the sands are records of gladiators, great walls rumoured to be inscribed with their names, victories and their fates beyond the great arena, similar to the legion's tomb you found.'

'So why can't we see them?' I ask.

'The Italian government values its past and history

higher than many other nations. They keep this particular treasure locked away. Only those deemed worthy are allowed admittance.'

'You mean the wealthy,' I state.

'The privileged and those specialists within the Italian government,' she says. 'That's probably where Matt got his lead, from one of their historians he was able to bribe. We have tried, God knows how many times, to gain access to the Colosseum, officially as the British Museum, and unofficially, but we have never had any luck.'

I scan Matt's journal for more information, more clues, but the encryptions release no more secrets. A thousand ideas rush through my mind but one prevails over all.

'I have to report this to Charles,' Emma says. 'He needs to know so we can chase this up.'

'I'm coming with you...' I begin to say before she stops me.

'No, stay here,' she orders.

'What?' I reply, stunned.

'You didn't complete the tests.' All friendliness is now gone.

'You'll just leave me here?' I ask.

'I'm sorry, but you didn't make the team,' she says coldly.

'If you won't help me, I'll do it on my own,' I call after her.

'We can't let you do that!'

'I'd like to see you stop me,' I warn her.

'Stay here and don't do anything stupid,' she orders, heading through the door.

'Fine,' I say, a plan forming in my mind.

Once she is gone, I collect my belongings, those not destroyed in the crash, along with Matt's journal, and pull on my father's jacket. I hurry to the training facility where I failed the trials, hoping to *borrow* some of their equipment. Inside is Gabriel, standing alone before the firing range.

'You're going after him on your own, aren't you?' he asks without looking to me. His voice is filled with emotion. Gone is the cocky smart-ass from before.

'I can't just stay here waiting for Charles' permission.'

'I'd do the same,' he says, turning and throwing a card towards me. His eyes are red, raw with emotion. 'That'll give you access to the equipment in here and the lift back up to the main museum.'

'Why are you helping me?'

'Find Matt,' Gabriel says, ignoring the question. 'Find him and bring him home.'

Turning back to the firing range, he unleashes round after round, destroying the targets with ruthless efficiency. He screams in a rage until the weapon is empty, dropping it to the ground and standing there, unmoving.

'Don't let your brother join the people we've lost,' he says, distant, in a daze.

That's why he is the only member of Bravo Team, I realise.

22

THE CENTURION—Capua

'Fight, win, and see yourself gladiator of the House of Hader. Only then will word from your wife be gained.'

That was the order of my Dominus. Win or die upon the sands, forever lost to my dear Lucilla – wherever in this world she is. I have no choice but to embrace the path left before me. More blood. More death.

With rusted and blunt blade, the barest armour, holed by the blows that killed the last owner and sweating under the blazing sun, I am to step out into battle. I will not fight alone though.

'Noble Mercatio hosts these games and has deemed all bouts will be fought in pairs. Fortunate for Garus, but maybe not so for you,' Hader told me before taking his seat among the nobility in the arena. The boy is paired with me by a length of chain connecting our wrists. His face pales as our moment approaches.

'Mercatio hates me with passion known only by the gods,' Hader states.

'Why?' I dare to ask.

'Slaves are to answer questions, not ask them,' he says, a wry smile on his face. 'I may have enjoyed the company of his daughter one evening.'

I know he is not telling all the tale and he sees my look of doubt.

'Both of his daughters,' he concedes, pacing away and leaving Garus and I to our fates.

'Fight, win, wipe the smile off his face and earn glory for us both!' he shouts back before disappearing into the chambers of the arena.

Looking to Garus, I see his terror on his face. His fear buries my own.

'Keep your shield raised, protect your flank, and do not stray from my side,' I instruct him as Mercatio begins our introductions. We are named by the drunken noble, 'The Boy and the Centurion of Hader.'

'Do as I have instructed and you will survive this day,' I tell Garus.

'And our foes shall fall before us,' he says back, forcing a smile. 'Gratitude for all you have taught me, Centurion.'

'Show no mercy!' I shout to him above the growing

roar of the crowd as the arena gates open before us. 'For they'll show you none!'

We march out, few cheering us unknown men but heaping adoration upon those we will face. Obscenities are hurled our way and I see more doubt and fear creep into Garus's gaze. His moment will come. Fight or die.

Our arena is square formed of four banks of spectators, small in comparison to those I have seen throughout the Empire, but large enough to house at least three hundred. As is ritual, we salute the honoured guests, those belonging to nobility and who can afford the most expensive seats within the pulvinus, and of course, Mercatio, whose games this day belong to.

'Veterans of the House of Bravatos face the latest recruits of the House of Hader, boys barely old enough to know the love of good women. This will be a mismatch, I fear, but one sure to bring spectacle. No mercy is to be given in this bout to honour the gods. Watch as Hader's dogs are shown for the pitiful wretches they truly are.'

I can see Hader's smirk even in the bright light of the sun. Cold, clever, and gambler at heart. My Dominus sacrifices the lives of two men with ease, or sees greater glory from recruits beating seasoned gladiators and shaming the man who dishonours him. He knows I am no boy stumbling about, barely able to suffer the weight of sword and shield. I am a soldier: his secret weapon.

'Begin!'

We turn, our foes awaiting us, arms up to the crowds, encouraging them to bear witness to what they think will be victory with ease. Both are towering and strong; scars on their bodies mark many matches fought and won. One carries a trident and net in the fighting style of Retiarius, and the other, in the style of Hoplomachus, carries a spear and a round shield. Both men have strength and reach over Garus and I with shield and short sword, but their arrogance gives us advantage.

'Avoid the net!' I yell to Garus. 'Draw them in and rob them of their advantage of reach.'

I hope he understands, but above all, I pray he stands and fights.

I am shocked by his actions as he charges headlong towards our foes, roaring in rage. Our chain bonding us, I can only charge with him. It's a more aggressive strike than I would have made, but I thank the gods for his courage – we may yet come out of this both alive. The trident strikes the boy's shield as a spear hammers mine – the battle has begun.

The spear of the Hoplomachus strikes my shield again, the impact thundering up my arm but I hold balance, slashing the gladius round but without impact. My opponent is skilled with the spear, forcing me away and unable to bring my shorter blade to bear. A thrust too quick to block catches the shoulder of my armour but I am unharmed, ducking beneath the next attack and slamming my shield into his and throwing him back.

My glance catches Garus, blocking the trident and net as they seek to capture and impale. He is doing well, though a deep cut to his arm shows he is not without mistakes. The Retiarius laughs to the crowd as he forces the boy back again. His smile is wiped from his face as Garus charges and swipes his sword across the man's bare thigh to draw blood. Good, but I must jerk hard on our chain to pull him away from the falling net. In return, the trident flashes across my face, almost meeting flesh as I duck away.

Turning back to my foe, the Hoplomachus, who has rallied from the impact of my shield, charges me, enraged and eager to end my life. I turn and twist away from each thrust of the spear, angering him more, drawing him closer and closer, until I can go on the attack. Spinning off his spear as it hammers into my shield, I pull him close and seek to run through him with my sword. He knows what is coming, bringing his shield round in defence and then punching it across my face, filling my mouth with blood and sending me stumbling to the sands. I roll from the reach of his spear, its iron tip falling to where I laid. Rising up quickly, I block the spear again, spitting blood from my mouth in annoyance at my own foolishness. This ends now.

I draw the Hoplomachus in, feigning injury and

exhaustion and he strikes with increasing desperation and eagerness to end the fight. Taking my time, I wait until the right moment. When I sense he is off-balance, I drop my shield, grasping the spear's staff and bringing my blade down on the wood, shattering it in two. Before he can recover, I spin, ducking beneath his rising shield and tearing my sword through armour and flesh. Ignoring the wound, he tries to draw his dagger but my blade finds him again, ending the attack as the fire in his eyes begins to fade.

Turning, expecting to have to rush to the aid of Garus, I am stunned when I see him standing over his foe. Blood covers them both but it flows only from the fallen. Garus looks to me, his smile growing in elation. The crowd around us is cheering louder than any I have heard before. Garus stands, no longer a boy, but a man.

Mercatio rises to address all, scorn and anger on his face.

'That was far too brief!' he declares. 'Send another pair to face Hader's boys!'

Two men charge from the arena gates, and in that instant, cheated of our victory, rage takes me. For all the injustices, all the dishonours I suffer, this is to be the last this day. It is my turn to charge, Garus dragged by the chain. I care not for the men I face, only that they suffer my wrath. They are skilled in combat, fighting with weapons still stained by the blood of their earlier kills – but I am filled with righteous anger.

In my fury, I call forth on my years in the legion and with sword and shield, Garus beside me, I strike down both men, cleaving them almost in two such is the strength of my rage.

'Another!' Mercatio orders, but the result is much the same. 'Cast these wretched boys down!'

When, finally, eight men are fallen to our blades, three defeated by Garus, the rest by my sword, an end is at last called, the crowd cheering ever louder, chanting the name of centurion to the heavens. We raise bloodied swords in salute, the day is ours and my word kept.

I can only pray Hader keeps his.

23

ADAM—Terminal 5, Heathrow Airport, London, England

Only the worthy. The words echo in my head again and again. Only the worthy.

Four hours after leaving the British Museum, I am on board a plane, waiting for take-off. My destination is Rome. As I wait for the rest of the passengers to take their seats and the crew to make their pre-flight checks, I read through the messages on my phone, from Duncan and Sara first, saving my mother's until last.

> Mate, I wish you would get in touch. Let me know where you are and I will help you find Matt. You need anything, let me know and I'll help all I can. Keep safe.

Duncan.

He is a good friend and I knew he would offer help. There is nothing he can do though, finding Matt is my mission.

Hey Duncan. I'm still searching for Matt. Cant stop until I find him. I'll they to keep you updated but it's proving difficult. Speak when I can. Thanks again.

Next is Sara.

Hi stranger. Starting to worry you're avoiding me. Duncan says you've been away, trying to find Matt. Need anything, please let me know. Stay safe. Sara Starr. x

No mention of shopping, clothes or make-up this time she must be worried. I smile briefly at her show of concern, before I come to the last messages, my mother's. There are many.

Come home now! I am so angry. Why can you never do as you're told or listen to me?

You are a child!! Ring me!!

Why are you doing this? Is it just to hurt me?

The last message surprises me most of all.

Please, come home. I'm sorry. Please call me, text me, anything. Just let me know you're okay.

It has been almost a week since I left. I should speak to her. She deserves at least a call before the plane takes off and I leave the country.

She answers immediately, though any sentiment and apology from her last message is completely absent. 'Where the hell have you been?'

'Hi,' I reply.

'You run away just as your brother goes missing. I have been worried sick. I have never been so furious, so disappointed...'

'Yeah I got your messages,' I interrupt.

'Then why didn't you reply?'

'Didn't have much of a chance...'

'I want you home, now!'

'I can't do that.'

'Why the hell not?' my mother demands.

'Matt...' I try to say but she cuts me off.

'I want you home, now!' she repeats.

'I have to find him...' I begin to say but am interrupted again.

'For once, do as I say, Adam!'

I feel the frustration bubbling up. 'Listen to me!' I shout down the phone, drawing startled looks from other passengers on the plane. 'Listen to me for once. Matt is out there. I can find him. I can bring him home.'

'You're just a boy,' she says after a few moments silence, her voice broken. She's almost crying.

'Not anymore,' I tell her.

A stewardess waves a hand in front of me, urging me to turn off the phone, take-off fast approaching.

'I will find Matt,' I say. 'I'll find him and I'll bring him home.'

'I don't trust Charles Lovell,' she says.

'Then trust me,' I tell her.

There is silence. Just as I'm about to click off, I hear her voice, unusually fragile, 'Please be careful, Adam. I love you.'

I hang up then, closing my eyes as a thousand thoughts flurry through my head.

'You know the stewardesses have already asked for all mobile phones to be turned off,' a military tone says from the man behind the newspaper in the seat next to me.

'How did you track me down?' I ask, recognising his voice without opening my eyes.

Dave Conway nods to my phone.

'You bugged my phone!' I state. It was stupid of me not to consider it.

'When we saw you were headed for the airport, it wasn't a stretch of the imagination to guess where your destination would be. How did you afford the ticket?'

'It's an economy seat and I have an emergency credit card,' I explain. 'Look, if it's about the equipment I took, I was only going to borrow it. I was planning on returning it.'

'Sure you were,' he replies.

'You can't stop me from going after Matt and the Eagle,' I tell him. 'He is my brother and I will not let his name join those upon your stupid plaques to honour your dead. You can't stop me.'

'I know, that's why I am not going to try,' he says, securing his seatbelt.

'What?' I ask, confused.

'You remind me so much of Matt,' Dave begins to explain. 'You're clever and determined but stubborn and foolhardy, just like your brother. He thought nothing of charging up to Scotland in search of the legion and its fabled Eagle. Now you are doing the same, rushing off on your crusade.'

'What other choice do I have?' I argue but he holds up his hands to quiet me and apologise.

'I meant no disrespect,' he says. 'I simply wanted to illustrate the similarities. You are both good liars too, but I knew you were not telling the truth in the operations room when you said you had already spotted mentions in the journal about the legion and the Eagle.'

'Whatever it takes to get Matt back,' I say, justifying my lie. 'Besides, I was right, there were leads to the Eagle.'

'You *think* there are leads,' he corrects me. 'This centurion, it could all be a wild goose chase.'

'It doesn't matter,' I argue. 'If there is a chance to find my brother, I will take it.'

'I don't blame you.' He sighs, leaning back in his chair. 'That is why I'm going with you.'

'What?' I ask in disbelief.

'You would've passed the last physical test of the trials if it wasn't for your fear of water,' he tells me. 'Besides, accessing the crypt in Scotland, evading Matt's captors, those were trials in themselves that you passed alone without any advice or support. I am going with you to Rome though, on babysitting duty again.'

He hands me the headset I wore during the trials, urging me to put the glasses on.

'I'm going with you, too,' Abbey says, her slight Irish accent speaking to me through the earphones of the glasses. 'You didn't take any of the mental and psychological evaluations I had ready for you but I can give you all the information and research you could possibly need.'

'What of Charles?' I ask. 'Does your boss know about this?'

'Officially he and the British Museum cannot support

your travel to Italy or whatever activities you undertake there,' Abbey says in her sternest, stiffest British voice to mask her Irish accent.

'And unofficially,' Charles' voice interrupts over the headset, 'find your brother, Mr Hunter. I will be watching.'

'As will I,' utters a voice from the seat in front of me, Emma's. 'I told you not to do anything stupid, yet here you are.'

24

THE CENTURION—Capua

Marcus,

I cannot believe it. I was certain you were dead. To have word from you, alive and well, it lifts my heart beyond belief. The gods finally hear my prayers.

When I received word that you and the legion were returned, I hurried to the Campus Martius but all I found were the slain, the legion desecrated. I thought you among them, certain of it, taken from me by cruellest fate.

I have joined Mother and Father in Pompeii, fearful of

reprisal from the emperor after turning on you and the legion. I do not believe what they say, that you turned traitor and fled your brothers in Britannia. That is not the man I married.

Your messenger found me by your instruction after discovering our home empty, his words bringing untold joy of your survival. I await you in Pompeii should you ever gain freedom. My heart belonging to you for all eternity. You are a strong and fierce warrior. I know we will be reunited, in this lifetime or the next.

Eternally I wait for you.

Lucilla.

I read her words again and again, the letter given after my latest victory in the arena, hands still marked by my foe's blood. She is alive and she is safe. Nothing matters more than that.

Folding the letter and securing it within my armour, I turn to the gates, watching Garus stand alone on the sands, on the same spot where we first fought. We are now nine victories further on our journey. My ascension in the House of Hader has been swift; I am now a trusted brother and gladiator amongst the warriors of the ludus. I am offered women and wine in exchange for the coin I earn with each victory, but I ask for neither. I stash my coin, saving for my freedom. Lucilla's letter gives me all motivation needed.

Watching Garus, I stand amazed at how he has grown since first standing alongside me as a recruit. Under tutelage of Hader's Doctores and heeding my words, he has become a fine warrior. He does not rush or fall to feint, waiting for his opportunity to strike. Catching his foe off balance, he draws blade across stomach, the man falling to his knees as Garus stands over him, tip of gladius raised to his throat.

'Mercy,' the man calls; his wounds are not grievous enough to kill, but the fight is ended all the same. Two fingers rise to offer missio.

'Poor showing indeed,' nobles call out, thumbs down in irritation, the fallen man's judgement and sentence given.

'Please, don't...' the man pleads, and I see Garus waver with uncertainty.

'Don't be foolish,' I shout, although he is too far away in both body and spirit to hear my words.

The crowd begins to show its displeasure as the victor continues to falter.

'He is defeated, is that not enough?' Garus yells from the sands.

'If you do not end this man, your life will end, too,' warns a noble. Garus does not act until he throws his blade away, falling to his knees, tears streaming from his eyes.

'I... I cannot...' he mutters before screaming to the heavens. 'I CANNOT KILL THOSE WHO BEG FOR MERCY!'

'NO!' I yell, pulling at the gates, trying to reach him as the arena guards circle the pair, weapons drawn.

My brother gladiators and guards from the House of Hader grapple with me, pulling me back, trying to stop me from joining the fate of those on the sands. I fight them off, reaching the gates as I see the blades fall. Garus cries out with his final breath, damning them all. Brave but foolish.

Hader's Doctores are upon me, striking with club and lash until darkness claims me, body bruised and broken – and now I have lost another brother.

25

ADAM—Somewhere over Italy

My new companions don't speak much; Dave sleeps most of the way, and Emma wears a large set of headphones with music loud enough for me to hear every word clearly. She has not spoken a word since the plane took off, annoyed at my presence. I don't really care to be honest. I will find the damned Eagle, and with it, hopefully, I will find Matt. *Only the worthy.* It runs through my head again. I will prove my worth and show Emma, Dave, Abbey, Charles, my mother... all of them.

Looking out of the plane window, I see the expanse of the channel below us. I try to start conversations with Dave to take my mind off the waters below, but he doesn't stir.

'You'd have better luck waking a bear from its hibernation,' Abbey tells me through the headset. 'You dislike flying, too?'

'How can you tell there's something wrong?' I ask.

'You're trying to wake an ex-commando and your hands have turned white from gripping the arms of your seat so tightly.'

'It's not the flying, it's what's below the plane.'

'Only another few minutes and then you'll be over mainland Europe,' she tells me. 'Then, if the plane should crash, you'd just be flying into the ground in a great fiery ball of death rather than plunging into water.'

'Very reassuring,' I say sarcastically.

'I try.' She laughs.

I spend most of the flight trying to decrypt more of Matt's journal, forcing the water beneath the plane from my mind by focusing on work. A pen twirls between my fingers as I read, the motion helping me to settle and focus on my task. Abbey asks lots of questions, unable to understand the encryptions even with the help of all her computers. I can see them though, the patterns and intricacies. There are mentions of golden palaces, sunken and missing ships vanished from the seas, lost civilisations and more. There are even references to old legends; Atlantis, the Holy Grail, and Shangri-La to name but a few. Matt has been busy, but all that is featured is the slightest of clues and nothing of certainty. There are no more mentions of the legion or the Eagle, apart from that of the centurion I uncovered before.

After working on the journal for another hour, I give up, looking out of the window and seeing land beneath us.

'Whereabouts are we, Abbey?' I ask.

'Over northern Italy at the moment,' she says quickly, as if she's been watching my progress constantly. 'At most, another half hour to go.'

'So tell me about you,' I ask. 'I know Dave is an ex-soldier who likes to torture people through assault courses. Emma hates that I'm here. Charles is a pompous government type with some frustration issues. Tristram is a techie a little too proud of his equipment, who I suspect you might be dating or at least have a crush on...'

'What? Abbey splutters. 'What makes you say that?'

'...and Gabriel is a drunk with a... a dark past. You though, remain a mystery, apart from that you do the work of an entire team of analysts.'

'Not a whole lot to tell,' she says, seemingly glad for the subject to move away from her and Tristram. 'I was top of my class at school, skipped ahead a few years and flew through college and university. I don't know if it's an eidetic memory or what, but I just seem to be able to remember and process things well.'

'Such as Latin, a dead language,' I add.

'Exactly.'

'What led you to join the museum?'

'Charles found me,' she explains. 'He had a team down in Dover who had uncovered scriptures all in Latin. He was seeking out the best historian who could translate for him and his team.'

'And got more than he bargained for,' I finished for her.

'I was assigned to Echo Team along with Matt, and until now, I was the youngest recruit.'

'I am not one of your recruits,' I tell her.

'Not yet,' she chirps.

'So, youngest recruit, how old are you anyway?' I ask.

'You're never supposed to ask a lady that,' she replies with mock horror.

'But you're going to answer anyway,' I tease.

'Not that much older than you,' she says.

'Eighteen,' I guess.

'Maybe,' she says after a long pause. I know I'm right.

'I thought you would want to know about Em?' she asks, Em short for Emma.

'Why's that?'

'I saw on the monitors you two talking in the garage at the museum. She's usually very closed off, rarely speaking to new people.'

'It was mainly shouting at me,' I reply, lowering my voice just in case Emma might hear over the sound of her loud music.

'Sounds about right.' Abbey laughs.

'She helped,' I admit. 'I haven't spoken about my fear of water to anyone for a long time.'

'Yet you told Em?'

'Before she started shouting at me again.'

'She's not always like that. She has her own fears, too.'

'Fire,' I say. 'She told me. Fire and water. Quite the pair, opposites attracting and all that.'

'That is a terrible line,' Abbey teases.

'I've used worse,' I admit.

'Did she tell you why?' she asks.

'Why what?'

'Why she fears fire?'

'It is her secret,' I reply. 'You can tell me one thing though – what are your surnames? Yours and Emma's?'

'Before I tell you, you have to know that Em was chosen for this team for being very, very good at what she does,' Abbey says, Irish tone showing as she rushes her explanation. 'She passed all the tests and trials and is as good a hunter as your brother...'

'Get to the point, Abbey,' I say.

'Lovell,' she reveals, the same surname as Charles.

'Ah, so daddy's little girl was helped into this job,' I say, taking joy from the revelation.

'He's her uncle,' Abbey explains.

'Same difference,' I retort.

'No, it's not,' she says, suddenly becoming very defensive. 'Charles is the only family Em has.'

'She lost her parents?' I ask, my voice barely audible.

'Yes.'

'Fire?' I ask.

'Car crash,' Abbey explains, sadness in her voice. 'Her father pushed her out but she saw them...'

I know what the final word is without it being spoken. Burn.

'It's okay, Abbey. You don't need to say anymore.'

'Please don't tell her I said all this.'

'You have my word.'

There is silence between us for a long while and I look out of the window again.

'How are the injuries?' Abbey asks, breaking the silence.

'I barely feel a thing,' I reply, before something in my memory suddenly resurfaces. 'About a year ago, Matt sprained his ankle skiing. That wasn't true was it?'

'It did involve snow in a way,' she says.

'And the truth?'

'Caught up in an avalanche climbing Everest.'

'And the concussion from a car crash six months ago?' I ask.

'Run in with a tribal leader in Kenya.'

'Cuts to his arm from a neighbour's dog?'

'Shark bite whilst deep sea diving.'

'Little liar,' I say, astounded.

'He did struggle with lying to you all this time,' Abbey says.

'Really?' I ask suspiciously.

'Nope, he actually found it quite funny.' She laughs.

Standing up from my seat, I move towards the toilets, a quick shout from Abbey reminding me that whilst wearing the glasses she can see everything. I take them off and tuck them into my pocket. When I return to my seat and put the glasses on again, I can see the mainland of Italy in the distance through the windows.

'Not long now,' Abbey says through the headset. 'Rome. The heart of an empire that spanned from northern England to Egypt, the Black Sea, and everything in between. One man stood emperor, Julius Caesar, although technically he held the title of dictator. His successor, Augustus as he was formerly known, became the first man with the title of emperor.'

The image of Julius Caesar appears in my glasses, enactments and films depicting his life. Abbey gives me a full commentary of it all, of Caesar's rise to power as a victorious general, of his rivalry with the senate and his march on Rome to become dictator. Lastly, I see his infamous assassination on the Ides of March.

'Wasn't it Titus who was emperor during the time the Eagle would've been returned to Rome?' I ask, showing my own brief research carried out as I waited for my flight via mobile phone and online encyclopedias.

'His father Vespasian, actually.' I can hear the joy in her voice at correcting me.

'So why did you tell me about Julius Caesar?'

'Because he was one of the most famous men who ever lived and his past and history is interesting,' she tries to explain herself.

'I see why Charles has to tell you to keep on track,' I say with a smile, shaking my head. 'So none of that was actually relevant to what we're doing here.'

'Anyway, on your right in the far distance,' Abbey says, putting on her best tour guide voice, 'you will see Mount Vesuvius.'

On the lens of the glasses appears a crosshairs, directing me towards the mountain.

'The mountain that blew,' I say; the image of an erupting volcano appears in the lens.

'Yep,' says Abbey. 'Another terrifying piece of history. It was also the site of a great triumph by a group of escaped gladiators and house slaves over the forces of Rome.'

'I am Spartacus!' I reply with a grin, already knowing the story.

'Sorry, Sir?' a nearby stewardess asks in confusion.

'Oh, er, nothing,' I quickly say, looking back out towards the horizon.

'Where are you, Matt?' I whisper to myself.

'We'll find him, Hunter,' she says, trying to reassure me and forgetting herself for a moment.

'That was what you called Matt, wasn't it?

'Yeah, sorry. Old habits.'

'You call the operatives hunters,' I say. 'Is that where you got the name from? Matt?'

'No, that was in use long before Matt came along.'

I hear it, the emotion in her voice. She really does care for Matt

'We'll find him, Abbey,' I try to reassure her.

'I know you will, Hunter. Sorry, I mean, Adam.'

I let her off this time and look through the plane's window towards Rome, the capital city of what was once the most powerful empire in the world.

'Hang on, you never told me your surname,' I say.

'And it will remain one of life's great mysteries,' Abbey laughs.

26

THE CENTURION—Capua

For many days, I am confined to my cell within ludis, healing and seeing out my punishment, never setting foot beyond the bars, not even to train or fight in the arenas. No further word is received from my wife, and by order of the Dominus, my coin earned from victories is taken, to cover the cost of hiring new guards to replace those wounded by my hands at the arena. The other gladiators shun me also, respect earned since joining their number lost in my maddened attempt to save Garus. In my darkest days, I realise I will never escape this place; my fate is to die in the darkness or fall to the amusement of the crowd.

One day, after my meagre meal of mouldy bread and cup of water, Hader comes to my cell.

'You should not have acted so foolishly,' he tells me.

'You had the crowd chanting your name, the interest of the nobility for all their games, and a portion of the coin raised for your freedom; long sought word from your wife was gained – so why, for the love of the gods, why did you act with such recklessness?

'Garus did not deserve death,' I mutter in reply.

'So you were to charge onto the sands, slay all the guards of the arena and carry him to safety? What fever seized your mind?'

'He was a brother.'

'As are all gladiators within this house. It is an honour to fall upon the sands.'

'Not after claiming victory,' I argue back, forcing myself to calm as I see the guards take a step closer.

'The boy was as foolish as you,' Hader states with frustration. 'He should have finished; the man was already defeated. His weakness surfaced in his lack of action.'

'You see mercy as weakness?'

'Did he not lose his life?'

'Life taken at the whim of others. We are of equal worth!'

'You are a slave! Your lives belong to me and all with position as long as you remain under my ownership and still draw breath! You talk as if you are free!'

'I was!'

'But no longer! You are a slave!'

We both fall silent for a moment, the heat of the argument settling.

'Your actions force me to make a difficult choice,' the Dominus says, breaking the tension between us. 'The games to honour the naming of Titus, son of Vespasian, as emperor, fast approach.'

'Vespasian is dead?' I ask in shock.

'I thought that would banish some gloom. Disease claimed his life, yet others say it was poison. There were many who wished to remove the tyrant. In his final moments, he declared he was ascending to join the gods. He died with his mind utterly lost.'

By disease or poison, Vespasian is dead, my legion avenged. It brings little joy as I still languish in this cell, and my wife is far away.

'The games to honour Titus will see gladiators from all across the Roman Empire summoned for the greatest battle ever witnessed in an arena, a spectacle unlike any seen before. Request has been made for three of my best fighters. Two spaces are filled already, but the third... the third causes me struggle. In your absence, I have lost many of our best to injury or death. I have a mind to name you my third champion.'

'I do as you command,' I say without emotion.

'Do you? I cannot recall ordering you to storm the sands in vain attempt to rescue Garus.'

'As you said, Dominus, a fever-seized mind.'

I say no more, silent as he judges my worth once again.

'I cannot think now without wine in my cup,' he says in frustration. 'You irritate me more than any other, Centurion, but the gods for some inexplicable reason, seem to favour you. With a sword in hand, you are like Mars, God of War himself in battle, possessing skill far beyond your years. Perhaps together, we will march to Rome to honour Titus our new emperor. And this spectacle is to be held in the new arena; the greatest ever constructed – sands untouched by blood and death. We will achieve glory unlike any ever seized before – or we will baptise the ground with your blood.'

27

ADAM—Rome, Italy

Hundreds of people are gathered outside the Colosseum; tourists, tour guides, families on holiday of a dozen nationalities.

Images flicker across the lenses of the glasses, depicting the Colosseum in all its glory. Audiences of sixty thousand people, games lasting a hundred days – death always the spectacle. Now, the Colosseum stands a deteriorated tourist attraction, vast sections of its walls long gone. Strikes of lightning and earthquakes have taken their toll but the hands of man even more so, having used much of the stone for other constructions.

Even in its current condition, the Colosseum is impressive, towering over the surrounding area. It's easy to imagine thousands of people flocking to see the grand spectacles held by the emperors and nobility of Rome. The greatest fighters in the world fought inside those walls.

'I've always wanted to see it,' I say in wonder, thinking of the map on my wall at home; Rome and the Colosseum marked as future destinations. 'I can see why Matt took this job.'

'It's why most of the hunters join up,' Abbey says.

'Tell me more about it,' I ask of her.

'The construction was begun by the Emperor Vespasian in 72AD but he was to never see it open. Completion was overseen by his son, Titus,' Abbey explains as images on the headset match everything she says; names, dates, maps, and more. 'The inaugural festivities lasted a hundred days with five thousand wild beasts said to have been killed in a single day; ostriches, tigers, lions, panthers, bears, and even hippos. Combat between gladiators and wild animals was said to be the most popular event, but there were many variations, and without exception, all were fights to the death. It saw one million animals slaughtered and half a million people, all to keep the mob entertained. All kinds of weapons were used; swords, nets, tridents, daggers, and offensive shields, and the people involved were formerly listed as including professional gladiators, convicted criminals, Christians, hunters, dwarves, and women.'

'You're better than any tour guide,' I tell her.

'Thank you,' she replies politely.

'It still doesn't answer how we get inside,' Dave mutters beside me. 'Especially with all those civilians.'

He and Emma are fully kitted out in the dark grey uniforms with blue lining, as am I, all of us wearing ordinary jackets over the top so as only the trousers are visible. They each wear their own earpieces and mics so all of us can communicate, only I am wearing a headset.

Standing in an abandoned office building across from the Colosseum, we watch the circuit of the security guards and plan our infiltration.

'Looking at the schematics I gained from the Italian national records...'

'Which you hacked into their Government system to gain,' Emma interrupts, talking with pride in her voice.

'Maybe,' Abbey admits. I don't need to see it to know Abbey is most likely throwing one of her scowls. 'Anyway, from the schematics, there are two main sets of iron gates that lead to the closed off restricted areas, including the lower levels you need to access. The nearest to you is the east gates. They are generally used as a secondary entrance but right now they're already locked shut. The gates reach ceiling to floor and they don't have typical locks, requiring unique keys to open. Each gate has a sensor that will sound if anyone stands at the gates for too long without passing through the walkway. Basically, picking the locks is not an option so you need the keys. Then you need to get through before entering the lower levels, which is where the animals were caged and gladiators prepared for combat. No members of the public are permitted, but it is where you will find the records of victorious gladiators carved into the walls.'

'You're enjoying this, aren't you?' I tease Abbey, sensing the rising excitement in her voice and the broadening of her brogue.

'Maybe,' she repeats.

'Enough,' Dave mutters. 'So, first of all, we need the keys.'

'Who would have them?' Emma asks.

'Not likely to be the guards patrolling the outside,' Abbey says. 'We will need whoever is in charge of tonight's security detail. I bet a hundred pounds they'll have the keys on them.'

Dave, Emma, and I have been watching the security of the Colosseum since dawn. There are teams of three circling around the structure, passing the entrances every three minutes. One person seems to be in charge, a woman, standing near to the entrance we planned on using.

I scan the area and see her. She's in her mid-thirties; dark hair, and wearing a smart uniform. A firearm is sheathed at her hip. The serious expression on her face gives the impression she is skilled in its use.

'That looks like our girl,' Dave says, drawing his own handgun and checking it's loaded.

'Whoa!' I say, ushering for him to lower the gun. 'You're not going to kill her.'

'Who said anything about killing,' Emma says with a dark grin, drawing her own firearm. 'Maybe just scare her a little.'

'I still can't believe you managed to get them and the rest of the equipment through customs,' I say, looking back to our target. In Dave's rucksack are handguns, a dozen of Tristram's gadgets, smoke grenades, flash bangs, and bolas among them.

'You wouldn't believe what Lovell is capable of – he's a *very* influential man,' he replies.

'So what's the plan then, Adam?' Dave asks. 'This is your show after all. We're just here for the ride.'

Emma catches my gaze with hard eyes; she is unimpressed.

I think for a moment, weighing up a few options. If what Abbey says about the gates is true, then picking the locks will be impossible. I need the keys.

'We could wait until nightfall,' suggests Dave.

'We don't have the time to wait,' I say. 'Matt's captors could be on their way, if they aren't already here. Besides, the quicker we find the Eagle, the quicker we find Matt.'

'What about all these people?' Emma says, her eyes assessing the crowds of tourists.

'There's only one choice,' I say to them. 'Why postpone what can be done today.'

'Now you're beginning to sound like Matt,' Emma says with a slight smile on her lips.

I zip up my father's biker jacket, brush my hair down out of nervous habit, and take a map of Rome from my pocket. I tighten the straps on my rucksack as much as possible, trying to give the impression of an ordinary lost tourist.

'I will go and have a talk with her,' I say nodding in the direction of the woman in the uniform. 'You never know, she might just kindly hand the keys over to me.'

I leave them bemused, weaving through the masses of tourists. Emma makes a small effort to call after me from the empty office but I ignore her.

'Do you know what you're doing?' she demands over my headset.

'We'll soon see,' I tell her.

'If not, you'll be arrested and of no help to your brother,' Dave warns angrily via his earpiece and mic. 'Just be ready for when I need you,' I tell them. 'Distract and act. Dave, be ready. When I say the word *Hunter,* I need a distraction. Emma, at the same time, I need you to make your way to me as quickly as possible.'

'Can you even speak Italian?' Abbey asks as I near the security guard.

'Nope,' I admit.

'Not a word?'

'Not a word,' I confirm.

'Say what you want to tell her and I will repeat it in Italian for you,' she says.

'I'll try,' I tell her.

'You're going to get arrested,' she warns. 'Or shot.'

'Probably both,' Dave adds.

'Definitely both,' Emma agrees.

'Where's your optimism, guys?' I ask. 'No wonder Matt went to Scotland without you.'

I walk across the road and force my way through the crowds. As I near, I see that she has already spotted me, eyeing me warily as I make a beeline straight towards her. She wears a badge saying 'Chief of Security' according to Abbey.

'Hi, sorry,' I say as I approach with map already open. She nods a greeting, already annoyed at my intrusion and speaks briefly into the intercom at her shoulder.

'Can you please tell me how to get to the Pantheon?' I ask her, naming one of the other landmarks I can remember on the spot.

'Per favore mi puoi dire come arrivare al Pantheon,' Abbey says through the headset, pronouncing the words as they appear across the lenses.

'Por favour my pui dire come arrivei all Pantheon,' I say in terrible Italian. The security guard eyes me suspiciously, clearly not understanding a thing I have said.

'My God that was simply awful,' Abbey says. 'You're

definitely going to be arrested. Try; in quale direzione è il pantheon.'

I try to repeat the words again but the woman is even more confused until suddenly she understands one word.

'Pantheon?' she asks.

'Oui, oui,' I say.

'That's French, you idiot! You mean *si*,' Abbey says, barely able to contain her laughter.

'Si, si,' I repeat, pointing at my map. The security guard looks at the map and starts indicating the route to the Pantheon, but as she does, she leans forward and I can see straight down her top, flashing me an eyeful of white girlie lace – a stark contrast to her masculine and authoritarian uniform.

'Uh, Adam,' Abbey warns, 'Remember I see whatever you're looking at. Be a gentleman.'

'Hunter,' I whisper.

A loud bang sounds from farther up the street, followed by crashing glass. Youths are shouting at the top of their voices and cheering. The security guard forces the map back into my hands and hurries away, shouting and calling into her intercom for back up.

'Good distraction, Dave. Now hurry up and get over here,' I tell him, backing away towards the Colosseum's secondary entrance and the iron gates we need to overcome. There are still hundreds of people around me but not for much longer.

'What's the next part of your brilliant plan then?' Emma asks as she hurries over to me.

I lift up the security guard's intercom, taken from the guard whilst Abbey thought my gaze was wandering. Emma smiles and snatches it out of my hand, knowing the rest of what I have in mind. Her Italian words come fluent and clear, impressive. It doesn't take long to hear the results. Across the Colosseum loudspeakers, announcements flood out and a general evacuation begins.

'The people may be going but we still can't get past the gates,' Abbey warns.

'We can with these,' I say, holding up the set of keys and an identification card I lifted from the guard as she inspected my map.

'Francesca Visiers, Chief of Security,' I say, reading the ID badge. 'And you thought I was just eyeing her...'

I'm silenced as a young, attractive woman, marches straight towards me, her face flushed with anger. My God, she's beautiful. Her words come fast and furious.

'What's she saying?' I ask.

She's very annoyed. She's asking if you know why there has been an evacuation called. She's spent a lot of money and she wants reimbursing. She's going to blow our cover if she continues ranting like this,' Emma warns. 'We're losing time.'

'Why don't you speak to her then,' I encourage Emma.

'No way,' she says, backing away. 'It's you she's yelling at. Come on. Use some of that Hunter charm.'

'How do you say you're very beautiful in Italian?' I ask.

'What?' Abbey replies. 'How does that help?'

'We don't have time for this,' Emma warns.

'She's Spanish anyway, not Italian,' Abbey adds.

'Abbey?'

'Fine, what do you want to say?'

'Something like, you have my sincerest apologies. If there is anything I can do to help such a stunningly beautiful woman such as you, you need only say.'

Abbey translates everything and I repeat it, laying on the charm despite my woeful attempts at the language. It doesn't go down well; the furious woman slaps me hard across the face, shouting a tirade of what I imagine are insults before storming off.

'What did she say?' I ask, rubbing the sore, red cheek and my wounded pride. 'Okay, Abbey, you can stop laughing so hysterically.'

'No, no, I can't! You were *so* rude to her.' She continues to howl.

'What did I say?' I'm beginning to realise that my usual Hunter charm had got woefully lost in translation.

'I really can't repeat what you said, but it was hilarious!'

'C'mon, lover boy,' Dave says as he reaches us, hurrying us through the evacuating crowds towards the secondary entrance and the vast locked gates.

'What the hell was that, Adam?' Emma asks me as we hurry towards the gates.

'Improvisation,' I reply. 'It was worth a shot. Why? You jealous?'

'Amateur,' she says back.

I stop just before we reach the iron gates blocking the entrance. There's a security camera overhead, turning in its surveillance. Once it's facing away, we sprint forward and beneath it. Dave takes a small electronic device from his pack, and with a boost up from me, connects it to the casing of the camera. Thankfully, it doesn't take him long. He's a tonne of solid muscle.

'An electro-magnetic pulse device,' Abbey explains over the headset.

'EMP,' I reply in a whisper. 'Another gadget of Tristram's?'

'Yep. Attached to the camera it'll short-out their security system, requiring a full reboot.'

'Whatever you guys pay Tristram, it's not enough,' I say, impressed.

'He agrees wholeheartedly,' Abbey says, conveying the technician's message.

Dave activates the device, and though it doesn't give a sound, I feel the pressure increase in my ears for a brief second before the camera stills, its lights dimming.

'Shouldn't the EMP have knocked out the glasses and earpieces?' I ask.

'Please, our equipment is far too advanced for that,' Abbey states proudly. 'All the shielding money can buy.'

'Again, tell Charles to pay Tristram more,' I tell her. 'How much time does that buy us?'

'Ten, fifteen minutes max,' Dave states as we rush on towards the gates. 'It'll only affect those security systems in circuit with it though, so whatever other surprises they have in wait we will have to overcome.'

'At least they won't get our image on the cameras,' I say.

'I can't imagine anything worse than your ugly mugs being shown on worldwide news,' Abbey taunts. '*Have you seen these men, international criminals Adam Hunter and Dave Conway?*'

'What about Emma?' I ask.

'She's too good to get caught,' Abbey says.

'Damn right,' Emma agrees.

'Quiet,' Dave silences us as we reach the gates.

There are two locks to the gate and I size them up with the keys in my hand. Thankfully, they click into place without effort or alarm. It takes all three of us to pull the heavy iron open, closing the gate again once we are inside. Beyond the gate, we enter long, dark passages that wind around the Colosseum.

'Not going to be able to see much in the dark without torches,' I say. 'The light may give away our presence to any guards wandering by.'

'As you seem fond of saying, 'No worries',' Abbey

replies. The lenses of the glasses flicker for a moment and my vision is bathed in green, able to see as clear as if it was the middle of the day.

'Now where?' Dave asks, one eye on his watch. He's not wearing glasses, nor Emma, but I can see their eyes surveying our surroundings with ease, military experience and training.

A map appears before my left eye, a full layout of the Colosseum with a single blue dot representing where we stand. A red cross shows our destination.

'You need to circle around the arena to avoid the security rooms,' Abbey explains, the route appearing on the glasses. 'They will have their hands full with the evacuation and trying to get their cameras back on, but that doesn't mean they won't still be patrolling the area. You then need to descend into the lower levels beneath the arena. I am afraid you're on your own after that; there have never been maps or schematics published of what is down there.'

'But the engraved walls, the records, they're down there?' I ask.

'Supposedly,' Abbey simply replies.

'That doesn't exactly inspire confidence,' I tell her.

'Where's your optimism?' she mimics me.

'Enough, you two,' Dave says, hurrying on in silence, Emma and I close behind.

We continue onwards, in the dark walkways of the

Colosseum. There are security cameras covering all areas, but they still show no signs of activity.

We hurry, the heat of the Italian night and the weight of our equipment making us sweat. Quicker than I thought possible, we reach the red marker on the map – it marks the stairwell down into the dark heart of the Colosseum. Standing at the bottom of the stairs, as if waiting for us, are two guards, handguns holstered at their hips. As Dave indicates to me, they are both wearing ear piece communicators, an easy way to call for back up.

'There's no other way into the lower levels than this,' Abbey explains.

'We'll have to go through them,' Dave mutters in a whisper.

He pulls another EMP device from his rucksack and activates it, the pressure in my ears building for a moment again, knocking out the guard's earpieces. Dave then shows me something else, a canister with a ring pin, the word *GAS* across its length.

'Ready, Em?' he asks her.

'Yep,' she says, then turning to me, she adds, 'Stay here.'

'Take a deep breath,' Dave tells us.

Dave pulls the pin and rolls the canister down the stairs. Smoke billows out to cover the stairwell. The guards cough and splutter, trying to raise the alarm but with no luck. Dave charges forward, thundering down the stairs and barging one of the guards to the ground. Emma follows, leaping down and propelling herself off the wall to the side, landing a hard kick to the back of the legs of the remaining guard. His knees buckle and she catches him, holding him in the smoke until he falls unconscious.

As the smoke clears, Dave emerges, victorious, with the guard lying limp at the foot of the stairs. He has the guard's firearm in his hands, and unloads and dismantles it in a matter of seconds. I look to Emma, a broad smile across her face. She enjoys all this. Only when the smoke clears do they take a breath.

'They're still alive, right?' I ask.

'Yes, don't worry,' Dave states, dismantling the other guard's gun.

Suddenly, from around the corner, another guard emerges, cups of coffee in his hands. He is young, younger even than me, and seeing his colleagues down, he starts to turn and runs without a word.

'I've got him,' I say, running after the guard and taking from my pocket a single bolas. Throwing it, the wire wraps quickly around the guard's body, his arms and legs entangled. He collapses, crying out as he lands hard on the stone floor.

'Nice work, kid,' Dave says as he catches up to me and silences the man with a cloth soaked in what smells like petrol. The guard falls limp instantly, though I can see he is still breathing fine.

'Now where?' Dave asks.

'Your guess is as good as mine,' Abbey admits. 'Remember I have no records of what is down there.'

We continue on into the dark lower levels, seeing little of interest except more passageways until Dave suddenly grabs Emma and me. Slowly, he lowers down, pointing out what we were just about to step through. Barely visible to the human eye is a single red laser.

'Good spot,' Emma says, kneeling down and taking a closer look. 'Break the laser and it'll trigger a mass alarm.'

'I can help with that,' Abbey says. The vision on the glasses flickers to red, the faint lines of the lasers now visible. They cross the passageway, some covering vast areas and creating difficult obstacles at different heights.

'There's something beyond this that somebody didn't want found,' Dave says.

'No worries,' I reply, flashing him a grin that draws a roll of the eyes from Emma.

I back up before taking a long, deep breath. I sprint forward, leap over the first few, ducking under the next and then, grasping a stone column across the ceiling, pull myself up and around the next. All those school escapades have trained me well. I pause briefly, on tips toes as I try to keep my balance and stop myself from tumbling forward, then leaping on and over the next set of lasers. I duck under the next, rolling across the floor and to the end of the passageway.

'See, no worries,' I say as I rise up, lifting my arms in triumph. 'Your turn.'

I throw the glasses to Emma, narrowly missing the lasers, and she travels down the passageway the same as me. I have to admit that her reflexes and agility are far superior, leaping and moving without effort. Within no time, she has crossed the corridor without setting off the alarm.

'Your turn, old man,' she taunts Dave.

He shakes his head, draws his handgun, silencer already attached to its barrel, and fires a single round. I duck away but the bullet is nowhere near me, striking a fuse box against the wall halfway down the passageway. The lasers disappear instantly.

'And you couldn't have done that before?' I ask, feeling like an idiot.

'You didn't ask,' Dave says, briefly showing a smile as he begins to walk towards me. It disappears instantly as we hear another voice call out from behind us.

'Ferma qui!' two security guards yell, handguns raised.

'Stop there!' Abbey translates.

'Yeah, guessed that,' I reply.

Before we can say or do anything, gunshots sound, the noise deafening in the tight passageway as the two guards fall to the ground. Emma and I duck behind a wall, peering out and seeing Dave taking cover behind the remains of a stone statue.

'What the... you shot them!' I say, turning on Dave.

'No, I didn't,' he says, looking at his gun. 'I didn't release the catch.'

'Then who did?'

As I'm staring at the shapes of the men on the floor, a familiar Australian voice calls out,

'Well, if it isn't Matt's little brother again.'

'Come here, punk,' an American voice adds, 'I owe you a great deal of pain.'

'Is that Dave Conway as well?' the Australian says with joy. 'Oh, we've been looking forward to the next time our paths cross again. This time, I'll be putting a bullet in you!'

'Leon and Bishop,' I whisper. Dread ripples through me as, peering around the corner, I see the red eye, the still healing spear wound across its face and ruined eye. The wolf sees me, too and unleashes a terrifying roar.

'Em, Adam, get out of here,' Dave orders me. 'I'll hold them off. Keep going. Get to the records.'

'We can't leave you!' I protest.

'Do as I say, kid!' he yells, firing two rounds, forcing Leon and Bishop to duck away before throwing a smoke grenade to cover our escape. 'You're no use dead! Em, get him out of here! I'm not going to tell you ag...'

Dave's words are silenced as the wolf charges through the smoke and knocks him away in its haste to get to me.

'Run, Hunter, run!' Abbey screams.

It's the only choice we have. I grab Emma and drag her

away into the unknown. In the next room are more laser sensors and we manage to trigger every single one of them in our escape, the alarms echoing through the Colosseum. With two guards gunned down, and a battle still ongoing behind us as Dave holds off Leon and Bishop, it's too late for subtlety anyway. I hear the wolf's jaws snapping behind me, gaining on me as we enter the next room, which is filled with tables, computers and all manner of equipment for excavation and analysis.

We split then, Emma running to one side of the room and me the other. The wolf has only one target. Leaping at me, it thunders into my back, forcing me down as its claws tear into my leather jacket. As I hit the ground, I roll, ducking beneath a table and pulling it down after me, table and computer equipment striking the beast but it doesn't slow. I strike it with a chair but it doesn't stop – it has one and only one aim – to tear me apart.

Suddenly, a gunshot rings in my ears, the bullet striking near to the beast but missing and ricocheting. Stopping and turning, the wolf hurtles towards its attacker, Emma. She fires three more rounds, striking the animal twice, but it doesn't slow. That's when I understand – the wolf isn't of this world; it is something else – something supernatural. Leaping towards her, it snaps its jaws savagely. Diving away, she only just clears the beast, smashing through more equipment and sending sparks flying before a loud boom deafens us both. The shockwave of the equipment exploding throws both of us to the ground.

I feel the heat before I see it, flames covering the room, but its Emma's screams that rouse me. The wolf has her, jaws clamped tight around her leg, the wound already bleeding heavily. Without thinking, I rise up and charge it, leaping over debris to slam both boots into the beast's side and send it crashing into the flames. It howls loudly, the fire burning through its fur. It rises out of the blaze, a demonic hound, fleeing back down the dark corridors.

Emma's screams fill the space; pain and fear.

'Come on,' I urge, but she's not hearing me. She is seeing only the fire, the growing inferno. I see in her eyes that she is no longer here, but lost somewhere in the horror of her past.

'We need to get out of here,' I coax, kneeling at her side.

'I... I can't.'

'Close your eyes,' I say, taking her trembling hands in mine. 'Listen to me. Close your eyes and listen to my voice. I will get you out of here.'

At last, she meets my gaze. She is terrified. Tears stream from her eyes.

'I will get you out of here,' I repeat. 'Close your eyes.'

She nods, summoning her courage and closing her eyes. With an arm around her, I help her to stand, taking most of her weight from the injured leg.

'Come on,' I whisper. 'One step at a time.'

Suddenly, blue flames join the rest, rising ever higher around us.

'He's here,' I whisper under my breath, trying not to panic Emma further.

I guide her through the room, her body still trembling in fear; the heat of the flames is still too close. Every step she takes on her injured leg draws a cry of agony, but she doesn't stop; the need to escape overwhelms any pain.

'Nearly there,' I say calmly, despite the flames all around us.

'You're not a good liar, are you?' Emma forces a joke.

It's only when we are clear and into the next corridor that I tell her to open her eyes. Her legs buckle instantly and I lower her to the ground. Looking back, I see the trail of blood in our wake. She's badly injured, and we don't have much time – I know he is here. Quickly, I take the first aid kit from my rucksack, hoping there is something I can use as a tourniquet. I thank God for the team back at base when I discover, nestled at the bottom of the bag, a length of black cloth. I tie it tightly around her leg above the bite, drawing another cry of pain from her lips before wrapping the wound in more bandages.

'That'll slow the bleeding,' I tell her, 'but we need to get you to a hospital.'

'Later,' Emma says. 'You need to keep going.'

'I can't leave you.'

'Go. If not, this will all have been for nothing.'

'What if Leon and Bishop make it this far?' I ask, still hearing distant gunfire. 'Or the flames keep spreading?'

'If they come, I will deal with Leon and Bishop,' she says with a smirk, her handgun ready.

'The sprinkler systems in that room have been activated,' Abbey's voice says, breaking through static. 'Took their time too.'

'I thought we had lost you,' I reply.

'Something in there interfered with my comms. That shouldn't have happened. I could see everything though. Got pretty heated in there.'

I can't tell if she's trying to crack a joke or not, but I'm not in the mood. 'Have you heard anything from Dave?' I ask her.

'Nothing good,' Abbey replies.

'We need to get back there and help him,' I say. 'We need to get Emma out of here.'

'No, Adam, you need to keep going,' Emma orders me. 'Find out what happened to the centurion. Find the Eagle. Find Matt.'

'She's right,' Abbey tells me. 'The police have been alerted and you will never have a better chance than now. Dave can handle himself. He's survived worse.'

'All right,' I concede, turning then to Emma. 'I'll find the records first, then I'll come back for you and Dave.'

'Go!' she orders me. 'And thank you.'

'No worries,' I tell her, lingering for a moment.

'Go!'

I want to stay, to look after her and get her out of this place, but I know she and Abbey are right; I need to continue. I hurry on, running from room to room but find nothing until I enter a vast chamber, directly under what has to be the arena. Looking up, I can see the wooden beams of the arena floor, the old beams marked with age and blood. Light from the Colosseum's arena seeps through the gaps in the beams, illuminating the chamber, the glasses reacting to give better vision. In the vast chamber is more equipment and several glass cabinets housing excavation gear in storage and others containing relics recently discovered. Around me are smaller cells with doors made of aged iron bars.

'This must be where the gladiators and animals were kept,' Abbey tells me. 'And there directly before you in the centre, that must have been the lift to raise those who would fight into the arena.'

I can see the vast mechanism, still in place after all this time, but it's not that which catches my eye, nor is it the impressive statue, still completely intact, of Mars, God of War. It towers over me, sword and head of defeated foe held high, pelt of a bear draped around the god's shoulders. The statue stands on watch over the area, as it would've greeted all gladiators about to take to the arena.

The walls capture my attention; across every inch of

them is Latin inscriptions. On a marble arch, at the heart of the walls before the lift are the words *HIC STATIS HONORATUM VICTORES.*

'Here stand the honoured victorious!' Abbey translates, her voice a higher pitch than normal with excitement, her Irish tone more pronounced than ever. 'Oh my God, Hunter, you've found it!'

'Why would anyone want to hide this?' I ask in wonder. 'It is a testament to the men who fought and died here.'

'The Colosseum is just a tourist attraction these days,' Abbey replies. 'Perhaps they wanted to hold onto this, this one piece of their history, keeping it as theirs.'

I can understand that. From the outside, I can see the decay and ruin inflicted on the great structure by man over the years. They wanted to keep just one piece of their history as it was in the days when gladiators fought on the sands above. They wanted to preserve the heroes of their past.

'Take as many images as you can, Abbey, so you can translate it later,' I say, slowly turning my head so that the glasses see as much of the walls as possible. 'I need to get back to Emma and Dave.'

The glasses highlight each and every inscription, red crosshairs centring on each with images stored for later analysis.

'No need,' Abbey says, voice more excited than ever. 'I've found it!'

28

THE CENTURION—Capua

My fate leads me to the Colosseum. It is the greatest structure I have set eyes on; the biggest and grandest in all of
Rome. Vespasian was a madman but this, his creation, is
certain to be the pinnacle of his achievements and could
almost banish the memory of his tyranny. Forty thousand
people are attending the Games of Titus, son of Vespasian,
to honour his ascension to emperor. Forty thousand
people and the arena is not even complete yet; the upper
echelons are still under construction.

Standing with me, awaiting our turn upon the sands, is
the Celt Machonus and Onyxx of Gaul, skilled warriors
with dozens of victories between them. They are good
men, cursing me as a recruit but each showing respect
after my worth was proven.

Machonus, the long fire-haired Celt, carries gladius and shield as I do, whereas bald-headed Onyxx, tallest and stoutest of Hader's gladiators, is armed with twin battleaxes. We wear the armour of the legion, breastplate, greaves, helms, all of it to give further credence to my title as the Centurion. Despite my initial distaste, I must admit there is comfort in wearing the armaments of the legion once again.

Against the three of us will be the champions of five other ludises, each fighting for the glory of their house. The melee, as it is known, will only end when a single man stands alone victorious. That man will be me. I will be fighting for Lucilla.

'Stay together and we may yet survive this,' I tell the Celt and giant Gaul at my side.

'Agreed,' says Machonus, Onyxx remaining eerily silent.

Executions of escaped slaves are greeted first, then bear and lion fighting, the animals losing every time to the spears of their hunters. After the carcass of the last beast is dragged away for the butchers, the gates open before us and we march out onto the already bloodied sands. The crowd's chants are so loud they shake my bones. The arena is beyond imagination, and we, the gladiators of Hader, cannot help but smile broadly as the roar of 'CENTURI-ONS' ripples through the spectators. In the centre, we stop and face our opponents, twelve of them, eager to spill any blood that is not their own. Even when they are defeated, I will need to face Machonus and Onyxx. There will be a moment that will transform us from brothers to enemies; it is a moment I do not relish.

From the pulvinus balcony high above, we see the nobility of Rome. One man stands before them, addressing the crowd. He stands tall and strong, veteran of campaigns, and surprisingly, he is wearing armour on such a hot day. He is Titus, our newly crowned emperor, already wearing the golden laurel wreath upon his brow as his father did before him.

'We come now to the most anticipated event of this honoured day,' Titus announces, enthralling the entire crowd. 'The Primus, the greatest event of any games has yet to be named. That is by my choice and its name will be announced upon completion of this melee. Fifteen men will fight from the Houses of; Ramis, Hader, Bollunth, Minthula, and Omanus. Your Dominuses do you great honour choosing you as their champions, as they honour me in their attendance at these games. Gratitude to all, for it shall not be forgotten.'

As he speaks, two men circle around us gladiators, pouring black liquid in a vast circle with us inside. With aflame torch, the liquid is ignited and the flames of Hades surround us.

'Any man finding himself outside the flames is eliminated from the contest, bringing shame upon his house.

The victor is the last man to be left standing within the circle of fire, all others fallen or eliminated. These men, these gladiators, are the greatest in all the lands. They fight to prove who is the greatest warrior in all of Rome. It will be a sight to be remembered for all eternity, gratitude paid to those men who give lives to honour me so.'

'FOR THE GLORY OF OUR EMPEROR AND ROME!' we gladiators roar back. I stay silent.

'Let it begin!'

It is chaos the moment the order is given. Blood and death. It is battle, no melee. Machonus and Onyxx are at my side at first, hacking and slashing at any in our path before they are lost amongst the carnage. I cannot look for them, I can only face and fight what is before me.

I kill the first man standing in my way, ending his suffering as his throat has already been ripped open. Hammering my shield into the next, I eliminate him, sending him falling through the flames as I cross blades with another. He reacts too slowly and his stomach is impaled. Without waiting to see him fall, I move on, leaping over Onyxx as he is thrown back, slamming his shield into his attacker and forcing him into the flames where his screams drown out the cheers of spectators.

Onyxx does not thank me, instead, hurling an axe towards my head. I raise my shield to deflect the blow. The moment has come. We are brothers no more. Then he is on me, thrashing axe upon shield, his strength greater than any I have faced before. Ducking away from his falling sword, we are separated as others attack.

The blade of a new foe catches my arm and draws blood, but I am not dazed, only angered. I sweep his legs from under him and lower my blade to his throat but he offers the missio, begging for his life. Kicking his gladius away, I leave him, letting others finish off the coward.

The next man to attack dies quickly, as does the next man, and the one after that, until I face Onyxx again. Both of us are covered in the blood of the slain. He holds a man by the throat, his head forced into the fire and his screams piercing the roar of the crowd and chaos around us. When the cries stop, Onyxx drops his victim's charred body and turns to face me. My blood is raging fire. I am eager to end it.

'Centurion, now you die!' Onyxx bellows. He has axe in one hand, raised spear in the other.

'Not this day!' I roar back in defiance, charging my towering opponent.

He hurls the spear and it glances off my shield to strike the man behind us. Onyxx's axe swings towards me in wide arcs. I stab at the giant but he parries everything before grasping hold of my shield and tearing it from my arm. I slash my gladius across his chest but he merely roars in defiance. His fists, like hammers, strike my head and send me to the ground.

My world is stars and blood.

'Lucilla...' I utter as Onyxx lowers his gaze to me. There is death in his eyes.

'CENTURION! CENTURION! CENTURION!'

The crowd is roaring for me, urging me to fight on.

'Lucilla,' I say, eyes focusing and my vision returning.

Machonus appears before me, breathing hard, bleeding from his wounds. He could kill me easily with the swing of a blade, but instead, he turns to face Onyxx. He dares to defend me. He shouts at the Gaul, who merely laughs before effortlessly knocking Machonus's blade away and tearing the man almost in two.

Onyxx laughs loudly in the slaughter of a brother. He is deranged by the horror of it all. Another gladiator approaches me, eager for an easy kill. He does not see my anger and rage.

'Lucilla!' My wife is my battle cry. I force myself up, and grasping the fallen gladius, I ram it into the man's stomach.

I charge Onyxx as he knocks Machonus's dying body away. We are the last two. He sees me coming, battleaxe already swinging, but I leap, swiping my blade across his chest again. The wound is deep but he still will not fall. We clash sword on axe, trying to gut each other, but neither will relent until I see the opportunity to slash his arm holding the axe. The gladius cuts through his flesh and bone until the limb is sent flying into the flames. Onyxx yells with untempered fury, transformed into an enraged beast. I silence him with my blade.

The crowd erupts around me but I cannot hear them. I fall to my knees in astonishment and exhaustion. Their cheers give me a new life and I rise, drawing the gladius from Onyxx's corpse and raising it high to all in salute.

I do not notice the crowd has hushed to silence until I see through the flames, the figure of the emperor approaching me, sword in hand. Guards are circling, dampening the flames, and giving me a clearer view. Through the trails of smoke, I see him grinning.

'Well fought, Centurion!' Titus, the emperor of Rome, yells from the sands so that all can hear. He never once takes his eyes from me.

'The House of Hader is blessed to have you among their number,' he says. 'I know more of you than most. Your Dominus tells me of your past with my own father – a story that leads to your slavery and this arena, where you have been – so far – victorious.'

My stomach lurches. I have won. Surely the rules are not to be so unfairly swayed. I'm about to protest, but he has started to address the audience once more. 'But, Centurion, your victory is short, your battle not done. This day, you will face one more test. You will fight in the primus.'

There is a mixed response from the crowd, and clearly it is not the response the emperor had been hoping for. I take advantage of the quieter moment to ask,

'And who will be my opponent?' I can barely get the

question out. My breathing laboured and my body screaming in agony and exhaustion.

'Your emperor,' he replies with a dark grin.

The sound of thousands of spectators gasping sounds like soughing reeds. This is the end of my story; this glorious moment. There is no way I can win, whatever I do. Death is the only victory on offer to me today. I am exhausted. The Emperor's victory is assured – and with it, his fearsome reputation.

'Fail to do as commanded and my guards will see you from this life Centurion,' Titus warns me quietly, not wishing to break his well-choreographed play. 'Fight me with the skill and wrath we have all witnessed. You have proven yourself a mighty warrior. If I should fall, it is my dying wish that your freedom be granted and ten thousand gold coins your prize.'

What am I to do? For one moment, I consider falling on my sword, taking a noble way out – but Lucilla...

'With the gods as my witness,' the Emperor swears. 'Fight me and do not hold back for I shall not.'

There is a murmur running through the stadium, which builds into an almighty roar of excitement.

I look to the praetorian guard, hands upon blade and spear, ready to strike me down. The prefect is among them, the man who tortured me, who executed the last of my legion. I see in his eyes, the same anger and hatred still burning.

No matter what Titus offers, his guard will not let me live.

'We shall stand as equals this day,' the emperor declares, raising his hand to the golden laurel wreath upon his head and throwing it to the ground. 'Let me prove myself as an equal to your skill, or fall in glorious attempt.'

This is my chance to claim freedom, but doubt remains if his words will be honoured. If Titus falls to my blade, surely my life will be forfeit. Choice is not given to me as he paces closer, shield and gladius raised.

I hurriedly grab my armaments from the sands before he can close, our shields slamming as we both reach for vantage; blades probing, but neither finding purchase. He barges his shield again into mine, forcing us apart before bringing his blade round in a wide arc and striking mine from my grip, sending it clattering to the ground. I am so tired. With all my last remaining strength, I charge with my shield, catching him unaware and striking him in the face, sending him sprawling to the ground with a broken and blooded nose.

He does not surrender. The fight is real. Rolling away and swinging out his blade, he catches my thigh, cutting it deep. I stagger back, picking up a fallen spear and hurling it at him as he begins to rise to stand. The emperor, still fresh in battle, leaps at the last moment over the missile, garnering an almost deafening roar from the crowd. I gather my sword from the sands just before he is on me again. Blades and shields clatter dozens of times as we fight. We are both veterans of the legion, both eager for victory – and life.

Titus charges. I let him come at me, hammering upon his shield and striking back when opportunity is granted; I am defensive, and it will get me killed. We stumble over the bodies of the fallen and I use them to my advantage, leaping from Onyxx's crumpled form to stab down at my emperor. He reacts at the last moment again, blocking the attack and sending me falling to the ground. With momentum, I rise up, my shield lost to me, now armed with only my gladius. More wounds are taken, cuts to my arm, chest and face but none deep enough to end the contest. I draw blood from him also, cries of shock emanate from the crowd around us, but he is no longer my emperor – he is my death.

'You truly are skilled, Centurion,' he calls to me through his blooded grin. 'You do the legions great honour, especially for one so young in years.'

Something within me snaps. Blood of the man who tore my legion asunder, who now talks as if there is honour in him.

'Your father ripped the beating heart from my legion!' I yell back at the emperor, striking at him with my gladius. My sword is unpredictable and he loses his footing, dancing from it. 'He executed my men and desecrated all honour and glories of the Legio IX Hispana!'

'My father made many mistakes in his lifetime,' Titus says, regaining his balance. 'But by the gods, I am not my father!'

He charges, our blades clashing in what I know will be the final time. He strikes, catching my left arm above the elbow; the wound is deep and the limb numb. I roar in anger, summoning what little strength I have, and ignoring my wound, I ram the pommel of my gladius into the emperor's face. He falls, dazed, and I am on him, my blade resting on his throat.

'You did well, Centurion,' he states, spitting blood from his mouth to the sands at our feet.

'As did you, Emperor,' I state, barely able to keep my gladius raised.

'Emperor defeated by slave, it is a glorious tale for all to behold,' he says bitterly.

I see his hand twitch, two fingers about to rise in the missio. He surrenders.

The crowd is silent. There is to be no celebration in the emperor's humiliation.

Dozens of the praetorian guard fall on me, protecting their emperor. I defend myself for as long as possible before my gladius is torn from my grasp and I fall to my knees, weak with the loss of blood, as spears and blades are raised to end my life, the prefect at their lead. When Vespasian passed judgement, it was this man, commander of the praetorian guard, who destroyed the Legio IX Hispana and condemned me to slavery.

'Finally, I am to end you, boy!' he taunts, blade raised and already swinging towards my head. I close eyes and think only of Lucilla.

The sword never touches my flesh, the prefect's chest impaled from behind by a spear thrown by Titus.

'Leave that man to your emperor!' he bellows with his hand raised toward me. The praetorian guards part and fall back. I am left there, kneeling before the Emperor of Rome who, just moments ago, I attempted to kill.

'I gave my word,' Titus yells, loud enough for all to hear. 'I swore that this man, this centurion, would be free if he could best his emperor. I stand bested by the greatest gladiator seen upon the sands and I will not see him cheated of his prize. Rise now and stand a free man.'

I cannot believe what I have heard. With all that I have, I try to rise but I stumble and fall. He catches me, the Emperor of Rome, greatest empire in the world, helping me to stand. He raises my hand high to salute the crowd.

'You earned this,' he tells me, but all I hear is the crowd as thoughts drift to Lucilla, seeing her smile and feeling her touch again, soon.

29

ADAM—Rome, Italy

The glasses highlight a particular area along the wall to the right of the arch, zooming in to give a better view. Abbey translates for me over the headset.

'79. Marcus Aurelius. The centurion, Legio IX Hispana.'

Finally, proof that this man, this gladiator, was of the legion. The inscriptions on the wall of the legatus's tomb said the centurion returned to Rome with the Eagle, but no record existed of him or the standard ever reaching their destination. Before me, on this very wall, is the only proof he ever made it back to Rome. Matt's journal was right.

'Granted freedom in victorious contest with Emperor Titus,' Abbey continues to translate.

'A high honour,' I reply in surprise. To hear that the emperor himself fought a gladiator is shock enough, but that the gladiator, viewed as no more than a slave in the days of the Roman Empire, was victorious and won his freedom, is an even greater revelation.

'Returned to wife in...' Abbey continues before stopping her translation.

'Where?' I ask. 'Where did he return to?'

'Returned to his wife in Pompeii.'

'When was Pompeii destroyed?' I ask. 'When did Mount Vesuvius blow?'

'You don't want to know the answer to that,' she says after a pause. Her voice has sunk, betraying disappointment.

'Abbey?' I urge her.

'The same year,' she relents.

The chances of us tracking down this man were slim at best before, but now, with his destination the cursed city of Pompeii, all hopes of finding the Eagle are lost.

'Where does that leave us now?' Abbey asks after a few moments of silence between us.

'It doesn't matter,' I tell her, forcing the issue to the back of my mind. 'We can sort it out later. I need to get back to Emma and Dave.'

'I wouldn't worry about that now,' a male voice calls to me from above.

Peering up, I see *him* crouched atop a tall pillar. There

are no ladders or accessible routes to suggest how he got there. He rises to stand and jumps down, ricocheting off the wall behind and landing directly in front of me; a cloud of dust rises from the impact.

As he turns to face me I both recognise and see him properly for the first time. His long black trench coat has its collar raised, but I know what tattoos are hidden beneath. His shirt, with loosened tie, adds a strange twist of ironic comedy, as if he has walked straight out of working at an office – and there is that black crystal pendant swinging from his neck – which I am convinced holds some form of dark energy. With hands stuffed in pockets, he circles me nonchalantly, kicking a rock along the stone floor, as if he has not a care in the world.

'We meet again, my friend,' he says to me, eyes black as night.

'Adam, don't....' Abbey tries to warn before her voice is obscured by static.

'Enough from her, I think,' he says.

'Abbey?' I call, but there is only static.

'I am afraid you won't hear from her for quite some time.' He chuckles. 'Technical difficulties, shall we call it.'

'Makov,' I mutter, my hands balling into fists. 'Where is my brother?'

'So you know my name.' He smiles, ignoring my question. 'Of course you do. After all, how many times have I faced and defeated your friends of the British Museum? I guess there are not too many immortals running around out there.' He laughs lightly, gripped by his own amusement. 'Which is rather ironic when you think about it, isn't it!'

Moment of mirth over, his hands stretch out, blue flames dancing from his fingertips to the far corners of the chambers, illuminating everything. As the flames gather, I see the crystal pendant shining. Makov turns, looking towards the marble arch.

'Hic statis honoratum victores. Here stand the honoured victorious. This is truly a staggering find. No wonder the Italians didn't want the world to know of it.'

'You read Latin?' I ask and then sigh. 'Of course you do!' Rage is building. He has Matt. He is the one who threw me into the river in the cave – knowing my darkest fear.

'Latin and a great many other languages, my young friend, but I do not mean to boast. I have lived the lives of a hundred men, learning all that I can, becoming all that I can until I stand as you see me, supreme in every way.'

'Leon and Bishop? What use are those buffoons to you if you are so supreme?'

'They are acquaintances of mine,' he reveals. 'Not the kind I would usually associate myself with, but they get the job done.'

'Where's my brother?' I demand.

'You worry for dear Matthew?' he says, turning to look

around the vast chamber around us. 'Of course you do. You are surrounded by history, seen only by a few people in the world, and yet you are focused on only seeing your troublesome older brother. How you mortals disappoint me. Your concern might be seen as commendable by some, but not me I am afraid,' he says shaking his head. 'Human bonds are what keep the human species weak.'

'What have you done with him? If you have harmed him...'

'You are in no position to be making threats!' Makov laughs. 'Besides, you already know my acquaintances have had a few close, personal chats with your dear brother. I'm afraid they've not ended well at all. All I wanted was information on the treasure I seek, but he gives us nothing. He has tried to escape a few times and came pretty close, too. Very resourceful and clever your brother. Luckily enough, his loving younger brother, so worried for his older sibling, went on his own search for answers and led us straight to what we needed. You followed the clues, so we followed you.'

'How did you know I'd be here?' I ask.

'You never know who is listening, Adam.' He laughs loudly. 'Or who you can trust. On that subject, I have a question for you. Matt's organisation, the British Museum – you've known them, what? Three days? Four? How well do you trust them?'

'More than I trust the man who holds my brother

captive and threw me into a river,' I say back in defiance. 'You knew I was terrified of it. You knew I fear water, didn't you?'

'Maybe,' Makov concedes, grin growing. 'I do apologise for that. It must have been hard for you, what with your past. It is one of my gifts, to see into the heart and mind of someone, to see their fear and their tragedy, the sorrows of their lives. Yours was very easy, I must say, as was Matt's. We gave your brother a choice, an offer. Treasures and riches, all the resources he could possibly ask for at his disposal. He turned them all down, some sort of loyalty to the crumbling, forgotten relic that is your British Museum. I would make the same offer to you, for you have proven your worth already just getting this far, but I am afraid this is where it ends.'

'Why do you want the Eagle?' I ask. 'If you are immortal, if you are all you say, then why do you need it?'

'The same reason mankind wants for anything,' he replies. 'Power and glory.'

'Power?' I repeat. 'The power of the Eagle? What if it's just a myth? All this, kidnapping, murder, all for a story told centuries ago.'

'How is it they put it? C'est la vie,' he says with a smile. *That's life.* 'Not all ventures produce reward. This is far from my first endeavour and it certainly will not be my last. Oh, you would not believe what has already been achieved and is in the pipeline. Funny that this all began with a long forgotten vase, depicting the Eagle and its strength.'

'What does the Eagle mean to you?' I ask.

'Nothing.' He shrugs, his grin broadening; his eyes alive with fire and fury. 'Everything. Power and glory. It is the way of the world, is it not?' He turns to the point out the names on the walls. 'All these men... it was just the same, despite the eons passed. I have travelled the world a hundred times, and in that passage of time, I have learnt one fundamental truth; mankind is the only form of life that will lie, cheat, and betray one another to get what he wants, all in the pursuit of power and glory. It is this principle that drives us all. Look only to yourself for an example. You, Adam Hunter, were talked into working with a powerful organisation, to travel the world in search of a fabled relic. Why? For personal gain, to save your brother. I am not sure if powerful is the right word to use for the museum though. I mean, after all, they did send a schoolboy to do their dirty work.'

'I don't care,' I tell him, knowing he is trying to get into my head, to confuse me. 'You didn't answer my question. Why do you want the Eagle?'

He grins at me menacingly. 'You possess more wisdom than I gave you credit for,' he concedes. 'As I explained, I have travelled this world for a long time. I have seen a lot and learned a lot. I have lived long enough to notice that this world is spiralling out of control. The human race kills its own planet as readily as it kills one another. Mankind will destroy itself or this world, or more likely both. I will see that it fails in that destruction. Now, as the blood moon rises and beckons this new age, I will rise. Regardless of cause or reason, I will see this new age begin.'

'By taking command?' I ask in disbelief. 'You want to rule with a mythical Eagle as your standard?'

'I have seen much in this world that cannot be explained,' he says, a single blue flame igniting in his fingers. 'Can you not feel it? This is a time of change. Events are approaching, circling us like a coming storm. The blood moon is the sign. After all, the moon ran crimson when last the Eagle rose. Perhaps that is the source of its power.'

'You're insane,' I say, aghast at his madness.

'Perhaps. After all I have given, all I have sacrificed to become the man I now stand, perhaps it has turned me lunatic – or maybe prophet; the line between the two is faint. Maybe it is I who sees clearly. Perhaps it is I who truly understands the sacrifice needed to bring this world out of the darkness. The burning city in Morocco was but the beginning.'

'You could have killed thousands of people. You destroyed their homes, nearly killing one of the museum's teams. You did all that just for...'

'Power and glory,' Makov says manically, his eyes crazed for a moment before smiling broadly.

'All I want is for my brother to be returned,' I warn him. I take off the now useless headset, tucking the glasses into my jacket. 'Let Matt go and I will join you willingly.'

'What possible value could you hold over your brother?' He laughs.

'I know where the Eagle is,' I lie.

'Whether that is true or not, your loyalty to your brother is to be commended. No, I will only let Matt go for one reason; I will release him if you can stop me.'

He stares straight into my eyes, daring me to attack.

'Well?' he asks. 'What are you waiting for? Is not your family motto, *Why postpone what can be done today*?'

'How do you know that?' I demand.

'Your dear brother, Matt, told us ...'

All I see is a red sea of rage. I charge him, fists ready to wipe the smile from his face. I will beat his flesh until he gives Matt back to me. I will punish him for what he has done.

Nothing happens as I think it will. My fists hit nothing but air. Makov evades me, ducking away and to the side, kicking me hard in the chest before striking a fist across my face. There are stars before my eyes, but ignoring them, I fight on. He moves with a speed and agility I can't hope to match.

'You're making it too easy,' he taunts, but I kick out, forcing him back.

'Where is my brother?' I demand, rising up and charging him again.

Again, Makov evades me, stepping back and leaping up, propelling himself off the wall behind and sending me crashing into the bars of one of the cells. I turn just in time to see him attack again and I duck away, rolling clear and rising up before he forces me to the ground. He is on me with no moment to pause or recover, his fist striking me hard and splitting open my bottom lip. The rancid taste of blood, sweat, and centuries old dust coat my tongue. My enemy steps back, leaving me on the ground before the statue of Mars.

'My how you disappoint the mighty God of War,' he taunts as I struggle to rise up. 'Do you really wish to continue this?'

He doesn't breathe hard nor look as if any effort has been given, taking only the briefest moment to straighten up his jacket.

'Where is my brother?' I repeat, but all he does is smile.

I charge again, but this time he grabs me, turning and throwing me into one of the glass cabinets housing recovered relics. It shatters, the impact sending pain rippling through my shoulder, head, back, all of me. His hands are on me again, dragging me up and throwing me across the chamber, landing hard at the centre of the ancient lift. The floor beneath me begins to move, the lift activated by Makov.

'It is a testament to the craftsmanship that this lift still works after all this time,' he says, walking back closer as we rise higher.

He stands over me, shaking his head.

'You were foolish to accept my challenge, Adam,' he tells me. 'As I said, I have lived the lives of a hundred men. From each of them, I have built on their strength and speed. I have endured countless wars, massacres, and slaughters, yet I still stand. You had no hope of defeating me, especially in this place. I can feel the dead all around me, the fallen within this great arena. I can feel their lives, their hopes, their fears, and most of all, their anguished deaths. It gives me a strength you could not possibly understand or compete against.'

'In the end, there is only one reason you fell,' Makov continues to taunt. I try to rise up, to fight on, but he forces me down again with a boot pressed on my back. 'You are simply not worthy.'

The words tear into me, just as his pendant shines and he lowers a hand to my chest, letting searing blue flames engulf me. I cry out in agony, my screams unending.

'NOT WORTHY!' he screams before releasing me.

The ceiling above us opens and the lift rises out onto the arena. Around us is the grand Colosseum, our viewpoint seen by hundreds of men and beasts that fought for their lives upon the sands.

'Have you even seen anything so magnificent?' Makov

asks. 'Ravaged by nature, man and time, yet it still stands impressive to all.'

He raises his foot from my back but then lowers a knee, leaning in to whisper in my ear, his weight pinning me down.

'This ends now for you. If you go any further, I will burn you and your brother and all those close to you. It was good to meet you, Adam Hunter. I hope for your sake, our paths do not cross again.'

And then he is gone and I am left alone in the centre of the vast Colosseum.

'Yeah, you'd better run,' I struggle to say.

The wind suddenly picks up around me, the sound of rotors growing until it deafens me, a spotlight bathing my body in light. My body aches, every movement is a struggle, and I am blinded by the spotlight of the police helicopter overhead. The headset crackles into life in my pocket and, though aching all over, I pull on the glasses.

'Hunter...Hunter...' Abbey's voice calls through the static. 'You need to get out.... run! Hunter, get out of there!'

'Emma,' I struggle to say, forcing myself to my feet. 'What about Emma and Dave?'

'You can't do anything for them now, just get out!'

I run away from the aggressive words shouted overhead by the crew of the helicopter. I am fleeing as fast as my legs can take me, ignoring the pain wracking my body. The map returns to the lens of my glasses, somehow undamaged in the fight with Makov. Abbey leads me on into the darkened walkways and beyond, until I reach what I can only describe as a staging area. There are ambulances parked and paramedics administering care to the injured security guards. I see police, too, co-ordinating their advance into the Colosseum, but none approach where I hide among the shadows.

Picking up a police jacket discarded by one of the wounded guards, I fasten it around me and walk on unhindered by others, just another officer of the law. If they saw my face or paid attention to my growing limp, a pain growing in my left leg, they would think otherwise. Thankfully, most of their efforts are focussed on what's happening deeper within the Colosseum, the battle between Dave, Leon, and Bishop. There is one who sees me though, the chief of security, Francesca Visiers.

'You!' she roars in accented English, tearing at the tails of my police jacket and forcing me against a pillar, only just out of sight of the police. Her words occasionally come in Italian as she struggles to translate.

'You were with them. You stole from me!'

'I'm sorry,' is all I can say.

'You caused this?' she demands. 'You shot my men!'

'No, that was...' I plead, trying to escape her grasp, but my body is still in immense pain.

'Who?' she asks, confused.

'Others.' I shake my head. There's too much to communicate and no time. 'They hurt my friends. A man and a young woman, they were down there. The woman is injured...'

I stop as I see the chief of security realise who I mean. They have been found.

'Are they okay?' I ask.

'I do not know.'

I look past her, seeing paramedics carry a body into an ambulance. I recognise the red and purple hair instantly, an oxygen mask over her face.

'She is alive, but...' the chief of security tells me.

'You need to let me go,' I tell her, trying to free myself and reach Emma. 'We tried to stop what happened here.'

She fixes me with a hard glare, but eventually relents, releasing me.

'Go,' she says. 'Stop those who did this. Stop whoever shot my men.'

'I will,' I swear, but no sooner have I stepped away do I see the ambulance has already departed. There are still police all around me, and to my alarm, one of them looks my way, seeing my injuries.

Shouts and warnings in Italian are yelled at me but I don't stop nor wait for them to arrest me. I run as fast as my beaten body will take me, reaching the nearest vehicle, a police motorbike. The keys are thankfully in the ignition already and its engine roars to life as the police begin to circle me. I charge them, not releasing the throttle until I am clear.

It doesn't take them long to continue their pursuit; cars, motorbikes, and even the helicopter again as I weave through the streets of Rome. Any injuries, doubts, or fear are forgotten. All I must do is escape. The crowds help, despite it now being late evening and the streets still being busy. I don't slow, hurtling over pedestrian side-walks and down stone steps where my pursuers can't follow. Each time I think I have lost them, the sirens suddenly grow and the flashing lights appear nearer.

I think of Dave, likely captured by the police, and Emma taken to a hospital. I failed them. I have to escape for them, to free them. It's my fault. I led them here and I abandoned them. I was not worthy.

I hurtle into a congested highway, narrowly avoiding the speeding traffic and death a fair few times. Behind me, I hear crashing metal and glass as one of the police cars ploughs headlong into a truck.

I exit the motorway and enter a construction yard, the workers shouting at me to stop. Hurtling on, I aim for the far road, evading the towering cranes and diggers, crashing through the gates as the police struggle to follow. Like me, they have to dodge the construction vehicles, the worker crews, and the vast massive machinery; two cars are lost in the chaos of the yard.

Crossing parks and storming through tourist-heavy

districts, gathered around statues, fountains, and other attractions, I lose more of the police in the chase. I only lose the helicopter once I am amongst the buildings. I ditch the bike once I know I am hidden amongst crowds of shoppers.

I travel deeper into Rome, listening and looking for any sign of my pursuers, but none comes.

'Are you... Are you clear?' Abbey's voice asks once I finally stop.

'I think so,' I say. The only sirens are far in the distance, their noise growing more distant.

'What happened in there?' she asks. 'When Makov approached you, we lost all visual and audio. He did some-thing to our comms. The glasses should have been shielded against any attempt to disrupt their functions, but we lost all contact. I had to change to a completely different frequency and bounce reception off a dozen other satellites just to get partial communications back. What happened down there? What happened with Makov?'

'He beat the crap out of me,' I state, collapsing down onto a bench near a flowing fountain. 'That was fun, as was evading the entire police force of Rome.' I try to force a laugh but cough from the attempt, my whole body hurting at once.

'Are you okay?' she asks, concerned.

'Not sure,' I say, feeling a sudden sharp pain in my

hand and seeing a deep cut across the palm, a piece of glass still embedded.

I pull the rucksack from my shoulders, drawing more discomfort, and take out a bandage from the first aid kit. I let out a quiet roar as I pull the shard of glass free of my hand, drawing more blood from the wound. I clean it up and wrap the bandage tightly around my hand. I know there are more wounds; cuts, scrapes, and countless bruises, but most will just need time to recover and heal.

'Where's Dave?' I ask. 'Did he get away?'

'They have him,' Abbey says after a pause, more a sob than an answer.

'The police?'

'No. Leon, Bishop, Makov. They have him,' she says, and I can tell she is crying. 'The last I heard was their voices as they beat him, the savages. Then all communication was lost.'

'What do we do now?'

'I don't know,' she struggles to say before another voice speaks over the headset.

'Mr Hunter,' Charles suddenly addresses me, tone devoid of all emotion. 'I am advising you to get the next flight back to England. This is too dangerous and I was wrong to send you out there. I will dispatch one of our other teams to Rome immediately. Gabriel or someone...'

'By the time they get here, it will be too late,' I say back. 'Besides, that drunkard wouldn't help anyway. He had his chance. I promised I'd find Matt and bring him home. I promised that to my family and to the girl carrying his child.'

'You should not make promises you cannot hope to keep, Mr Hunter,' Charles replies coldly.

I take off the glasses, angry with them, myself, everyone.

'I need time to think,' I speak into the glasses before closing them down.

I am on my own and have no idea where Matt's captors are. They want the Eagle, and based on what they did today, they will kill to seize it. The only option I have is to beat them to finding the Eagle and force them to release Matt and Dave.

Makov's words of power come to mind. Power and glory.

What if the centurion feared giving such power over to a man who was already emperor? An emperor known for his tyranny. What if, as punishment for not producing the Eagle, the emperor condemned the legion to fight on the sands of the arena? Sounds plausible. As proven by the walls within the Colosseum, he claimed his victory and returned to his family in Pompeii. If he truly returned to that city, there is a strong chance he was caught in the doom that claimed the lives of its citizens, the infamous event forever remembered for all of history.

An idea comes to mind and I recover the glasses.

'Abbey, tell me all you can about the bodies recovered after the destruction of Pompeii.'

She is silent for a moment, likely pulling herself together before beginning her explanation. Images of Pompeii and its ruin appear in the lenses.

'In 79 AD, Mount Vesuvius erupted, engulfing the city of Pompeii in fire and ash. Only fragmentary skeletal remains were found, filling hollow spaces within the hardened volcanic debris, revealing the forms of many deceased Romans. Suffocated by volcanic gasses and covered in flames, ash, and debris, their bodies eventually decayed inside the hardening matter, but the ash held their form, encasing their likeness forever.'

'Where are the recovered remains stored?' I ask.

'There are small collections all over the world,' Abbey says. 'The largest by far is located in the museums within the Vatican.'

'What are you thinking, Mr Hunter?' Charles asks.

'The only way Matt and Dave will be released is if we have what Makov wants,' I tell them.

'The Eagle,' Abbey and Charles say in unison.

'Exactly,' I reply. 'If the centurion still had it in his possession, he wouldn't have been in Rome, he would've been in Pompeii when Mount Vesuvius blew. Our only chance of finding the Eagle is with the remains of those lost among the fire and ash. I need to search the Vatican and any other places where the remains are stored.'

'Would the fires not have destroyed the Eagle?' Charles asks.

'I don't know – but let's hope they didn't,' I say. 'Besides, if the myths about it casting down fire and lightning and raising the dead are true, who knows what else is possible?'

'The museums will be closed by now but we can contact the owners in the morning and try to make arrangements for viewing,' Abbey suggests.

'It can't wait until then,' I reply with haste. 'We have to begin our search now.'

'This is ludicrous, Mr Hunter,' Charles tells me. 'I know you are desperate to find your brother but you will not gain his freedom by investigating the barest of leads, relying on chance more than evidence.'

'What other choice do I have?' I yell into the headset. 'Makov has my brother. They have Dave. They have the same information we do and could be heading for the Eagle as we speak. If the Eagle can do all the legends say it can, do you really want it to fall into Makov's hands?'

'Of course not,' Charles states firmly.

'You have two choices,' I tell them. 'Either you help me find the bloody Eagle and free Matt and Dave, or I take off this headset and do it on my own.'

'You want to infiltrate the Vatican?' Charles asks after a moment of silence. 'You want to infiltrate one of the most heavily guarded structures in the world? In the very heart of Rome it is its own country, possessing its own army and is home to the Pope himself. You are certain this is what you want to do?'

'Yes,' I tell him with absolute certainty.

'And what if Makov is already there?' Charles asks.

'Abbey, the pendant on his chain,' I say.

'What about it?' she asks back.

'It glowed when he summoned the blue flames.'

'It could be the source of his power, as I suspected before,' she says.

'And if I destroy it?'

'It could level the playing field.'

This at least gives me a plan of attack next time I face him. There is silence until Abbey's voice finally returns.

'Okay then,' she says, a tremor in her tone. 'Breaking into the Vatican.'

'Cursum perficio,' I say.

'Latin?' Abbey questions. 'It means I finish the journey?'

'It's the Hunter family motto,' I reply. 'We see it as *I finish the race*, but journey seems more fitting.'

'You are full of surprises, Adam,' Abbey remarks.

'Now it's up to you,' Charles says. 'Finish the journey that your brother began. Bring him home.'

'I need to visit one place first,' I tell her. 'I need you to give me a location.'

30

MARCUS AURELIUS—Rome

With coin from victories, and gifted by the emperor
himself, I walk free of the ludis after over two years under
its roof, three since I last fought the Britons. Sheathed next
to the gladius I carried onto the Colosseum's sands is my
rudis, the wooden sword engraved with my triumphs. I still
bear Hader's Dominus mark of H upon my wrist, but my
rudis is proof that I now live free.

Hader offered me vast amounts of coin and titles to
fight for him or be doctore to other recruits and pass on
my skills in combat, but no reward could sway mind. I set
course for the embrace of my loving wife – but there is one
task in Rome left to me.

Returning, I can see how much it has changed already

under the reign of Emperor Titus. The streets are clean, people are walking freely. The tyranny of Vespasian is already fading into memory. Titus was right, he is not his father. Perhaps if he were emperor when I first returned with my brothers of the legion then we would not have been cast to ruin and myself enslaved. No one can tell how the mind can be swayed by power. It is that power that I must retrieve.

Beneath an orange tree on the banks of the River Tiber, in distant view of the Campus Maritius, I dig. I cannot bring myself to look upon the camp; the memory of the lash and my crucified brothers is still fresh in my memory despite the passage of years. I dig with bare hands until I feel it, bundled in the same cloth as it was since Britannia, buried to keep it out of Vespasian's hands. Perhaps I should have let him have it. My legion would still live, my wife would be at my side, and I would not have had to endure slavery or the horrors of the arena. Perhaps I should have given it to him and saw him burn as it had the crazed Briton. Only the worthy, as the men of the legion had said.

Unfurling the cloth, I see the bronze still shining, but I dare not place a hand upon the staff or wings. I'm almost tempted to throw it in the river, but I cannot, fearful of discovery, washed-up on banks downstream. What I will do with it? I do not know, but it cannot remain within reach of those who might wield it in anger or for ill purpose. It must come with me. My path is set for Pompeii and its port, where Lucilla waits for me. Then we shall take to lands beyond the reach of Rome. *We.* I can scarcely believe it.

31

ADAM—Salvator Mundi International Hospital.
Rome, Italy

There is one police officer at the door but he doesn't look at my bruised and battered face; he only sees the white doctor's coat I stole. Stepping aside from the door as I approach, I nod a thank you, knowing my awful accent and attempt at Italian would easily give me away.

Inside the room, I see her with her eyes closed, an oxygen mask over her face, and her leg heavily bandaged and raised in a sling. Her skin is pale, especially against her red and purple hair, an effect of the heavy blood loss. She looks almost at peace, a far cry from the terror I saw in her eyes at the Colosseum. I look at her chart, as any doctor would, just in case the policeman is checking on me. A heart monitor beeps steadily in the corner; the room is silent but for the machine.

'Please tell me you're not my doctor,' Emma says, lifting down the oxygen mask, startling me and making me drop her notes. 'If you are I am definitely going to lose the leg.'

'Good to see your cheerful attitude remains intact,' I reply, taking the seat next to her bed.

'The coat?'

'A doctor Sch...Schmo...Schmal...something,' I say, failing to read the ID badge on the coat. 'How's the leg?'

'It hurts,' she says, wincing as she shifts in the bed. 'Painkillers help though. Where am I?'

'Salvator Mundi International Hospital,' I tell her.

'Still in Rome?' she asks, speech slow and almost slurred, the painkillers taking their effect.

'Yep.'

'Where's Dave?' she asks.

'Keeping watch outside,' I lie, knowing the truth would only worry her.

'What happened to you?' she asks, seeing the damage to my face.

'You should see the other guy,' I reply.

'Who was he?'

'Vladimir Makov,' I say, before lying again. 'Don't worry, I won.'

'You look it.' She laughs gently. 'The wall in the Colosseum, did you find it? Do you know where the Eagle is?'

'Yes, I think so. I'm going after it but I had to see you first, to make sure you're okay.'

'Thank you,' Emma replies, a smile at her lips for a moment.

'It's nothing...' I begin to say before she stops me.

'No, thank you, for what you did in there. The flames... the fire... I wouldn't have escaped without you.'

She winces then, the pain in her leg striking and she grabs my hand, squeezing it hard. I don't let go. She looks to me and our eyes lock for a moment, before hers begin to close from exhaustion, blood loss, and the painkillers.

'You need to rest,' I tell her. 'Sleep and recover.'

'Find it, Adam,' she says, her words becoming more distant the more she speaks. 'Find the Eagle. Save Matt. Make them pay for this.'

'I will, Emma,' I promise.

'Call me Em,' she says with a smile on her lips, still gripping my hand. 'Go get them, Hunter.'

She winces again as she moves her leg to get comfortable, eyes heavy and closing.

'Stay with me...' she whispers.

'I'm not going anywhere,' I say, holding her hand tight as sleep finally takes her.

I wait there a few minutes in silence, simply sitting with her, holding her hand tightly. I don't want to go. I don't want to leave her, but I know I must. I have to save the others.

'Go get them, Hunter.' The words ring in my head.

'Sleep well, Em,' I whisper, gently placing a kiss on her forehead as I let go of her hand.

32

ADAM—Rome, Italy, five yards from the Vatican

'You and me brother,' I whisper, thinking of Matt. 'What the hell have you gotten me into?'

I can't stop, not now. Injured, alone, I only have this chance to save him.

'Only an hour until dawn, Adam,' Abbey tells me over the headset. 'Two max.'

'I know.'

'Why are you up on a roof, Mr Hunter?' Charles asks me.

'It helps me think,' I reply, gazing out towards St Peter's Square, the Basilica, and the Vatican beyond.

'Waiting for the painkillers to kick in?'

'Yeah.'

Why it's known as a square is beyond me as the

columns and their adjoined roof form an almost perfect circle, leading to St Peter's Basilica at its tip.

The Basilica is one of the largest churches in the world, known as one of the holiest Catholic sites. Its vast dome is visible for miles. Though it's the middle of the night, the square and Basilica are illuminated brilliantly by hundreds of lights, giving the area a look of divinity. Just past the Basilica is the rest of the Vatican, including the museums I must reach.

Charles' voice breaks my thoughts. 'As soon as you cross that street, you will no longer be in Italy. Technically, you will be in a completely different country, beholden to their rules, regulations, and laws. If captured, the British Museum will be forced to deny all knowledge of you. You will be on your own.'

'It's good to know you have my back,' I reply.

'In short, don't get yourself caught,' he says.

'Charles, I've got to ask something before we begin,' I say.

'Ask away, Mr Hunter. This may be the last chance you get to.'

'Why did you do it?' I ask. 'Put me in the trials, send Dave and Emma out with me and order Abbey to provide support? I turn seventeen years old in two days, no experience of any of this or any historical background. I haven't even finished college. Why did you show faith in me?'

He doesn't reply straight away, the pause too long for my liking.

'I see a lot of your brother in you, Mr Hunter,' Charles explains. 'The same fire and intensity, the drive that the Hunter family seems to possess. You proved that in Scotland and in the trials, but there is also something unique about you; it's not something that can be put into words, but I know it when I see it. I saw it with each of my team. I think with time and focus, you can achieve great things.'

Saying thank you doesn't seem enough for such praise. It's the first time in a long time I have received any praise at all.

'Find the Eagle,' Charles states. 'Secure Matthew and Dave's release.'

'One thing though,' I say, doubt creeping into my mind. 'What if the myths and legends are true? What if the standard contains this godly power? We can't hand that over to known criminals.'

'I am not saying we would,' Charles replies. 'Besides, these tales are usually just stories told to entertain children.'

'What if they're not just stories?' I ask.

'If that is the case then it is even more imperative you find the Eagle first.'

'Does that mean I have your backing?'

'Unofficially,' he says, bringing a grin to my face.

'What about you, Abbey?' I ask.

'I still think you're crazy,' she says. 'But since crazy is generally the norm around here, I'll give you all the support I can. Let's bring our friends home.'

'Thank you, both of you.'

I check the straps of my rucksack and the rest of my equipment, ensuring it's all secured. Zipping up my jacket and pulling the hood over my head, I take a deep breath, calming my racing heart. I look up and see the moon high above me; it is completely crimson.

'The blood moon,' I whisper to myself, remembering Makov's words. *With the rise of the blood moon, I will find it.*

'You sure you're ready for this?' Abbey asks.

'Why postpone what can be done today,' I reply.

Standing, I feel the pain has already begun to subside. I walk back to the rear of the roof, preparing myself.

'If this doesn't pan out how we hope…' I begin to say into the headset.

'You, Matt, Dave, Em, all of you are going to return home safe,' Abbey says with certainty.

'Yeah,' I reply.

'I hear the Pope is a heavy sleeper,' she says, trying to joke.

'Let's hope so,' I simply reply back, 'because I am about to break into his house.'

'You know this is breaking like a hundred different laws?'

'And we haven't broken enough already?' I laugh.

'Sometimes you need to break the law to do the right thing, Mr Hunter,' Charles adds.

'None of this makes sense,' I say, more to myself than to Abbey and Charles. 'Last week I was a bored, fairly rubbish student. My brother was supposed to be at a dead-end job...'

'And now you can make the difference, Hunter,' Abbey tells me.

Only the worthy. The words still run through my head.

'Are you sure about this?' she asks one last time.

'Absolutely not,' I reply, looking over the edge of the roof and then backing up to the far side.

'Dave would've had one of Tristram's gadgets for this,' Abbey says. 'Crossing the rooftops, I mean. How are you going to do it?'

'The old fashioned way,' I reply, forcing a laugh.

'How?' she asks again.

'Jump!'

Breaking into a sprint, I leap from the roof of the building towards the pillars of the square. I barely make it, crashing onto the arched roofing atop the pillars, frantically grasping at the tiling until I can pull myself clear of the edge.

'You okay?' Abbey asks anxiously.

'No worries,' I say, the pain in my leg flaring from the landing.

'Then get going, Hunter!' she yells. 'There are cameras and guards all over the place, including that roof!'

I force myself up and run as fast as I can, despite my injuries. I see one guard ahead of me, oblivious of my presence as he absentmindedly talks on his radio. I circle around him, keeping clear of his gaze and keeping to the darkness atop the roof before leaping clear and beyond his sight.

Farther ahead is another guard, more alert than the first and spotting my approach. Drawing his handgun, he yells a warning at me in Italian. Without slowing, I throw a bolas at him, the cord entangling the man before he can reach his radio. I take it and the handgun from him, sending both tumbling from the roof before tying a gag across his mouth. He'll wake up bruised but he'll live.

I hurry, forcing the pain in my body to the back of my mind before emerging onto the roof of St Peter's Basilica, the dome high above me. I cross the roof, bypassing another guard by leaping atop a barrier and circling around him before jumping clear. He turns, stopping his patrol for a moment and I wait, hidden until he passes. Emerging, I look up and from my vantage point high upon the roof, I can see all of Rome before me. It's an inspiring sight, and for a moment, I wish I could stop and appreciate it for longer.

'You're enjoying this, aren't you?' Abbey asks, mimicking my earlier question.

'Breaking into one of the most highly guarded and holiest sites in the entire world, after already infiltrating the Colosseum of Rome?' At this moment, I have to agree with her. 'Yeah, maybe I am,' I admit, still staring in wonder across all of Rome from atop St Peter's Basilica.

'The entrance to the catacombs is in the far corner below,' Abbey tells me over the headset. 'From what I can tell, the alarm hasn't been raised yet.'

'It's just a matter of time,' I reply, thinking of the guard I left tied up.

'Time is exactly what you do not have, Mr Hunter,' Charles warns over the headset. 'Get moving!'

I drop down from the Basilica's roof to the next building, rolling as I land and quickly sprint on, wary of the cameras above me. Leaping from level to level and using the window ledges and drainage pipes, I drop further down before reaching the gardens below. I land, unseen by anyone, and rush on towards the gated entrance to the Basilica's catacombs and tombs below. With my trusty picks, I make quick work of the first and second locks upon the gate, shutting it behind me once I am inside to cover my tracks. I descend down the stone staircase, into utter darkness once again.

The glasses instantly switch to night-vision and I travel onwards through the tombs, always led by Abbey's directions. The catacombs go on for miles, far bigger than the Roman tombs in Inchlonaig, and without Abbey's instructions, I would've lost my way dozens of times. There are cobwebs, spiders, and rats throughout, but I ignore them all, always moving onwards, banging into walls and striking my head against low ceilings in my haste.

I pause only once, when I must cross a narrow bridge across a waterway. My breathing and heartbeat quicken, sweat covering me, the fear and dizziness threatening as I take my first steps towards the bridge.

'Just think of Matt,' Abbey coaxes me. 'Think of your brother. Save your brother.'

Her words help and I focus my eyes upon the far wall, forcing my legs into action until I have crossed the bridge.

Finally, I reach my aim, another entrance to the catacombs used by tour groups from the museum. Emerging into the darkened halls and corridors of the museum, I see no signs of guards or anyone else.

'There is a security station just at the end of this hallway,' Abbey tells me. 'Get access to their system and I can hijack it, shutting down the cameras and alerting you to any approaching guards.'

'Just got to get past the guards at the station,' I whisper back.

'Well, yes, there is that,' she replies.

I pace down the hallway slowly, silently, keeping close to the walls and anything I can use as cover if I am discovered. To my surprise, I find I need not have worried. The station is occupied by only one guard who is slumped across his desk. I assume he is asleep and quietly walk around him, connecting a USB device to the security computer and giving Abbey the access she needs.

As I wait for Abbey to break through the system's own security and firewalls, I notice the trickle of blood on the floor beneath where the guard sits. My heart thunders in my chest as I take a step nearer, seeing the man is not moving or breathing. I pull on his shoulder and he slumps back in his chair, eyes fixed in death's stare. There are two bullet wounds in his chest.

'Oh my God!' Abbey screams through the headset.

'Makov's here!'

'It's not just this guard,' Abbey says, her voice unusually panicked. 'I can see it with the cameras. Every guard in the museum is down! Get out of there, Hunter! Get out and away from that place!'

'Abbey, raise the alarm,' I tell her. 'Get medical and police services here as soon as you can.'

'They'll arrest you!' she protests.

'It'll be worth it if they are able to save the life of even one of these guards,' I tell her.

'Fine, but you have to get out of there!'

'You know I can't do that,' I tell her, but she still protests, Charles's voice joining hers until I take off the headset and stuff the glasses into a pocket.

'Alone it is then,' I whisper.

Walking on, I pass through storage areas and then on

into the main museum, with its vast displays of relics from ancient history. I pass more cameras, but there are no lights or movements signalling activation. The bodies of three more guards lay lifeless and bloody. Without the glasses, I use a torch to guide my way, knowing that any alarms will likely have been deactivated by Abbey or my predecessors.

I stop still as I hear voices in the distance, voices I know too well. Quickly, I turn off my torch and crouch behind a wall, listening intently.

'They've moved the exhibits around,' Leon's unmistakeable Australian voice states with annoyance and frustration. 'No idea where the Pompeii relics are.'

'Then I suggest you keep looking,' Makov's voice says with menace. Hearing them makes my blood boil.

'I've secured the doors, boss,' I hear Bishop announce from behind me, walking straight past and thankfully not spotting me in my hiding place. 'We shouldn't have any interruptions unless they suspect our presence.'

'With the cameras deactivated and their entire security detail down, that won't be likely,' Leon replies.

'Search for the exhibit,' Makov orders. 'Bishop, keep our guests company. If they move, kill them.'

'With pleasure,' the thug replies. The metallic sounds of a gun reloading is unmistakeable.

The guests might be Matt and Dave, but unarmed, I can do nothing to free them. All I can do is find the Eagle first and negotiate their release. I duck out of sight as footsteps approach, waiting until they pass before emerging from hiding. I must find the Pompeii exhibit first.

I search, my footsteps silent and with no light from my torch to guide my way. Keeping away from the others, the thieves and captors of my brother, I rush from display to display, checking every glass cabinet for the volcanic debris encasing the ill-fated inhabitants of Rome. From exhibit to exhibit, I search room to room, always mindful of the others, the men who tried to kill me, the men who have tortured Matt.

I stop once, almost caught as I see a silhouette approach, the black trench coat unmistakeable, as are those haunting, terrible eyes. Makov walks on past me, whistling without concern, casting his gaze about him as if he has all the time in the world. The rage and anger of his beating me burns but I hold still and silent until the right moment, continuing my search.

It's in the next room that I see them, barely visible in the darkness, but distinct to all other pieces of history in the museum. There, behind the thick glass, are the figures, encased in hardened ash. Men, women, children, all lost in the face of such utter destruction from the erupting volcano. Some are trying to hide, lying on the ground or huddled together. Others kneel, praying to the gods for a salvation that would never come. Many cling to one another, embracing family and loved ones in their final moments of life. It's shocking to see such loss and remember that before me is only a small portion of the tragedy. The entire city was lost within a day.

Suddenly, without warning, I am blinded by the main lights flickering overhead and illuminating the room.

'I had a feeling you would join us, Adam,' I hear Makov's voice taunt. 'I must congratulate you on reaching this far.'

As my vision slowly returns, I see him approach, a wide smile across his face. Leon is beside him wearing a skull mask and looking to me with maddening glee. In his hands is a large machine gun, the likes of which I have only seen in computer games. It is raised in my direction.

'No escaping a bullet this time, boy,' the Australian says before Makov places a hand on his firearm, forcing it to lower.

'No, my friend,' he says. 'After all the hardships Adam has endured, and all that he has overcome, he deserves to see his brother one last time. Bishop, bring our guests in here!'

The brute quickly appears, again wearing Matt's base-ball cap, pushing two men with the barrel of his own impressive firearm. There are hoods over their heads and their wrists are bound tight enough to draw blood. As they reach Makov's side, the captives are forced to their knees.

'Where are we, you cowardly snakes?' I hear Dave ask shortly before Bishop silences him with a boot to the gut.

'Let us see you reunited with your brother.'

The hood is removed and I see Matt, his eyes bloodshot and barely able to open, look to me with shock. Bruises cover his pale face. His clothes are torn and bloody. He struggles for breath, pained with each intake of air, ribs likely broken. There is a bandaged wound on his arm, the rags old and marked with the blood seeping through. His blonde hair is matted with more blood and there are wounds at his temple and scalp.

'Adam?' he asks in pained surprise, but there is no joy in his eyes. 'What the hell are you doing here?'

'Trying to rescue you,' I reply, forcing a smile to lift his spirits.

'And a fine job you are making of this grand rescue,' Makov taunts. 'I warned you, Adam. I warned you not to interfere.'

'He's just a kid, you bastard. Leave him alone!' Dave roars.

'Silence the fool,' Makov instructs.

Bishop turns his fists to Dave again.

'You should not have come here, Adam,' he says as Dave's beating continues. 'I gave fair warning. I told you I would burn you. Thanks to your efforts, my wolf has been horrifically scarred.'

'That beast should be put down,' I reply.

'He has his uses and is ever loyal, something that

cannot be said of humans,' he says as he takes Leon's handgun from him, raising it towards me.

'At the Colosseum, I told you to stop. There must be punishment for ignoring my warning.'

He turns on Matt and pulls the trigger, a bullet tearing into my brother's leg, just above the knee. Matt screams in agony.

'No!' I yell before Makov turns the gun back on me.

'Do not fret, young Hunter,' Makov says with contempt. 'The bullet struck no artery, but Matt will certainly need medical attention soon.'

'Even without the bullet, I think he'd need a hospital soon,' Leon jokes cruelly. 'They both will.'

Dave is on the ground, badly beaten, but he is still breathing as Bishop stands over him.

'It is just you and us my friend,' Makov says. 'The Eagle is here somewhere, I am certain, as you must be to have followed us, or is it just a bold undertaking?'

'Recklessness,' is my reply. 'So I keep getting told. That or stupidity.'

'Get out of here, Adam, please,' Matt pleads, but is silenced as Leon's fist connects with his face. He spits blood onto the floor and the anger threatens to overwhelm me again.

'You've had your moment,' Makov tells my brother before turning to me. 'Now, Adam, what is your plan? You must have one, or else why come all this way on your own?'

I pray that Abbey notified the police when she contacted medical services for the downed security guards. Either way, my only chance is to hold back Makov and his cronies for as long as possible. Stop them from finding the Eagle.

'You're going to release them,' I say, pointing to Matt and Dave. 'Then you are going to leave empty-handed.'

Leon and Bishop laugh loudly.

'You've got some guts, boy, I'll give you that,' Bishop says. 'Boss, why don't we just put bullets in him and get rid of the other two as well? Why did we even bring them here?'

'It always pays to prepare,' Makov says. 'I have learnt over the years that a few hostages can be a very powerful bargaining chip. That, and a blood sacrifice may be required to awaken the power of the Eagle.'

'You will release Matt and Dave and leave this place,' I declare.

'That is not going to happen,' Makov merely states. 'We have come too far to simply leave.'

'Then face me,' I challenge him. 'You beat me before and you deemed me not worthy. Give me a chance to prove myself.'

'Why would I do such a thing?' he asks, but there is intrigue in his voice.

'Because you want to,' I say, sensing his interest in the challenge.

'As my associate said, you do have guts, my friend,' Makov says. 'You have barely recovered from our previous encounter. Are you certain you want to go through it again?

'I will not be beaten so easily,' I state with confidence, removing my rucksack. My eyes focus briefly on his pendant, hanging from the chain at his neck. *I hope you're right, Abbey.* Destroy the pendant, take his power, and then I might stand a chance.

'Let us begin then,' Makov declares. 'Leon, Bishop, you are not to interfere. Give Adam the fair chance his courage deserves.'

He turns on me, stepping closer, and I wait, every moment of delay vital. I know I can't beat him, but I can buy time until the police arrive.

'Don't do this, Adam,' Matt tries to warn.

'It is too late for brotherly concern,' Makov states. 'I will not hold back this time, my friend.'

'I don't expect you to,' I reply, raising my guard. 'Let's get this over with.'

He charges me, wanting it over as soon as possible. I back away, trying to keep a distance between us but he is far too quick. A fist strikes my arms, then another, before he ducks round and hammers into my stomach. The wind is knocked out of me but I force myself to recover quickly, pushing on and attacking to force him back. A hand grips my shoulder, pulling me down towards a rising knee, but I lash out, driving both fists into his chest with all the strength and fury I possess. He falls back, rolling as he lands on the polished floor before rising up.

'Very good, Adam. Much improved,' Makov praises me.

I say nothing in reply, saving my breath. Makov flies forward again. There is no rage or anger on his face, only focussed determination to beat me. I do all I can to block his strikes and fight back, but he is too fast, twisting and turning, finding a way through my defences despite all efforts. I throw a bolas at him but he knocks the cord away with ease. I throw another as he leaps over a fallen table, and though the cord wraps around his arm, he tears free before it can fully constrict him. I am quick though, and somehow, by some miracle, the pendant is dangling from my fingers. Throwing it to the floor I stamp down hard, the crystal shattering beneath my boot.

Makov just laughs.

'You are not the first to make that mistake,' he taunts me as flames cover his fist and he strikes me hard, throwing me back across the room. 'I do not rely on trinkets or treasures, you young fool.' He continues to laugh. 'Have you not listened to a word I have said? My strength is built from the lives and souls of the lost, and you shall soon join them.'

Closing in, his fists strike me, again and again until I

barely have the strength to keep my arms up. Grasping one arm, he twists my joints and they crack sickeningly but remain unbroken. His boot stamps down on the back of my knee and he barges me forward, crashing through tables and chairs, collapsing before Leon and Bishop. My brother looks on in horror. Makov grabs me by the throat and he lifts me to standing, striking me hard across my face again and again until I am barely conscious.

'Leave him alone!' Matt roars, trying to rise up before his captors force him down and pull the hood back over his head.

The distant sounds of sirens can be heard, and for a moment I think it's just ringing in my ears.

'You alerted the police? Not very wise, my friend! Not wise at all!'

He throws me with all the force he possesses into the display cabinets, the glass shattering on impact. I crash through and into the relics within, the recovered remnants of the people of Pompeii, smashing the ash debris to pieces. My body screams in agony, old wounds reopen and fresh ones join them. Warm blood trickles down the side of my face.

'At full strength, and with a clear head, you may have stood a chance,' Makov says as he steps into the display, glass crunching beneath his boots. I let him talk, feeling a dangerously large shard of glass beneath me.

The drone of helicopter rotors grows, three of them

visible through the large windows, searchlights all focused on us.

'Vladimir Makov, you and your men are ordered to surrender,' the police declare over the loudspeakers from the helicopters. 'Release your prisoners and lay down your weapons.'

I use the distraction, sliding the shard of glass across to Matt's bound hands.

'Ignore that fool's threats,' Makov tells Leon and Bishop. 'He can do nothing from there. When we are done here, blast him out of the sky.'

Makov turns his attention back to me.

'Again, you have proven yourself unworthy, Adam. No one can help you. Not your brother or this soldier, and certainly not those fools outside.'

I see Matt pass the shard to Dave – it's almost time.

'A lesson must be taught to you all.'

'Distract,' I struggle to say.

'And act!' Matt roars, rising up and disarming Leon, wrestling the gun from the rogue's hands. Matt fires three times at Makov.

The bullets all strike at his chest, and for a moment, doubt crosses the fiend's face before his mocking smile returns.

'Have you learned nothing?' he asks before unleashing blue flames towards Matt, blasting him across the room.

Smoke rises from his body and he moans in pain before calling out to us with two words, 'Stop him!'

With a roar, Dave unleashes an anger I didn't know he possessed, taking vengeance as he quickly rises up and beats down Leon and then charges the towering Bishop. Dave strikes the American several times before turning to face Makov. I struggle to rise, to help him, the pair of us facing the lone immortal. We fight together as a unit, but Makov is still standing. He takes everything we have – still grinning.

'May I begin now?' he asks, before unleashing a blast of blue flames that knocks us all back.

We are floored but we rise again to attack this black-eyed demon. There is little hope against his supernatural powers, his fires wracking us with agony. We are smashed to the floor again, toppling one of the ash-cases from the display cabinet and onto the floor, where it splits to reveal a flash of bronze.

It still shines brightly after all these years. I try to stop Makov as he reaches out for the Eagle, the standard of the Legio IX Hispana. Then it is in his hands.

'Incredible,' Makov says as he gazes upon it. 'After all this time, it has survived. Even the fires of Vesuvius could not melt it.'

He stops for a moment, blinking furiously, fingers flexing around the Eagle's staff.

'I can feel it...' he murmurs, a smile growing across his

face. 'It was no myth. I can feel it! The wrath of the gods! The world should know of this! The world will see this!'

Makov begins to lift it high, the bronze wings of the Eagle catching the light brilliantly. I clamp my eyes shut but even then I am still blinded, ears deafened by the God-like scream. The building shakes and trembles, and there is a great tearing above me. Peering through barely open eyes, I see almost all the roof ripped from over my head, a great beam of light surging down from the sky above.

Gunfire sounds and bullets sing past us as the helicopters recklessly open fire. Everyone ducks for cover except Makov, the undaunted immortal. He lifts the Eagle high, calling forth the power of the gods to rain from the sky, striking the police helicopters. Great towering beams of light soar down from the heavens, a tornado of godly might. Smoke and fire pours from their rotors and the aircraft falls from the sky.

'Now you see the truth!' Makov declares, looking down on us with maddened glee. 'Myth, legend, all these stories are proved true by this one Eagle. The world will know, but I am afraid this is where your story ends.'

I close my eyes, expecting the wrath of the gods to descend upon us all.

I have failed. I am not worthy.

33

MARCUS AURELIUS—Pompeii

From the shadow of Vesuvius, where the escaped gladiator Spartacus defeated the praetor Glaber, I see the mountain's peak billow smoke. It is a bad omen, a damning sign from the gods and so I urge my stead on towards the city and its port. I must find Lucilla.

As I enter the city, the very ground begins to shake. My horse rears up, throwing me from the saddle before bolting. I land hard on the ground, body wracked with pain, wounds still healing from the melee at the Colosseum. The tremors grow until the buildings around me begin to fall. Screams of Pompeii's people echo all around. The smoke ceases to rise from the peak, and for the briefest moment, I think the gods' anger is calmed – then the mountain explodes before my eyes.

The sky turns black and blots out the sun. Day turns to night. Ash falls as if it is rain, falling like a soft blanket, covering everything in sight. Rocks and fire streak the night sky like falling stars, tearing through everything in their path; no building is left standing in their wake.

I must find Lucilla.

I'm running through the streets, screaming out her name.

'LUCILLA!' I shout again and again, until my throat is hoarse but I do not stop.

'Marcus! MARCUS!'

My legs stop running, stilled by the amazement of seeing her. Her long blonde hair, her sun-kissed skin, her eyes, which glitter with diamonds. And in spite of all the horror, the fear, she is smiling through her tears. My wife, Lucilla.

We run into an embrace, holding each other tightly, never wanting release.

'I knew you would find me,' she says with lips that seek mine.

'I could not rest until I held you again,' I tell her. 'I am so sorry...'

'Don't.' My wife silences my apologies with her lips.

'Where is your family?' I ask, horribly aware that we must act or die.

'I don't know,' Lucilla replies, her hands clutching mine tightly with fear. 'I could not find them.'

The ground shakes again, and more fire and rock strikes the city around us; ash settles in our hair and on our shoulders.

'The mountain...' she says with trembling words, drawing my eyes to Vesuvius.

We see the great tide of fire and ash surging from the mountain and destroying all in its path: the city and its people. Another roar sounds but this time from the ocean. A massive wave sends the harbour ships crashing through the dock and into the city. Around us, the people flee, some on horseback, others by cart, and others simply running for their lives. They will not escape. There is no escape from this.

'The gods have damned us,' Lucilla sobs, looking only into my eyes.

'No, they have blessed us for we are together,' I say, holding her tight. 'Death will not see us parted. Do not cry, my love. We are together, and we are free.'

'I love you,' she says.

'I love you.' We embrace one final time – the world and its destruction forgotten. She is all that matters, in this life and the next.

34

ADAM—The Vatican

I wait for the end but it doesn't come. I open my eyes, stunned that the world is still as it was. I am still breathing, and the museum is still standing, minus its roof. Matt and Dave remain captives and Leon and Bishop merely look on expectantly.

'No, that would be too easy,' Makov says. 'Open your eyes, Adam. See true power.'

All around me, figures flicker into existence. Men, women, children, people of all races, they stand around me, their spirits summoned.

'I am God of the Afterlife,' Makov declares with a cruel glee. 'This is the true power of the Eagle. Now, my brothers and sisters, dispose of these cretins – all of them.'

They move towards us, and though we try to force

them away, they cannot be stopped. Our hands pass straight through them, and yet I feel their cold, icy hands on me, around my neck, on my arms and legs, growing tighter. They're on Matt and Dave too, all focused on our annihilation – except for one.

A man clad in Roman armour, a soldier barely a year or two older than me. I know who he is. I have been following his trail for days. It is the centurion.

He looks to me sadly, then shaking his head, he screams silently, throwing himself at Makov.

'No!' he yells. 'What are you doing? I command you to kill them! Unhand me!'

Makov summons his flames but they do nothing against the spirit who grabs for the Eagle, wrenching it from Makov's hands. The Eagle falls to the floor, the bronze clattering on the marble with no sign of damage

'How can this be?' he growls. He is held by the centurion and unable to see me reach for the Eagle.

'No, don't!' he warns, but it is too late. I grasp the standard and lift it high.

I feel it first, growing within my hand and then surging through me. The very museum shakes as the remains of the ceiling and roof are torn apart; a blinding white light surges down and engulfs me with a deafening roar. I can't understand or explain it. All I can do is bask in the light as it surrounds me. I feel no pain, my own wounds forgotten. Then it ends.

My vision returns instantly, and my ears are once more filled with cries of pain. Bishop and Leon lie fallen on the floor, clutching at their eyes and screaming for help, blood running between their fingers. Makov staggers near to me, his eyes still clamped shut and fists clenched tight as he suffers his own agony.

'How did you do that?' he demands as blue flames gather around him, swirling, building bigger than ever before. 'How could *you* do that?'

I turn on him, the Eagle still raised.

'Tantum dignos,' I declare, feeling the Eagle's power build again before the light tears towards Makov.

'ONLY THE WORTHY!' I yell above the mighty roar of the Eagle's power. 'YOU ARE NOT WORTHY!'

He flees, stumbling with his blindness. Dave picks up one of the fallen firearms and fires, hitting the immortal twice, but it doesn't slow him. Makov runs through the nearest window and falls from view. I hurry after him and peer down from the windows, seeing a drop of over thirty feet. There is no sign of Makov, but the spirits still surround us, and they are all looking to me for command.

I see the centurion. He looks to me and says, 'Tantum dignos.'

'Rest,' I command. The centurion nods his thanks before turning to grasp the hand of the young female spirit next to him, her hair shimmering like golden dust,

'Adam,' Matt calls out to me and I hurry to his side. 'I can't believe you're here,' he says with a broad smile, hugging me tightly through the pain. 'God, you look a state, little brother.'

'You should see yourself,' I reply, assessing the extent to his injuries. 'I have to get you to a hospital.'

'I'll join you for that,' Dave mutters.

Dave picks up the hood that covered his head and tears it apart, forming a rough bandage which he wraps tight around Matt's gunshot wound. When this is done, he moves onto tying up the two injured thugs, unable to resist booting each one in the stomach before leaving them to face the police.

'That's it then?' Dave asks, looking to the Eagle. I nod.

'I can't believe it's actually real,' Matt says. He approaches but stops short of placing a hand on it.

'The spirit, the centurion, he fought Makov but not you?' he asks, to which I nod. 'And the Eagle burned their eyes?'

'But not ours,' I say.

'Because we weren't foolish enough to have our eyes open,' Dave says with certainty.

'No,' I disagree. 'It's because I willed it to save you.'

'Like the legatus probably did for his legion,' Matt says. 'Did you see the tomb in Scotland?'

'I followed your clues all the way,' I tell him.

He smiles for a moment before the hum of helicopters

sounds overhead again, joining the sirens. Looking up, I see film crews hovering above us, too.

'Time to go,' I say.

'You two head that way,' Dave orders, pointing towards the rear of the museum as he takes my rucksack from me. 'I'll tidy up here.'

'Won't you get caught?' I ask.

'Dave has found his way out of trickier situations than this,' Matt assures me as I help him to stand.

'Wait,' I say, stopping and hurrying back to Leon and Bishop, both still writhing on the floor in pain.

'Your baseball cap,' I say, taking the hat and throwing it to Matt.

'C'mon, brother,' he says, his smile broadening as he pulls on his cap. 'Let's go home.'

35

ADAM—Somewhere over the English Channel

'You boys look like you've been in a scrap,' an air stewardess says as she passes us.

'Stag weekend,' Matt lies, an easy explanation for our cuts, bruises and many other injuries. 'A little too much drink.'

'Who's the lucky groom?' she asks.

'Him,' I say, pointing to the snoring Dave seated in front of us.

'Sounds like he's recovering well,' she says, walking farther down the plane to check on the rest of the passengers.

Em is seated next to Dave, fast asleep as well. Her leg is heavily bandaged, painkillers easing the pain and helping her to rest. It was quite the reunion, all four of us in the same hospital for Matt's gunshot wound and the countless injuries Dave and I carry. Now, after several days recuperating, we are finally flying home. We could've left earlier, separately, but wanted to return together, as a team.

'So, why didn't you tell me?' I ask Matt, this being the first time we have a moment alone.

'What do you mean?' he replies with a smile.

'You know exactly what I mean. The British Museum, this life of yours. I still can't believe it. I always thought you were just some stuffy office worker, yet you do all this. It's a whole new you, one I don't know.'

'Hey, I'm still your brother,' he says. 'Think back to when we were kids. Rock climbing, abseiling, scuba diving, anything that could get the pulse racing. Is it really that much of a stretch? Besides, could you really see me stuck in an office? I am sorry for lying to you, I truly am, but...'

'You're afraid of heights.' I laugh in disbelief. 'How have you been able to do any of this?'

'You'd be surprised what you are capable of for the right cause. As you found out.'

'Why didn't you ever tell me?' I ask.

'I know you too well, little brother,' he says, still smiling. 'We were brought up on tales of myths, legends, and ancient histories by our mother, and especially our father. If I'd told you what I do for a living, I knew you would've wanted in. I didn't want you to just follow me. I wanted you to make your own decisions, your own life.'

'And I ended up following you anyway.' I laugh.

'Yeah. Funny how things happen sometimes. So, are you interested then?'

'What do you mean?' It's my turn to ask.

'This work,' he replies. 'My leg is in bad shape and I won't be up and running for some time. Somebody has to fill in for me and if what you and Dave have told me of your activities over the past few days is true, then I can't imagine anyone better suited for it. Call it a seventeenth birthday present if you want.'

'Why on earth would the museum want me?' I ask. 'I mean don't get me wrong, traveling around the world, finding relics, defeating the bad guys, sounds perfect to me, but I failed the trials. I stole their equipment, got Dave captured and tortured, and Emma hospitalised. Oh, and let's not forget that I was almost arrested for breaking and entering.'

'You can always retake the trials and Dave will hold no grudges for what he endured, only against those who captured him,' Matt reassures me. 'Besides, that wasn't your fault.'

'I have no background or qualifications in history or archaeology and I am supposed to be studying in college. Besides, I'm not exactly the ideal employee, especially for a government agency that has ties with MI-5.'

'True, but that's why I think you'll be perfect for this kind of work,' Matt says, smiling. 'On gut instinct alone, without any support or aid, you found the tomb of the Ninth Legion, and navigated your way into the Vatican. Historians go their entire lives without seeing what you have. You have more than proved your worth, Adam.

'I'll think about it,' I say, but we both know that my answer will be yes. All of this sounds perfect for me. Together, with my brother, hunting down relics and ancient artefacts, and if it's anything like the past few days, it'll certainly not be boring.

'I have to warn you though, people like Makov and his thugs, they are everywhere in this life,' he explains. 'You have entered a world of thieves and scoundrels, liars and cheats.'

'I'll fit right in,' I add.

'Probably,' he admits with a smirk. 'Seriously though, you've crossed paths with some dangerous people and cost them dearly. They will not forget that. Bishop and Leon have been imprisoned, but Makov is still out there and he will be gunning for us.'

Let him come, I tell myself. *I will be ready next time.*

'I just want you to know what you'll be getting yourself into,' he says, but my mind is already made up. 'The world saw you, us. They saw the Eagle risen and its power. The governments will try to cover it up, use the media to call it a typical bolt of lightning, a freak event of nature, but people have started to wonder. Myth is becoming reality after being kept secret for so long.'

'You really think the world saw me?' I joke.

'Abbey said several videos and images have been leaked online,' Matt replies. 'One is sure to have your ugly mug on it!'

We both laugh, drawing looks of annoyance from the other passengers. Em and Dave don't even stir.

'I see you're wearing Dad's jacket,' he notices, tapping me on the arm of the biker jacket.

'Yeah, sorry. I know I probably shouldn't...'

'No, it suits you,' he says, cutting off my protests. 'He would want you to wear it. You still ride his bike?'

'Not at the moment.' It's not exactly a lie, but the truth and the wreckage of our father's motorcycle can wait until we return home. A beeping sounds from my pocket, a red light shining on the headset. I put the glasses on, Abbey's voice instantly speaking to me.

'Thirty minutes until you land at Heathrow,' she says, tone filled with annoyance.

'Are you still angry with me for taking off the glasses in the Vatican?' I ask. 'If it's about alerting the police then you should know that it saved the lives of two of the security guards. If you hadn't summoned medical aid then both would've died.'

'Continuing into the Vatican alone and without our support was reckless and foolish,' she berates me. 'You could've been arrested, or worse, killed.'

'But it was the right thing to do,' I say, my voice trying

to calm her. She reminds me of my mother with her ranting.

'You cut me off,' she protests. 'The authorities were onto you and you went in on your own without back-up.'

'I knew you two would get on well,' Matt says, closing his eyes and leaning back in his seat, earpiece and mic in place to join the conversation. He smiles and laughs as Abbey continues her tirade.

'Okay, okay,' I say, trying to calm her. 'I'm sorry and it'll never happen again.'

'Promise?'

'I promise,' I swear to her, struggling not to laugh.

'I can tell you're chuckling,' she says.

'I am not,' I say, unable to stifle the laughter anymore. 'Okay, I'm sorry again.'

'I'll let you off, but only because it's your birthday,' she says. 'Did Matt offer you a place on the team?

'He did,' I reply.

'Welcome to the team then,' she says.

'I haven't accepted yet!'

'You will,' she says.

'And Charles is okay with all this?'

'He will be – eventually,' Abbey says before putting on her stiff British accent to imitate her boss. 'Welcome to Echo Team, Mr Hunter.'

I can't contain my smile. I began all this a kid in college, uncertain of what I wanted to do with my life.

Now, I have a path and a purpose set out before me. Even if it's just until Matt recovers, I will savour every moment. Though the past week has been terrifying, exhausting, draining, and often painful, sitting on this plane alongside my brother and with an exciting future ahead of me, I can honestly say I would not change any of it at all.

'Does our mother know about any of this?' I ask, keen to know more about his 'real' life.

'She does now,' Matt says uncomfortably.

'And Kat?'

'Some of it,' he replies with a grin. 'I try to leave out the being captured and beaten side of things though.'

I'm tempted to tell him that Kat has a secret of her own – but I resist. It's her secret to tell. My mind flicks to what lies in secure storage within the cargo hold of the plane.

'What is the Eagle? I ask Matt quietly.

'The standard of a Roman legion,' he states, though seeing my gaze he knows more is expected. 'To say anymore opens up a whole can of worms that I really don't want to go into now.'

'*Wrath of the gods* as the Romans and Makov believed?' I suggest with wonder. 'A power unknown by this world, able to cast down light and fire and summon ghosts? I mean that was what we saw, wasn't it? Ghosts, spirits of the dead?'

'Stop now before you make my headache worse.' He laughs.

'What will happen to it when we get back?' I ask.

'We will carry out a few tests on it,' Abbey explains. 'Then it will go into the containment facility. It's too dangerous an object to be let loose upon the world.'

'Exactly what I think the centurion feared,' I say.

'It's my job, our job, to find these relics but if they are as powerful and hazardous as the Eagle, it's our duty to protect the world from them,' Matt says.

'The Hunter brothers, saving the world,' I say. 'Who would've thought it?'

'I still can't get my head around how you were able to wield the Eagle yet the centurion forced Makov to release it,' Matt says.

'Perhaps it can only be controlled by the righteous,' Abbey suggests. 'The legatus, with his dying breath, saving his men. Adam, beaten and bruised, saving his brother and friend. Perhaps the centurion recognised that.'

'Adam is a lot of things,' Matt says. 'Crafty and reckless yes, but righteous? I don't know.'

'He cares for his family,' Abbey adds as if I am not listening in. 'Maybe that was all that was needed.'

My phone beeps with an incoming message, and I try to ignore it, sure that it will be our mother for the millionth time.

'Aren't you going to get that?' Abbey asks. 'It's your girlfriend!'

'Abbey!' I say a little too loudly. I drop my voice. 'Are you still intercepting my messages?'

'Standard procedure, Adam. Standard procedure.'

I ignore her invitation for a row. I'm going to have to get used to this – a downside of being part of a team. I glance down at my phone and read the message.

That was you in those photos, wasn't it? Duncan is sure of it. Everybody is talking about it at college. So, Mr Celebrity, your offer to go to the end of the year ball with me still open?
Sarra Starr. x

I'm vaguely aware of Matt and Abbey having a conversation – and joking around at my expense.

'She just asked him out!' Abbey says.

'Good on you,' Matt cheers, punching me on the arm. 'You're more like me than I thought!'

'Can you two just butt out?'

I read the message again. I know I should be pleased, overjoyed, a date with the most popular girl at college, but I'm not. All I can think of is sitting in that hospital, with Em's hand in mine, our eyes meeting and my lips on her soft brow as she slept. Em has barely spoken to me since. I've caught her gaze a few times, but she looks annoyed and angry at me more than anything, warning me away.

Looking up towards her seat, seeing her sleeping again, I can't help but wish the message was from her.

I sigh heavily, returning to matters at hand. Rummaging through my rucksack, I produce Matt's journal.

'I wondered if I'd see that old thing again,' Matt says with surprise, taking the notebook eagerly. 'Some of the things in here should not be seen by anyone outside the museum. You have no idea what secrets are encrypted.'

'I've read some of them,' I reply. 'The centurion is mentioned in there, your lead...?'

'An old friend of mine, an Italian historian,' Matt says, guessing my question. 'He was one of the first to unearth the wall in the Colosseum with the inscriptions. It took a helluva bribe to get him to tell me the few details he had taken notes of, among other things. You found it though, didn't you? You saw the wall of victorious gladiators.'

I smile without saying anymore. I see it in his eyes, how he longed to have been there and seen it for himself. I don't taunt him by speaking about it, nor do I tell him of my other beating at Makov's hands beneath the Colosseum.

'I knew you'd figure out the encryptions,' he tells me, then looks back to his journal. 'You are meant for this life.'

'So,' Abbey says over the headsets to Matt and me. 'What do we do next, Hunters?'

THE RELIC HUNTERS

RETURN WILL IN...

CURSE OF THE SANDS

HISTORICAL NOTE

When I began to write the first entry for the Relic Hunters
series I knew from the start that it would be focussed on
the Romans – or more specifically – the lost Roman
Legion. The disappearance of the Roman Ninth Legion
has been much discussed by historians and has featured in
many books, television series and films. I knew that this
mystery would be the perfect historical basis for the first
book in a mythical treasure hunting series.

The Roman Ninth Legion – The Legion IX Hispana –
was a real legion that is recorded as suffering a severe
defeat in 61AD at the hands of Boudicca at the Battle of
Camulodunum (Colchester). Emperor Hadrian (commis-
sioner of Hadrian's Wall) once stated that 'the Britons
could not be kept under Roman control.' The prevailing
theory is that the Ninth Legion met its doom on Britain's
northern frontier, never to be seen or heard from again.

The Legion did not return to Rome and no other mentions of the Legion, its soldiers or its Eagle were ever made.

Between 71 and 79 AD, much of the reign of Emperor Titus Flāvius Caesar Vespasiānus Augustus (Vespasian for short) is a mystery. Though popular in his early years as Emperor, Vespasian receded from the public eye as he survived several conspiracies against him. The Emperor sought to make Rome great again following civil war and ordered the construction of a great many buildings and structures that would stand the test of time (the Colosseum among them). After a short illness, Emperor Vespasian died with his final words being; 'I think I am becoming a God.'

Following Vespasian's death, his son Titus Flāvius Caesar Vespasiānus Augustus (Titus for short) succeeded him as Emperor. Though Titus was well loved by the populace of Rome and was a seasoned soldier in the Legions, he sadly did not participate in the gladiatorial arts (though several other Emperors are recorded as doing so). Titus did oversee the completion of the Colosseum and its inaugural games prior to his death merely two years after his coronation.

The wall within the Colosseum recording the victorious gladiators is a fabrication of mine, as sadly is the mythical Eagle standard. There have been many rumours of the location and discovery of a Roman Legion's bronze Eagle in the highlands of Scotland, but no proof has yet been uncovered of what really happened to the Ninth Legion.

As I said before, I knew that my first book in this series would be based on the Romans. The Roman Empire spanned for over 1500 years, reaching from Northern Britain across Europe to Egypt and the Middle East with over 60 million inhabitants. The Roman Empire was one of the greatest seen by this world, but it is only a small part of history. There is much more for Adam Hunter and the British Museum to discover, many relics to unearth and myths and legends to be brought to life.

ACKNOWLEDGMENTS

The completion and release of this book could not have been possible without the advice, guidance and assistance of a great many people. First are the family and friends who have helped me, listened to me when I have needed to talk through ideas and given their precious time to read through countless drafts. Of course a massive thank you to the proof-readers and editors too who have done a fantastic job with this book. I thank you all and am sure I will be knocking at your door soon to talk over Book 2.

A big thank you must go to the staff and volunteers of the British Museum, the Colosseum in Rome and the Vatican Museums. I visited each of these whilst planning out this book and they dealt with all the questions I had for them, no matter how basic or strange. The sites were indeed so inspirational that I made them settings for the very story I was to write.

This is just the beginning.

I thank you all.

Martin Ferguson

ABOUT THE AUTHOR

MARTIN FERGUSON

I live in Norwich, England and am currently working on the young adult adventure and historical series 'Relic Hunters'. Inspired by the myths and legends my parents told me as a boy and with the help of my ever-suffering wife, a teacher and history graduate, 'Eagle of the Empire' was the first entry in the 'Relic Hunters' series.

When not writing I am training or at least planning my next challenge. Following a serious knee injury, I was told by surgeons never to run or play sports again. Stubborn and reckless, much like the characters in my writing, I have not listened and have completed the Three Peaks Challenge, the Great North Run, the Greater Manchester Marathon and the London Marathon.